MW01130655

Ganymede

Lone Tree Press

First Edition

Copyright © 2019

All rights reserved. No portion of this book may be reproduced in any form without permission from the publisher, except as permitted by U.S. copyright law.

This is a work of fiction. Names, characters, and incidents either are the products of the author's imagination or are used fictitiously. Any resemblance to actual persons, living or dead, is entirely coincidental.

Cover by Cakamura

To order additional copies: ganymedenovel@gmail.com

to Isaac

for discovering this idea with me

PART 1

CHAPTER 1

World Zero: 2088

Standing in the kitchen, her preparations complete, Mary knew she should take a moment to enjoy the calm before the coming storm. Elizabeth was in her bedroom playing with her toys, the presents were wrapped and the cake was cooling on the counter. She was pointedly ignoring the swarm of news-drones at the end of the block. She would take a moment for herself and try to relax.

She knew she was too old to be the mother of a seven-year-old. But that was the whole point wasn't it? It was because she couldn't conceive that she'd chosen this route. The protests, the blaring headlines, the violence in the streets, none of that mattered, not when compared with the miracle of her daughter – her perfect seven-year-old girl. Of course she was perfect. She was a marvel of science, the shining outcome of the largest research project conducted in the history of mankind.

Mary placed her palms flat on the countertop, looked out the window over her garden and smiled. She was content. More than content. She was for all intents and purposes immortal. If that wasn't satisfying, she didn't know what was. When she'd been chosen as a participant in the human trials, she had felt unbelievably lucky. She could finally have the child she so desperately wanted. In a burst of exuberance, she'd nearly given her daughter the same name as herself. But it had seemed like a step too far, an expression of arrogance that might tempt fate and tip them both into disaster. In the end, she had decided that Elizabeth should be her own unique person, clones shouldn't be named after their parents, and so she'd been given her own name.

The view out the window flickered, interrupting Mary's thoughts, a panorama of dense, grey buildings suddenly bleeding through the garden and fruit trees in her backyard. The failure surprised her; she'd never been subjected to an unfiltered view without authorization before. She closed her eyes, focused her attention on her network interface, and reinstated her preferred filter. The buildings blurred and fuzzed then blinked out of existence, her backyard returning to greenery.

She watched for a minute longer to see if the filter would reveal additional instability. When she was satisfied that her preferred reality was solidly back in place, she turned away from the window. "Elizabeth! Come down! Are you ready for the party?"

When Elizabeth didn't respond, Mary's face creased into an unaccustomed frown. She walked through the dining room to the long, white-carpeted stairs, and called up to her daughter's room. "Elizabeth, can you hear me?"

Still no response.

This silence was unlike her. Elizabeth was usually so responsive. Maybe it had to do with turning seven? Mary thought back to her own seventh birthday. Had she been worried about turning seven? She honestly couldn't remember. Raising a clone could be confusing at times. It was hard to stay inside your own head.

Mary checked her watch. There was plenty of time, still thirty minutes until the first guests would arrive. She walked up the stairs to the second floor, trailing her fingers along the hand-rail. She stopped at Elizabeth's room and placed one hand tentatively on the door. "Elizabeth, can I come in?"

The room was silent.

A sharp pang of anxiety spiked through her. The feeling was there and gone in an instant, a liquid flutter in her stomach. She didn't know where the feeling had come from, but over the years she'd learned to trust her intuition. Right now, the silence emanating from her daughter's room seemed ominous.

"Elizabeth?" she called through the door, her voice louder and more concerned than she would have liked. She prided herself on her ability to remain calm under fire. Yet, here she was falling apart over nothing.

She waited a moment longer and when there was still no response, she made up her mind. She pushed the door open and entered the room to find Elizabeth sitting cross-legged in the middle of the floor, a doll in each hand, head down, hair falling in loose cascades over her face.

Mary took a deep breath, one hand on her chest to cover the frightened beating of her heart. "Honey, is everything ok?"

Elizabeth was oddly still, nothing like her usual boisterous self. Mary forced herself to stay calm as she crouched down in front of her. Revealing her anxiety would just scare her. Elizabeth was so sensitive and easily influenced by the feelings of those around her. But there was no reaction. No motion at all. Mary pushed her daughter's thick brown hair back away from her forehead, revealing her eyes while she surreptitiously checked for a fever with the palm of her hand.

Elizabeth didn't stir.

"Are you nervous about your birthday party?" Mary asked.

At first Elizabeth didn't respond, and for a long, pregnant moment the room was utterly silent. Then she lifted her head and looked Mary in the eye. "Who are you?" she asked, her face twisted with some intense emotion. It was an expression

Mary had never seen on her daughter's face before. Her anxiety returned, sharp and cruel, twisting within her. Something was wrong. She had known it all along. Elizabeth wasn't well.

"Honey, listen to me, do you feel sick?" Mary asked, tripping over her words in her concern.

Elizabeth's eyes darted around the room before returning to Mary. "Why are you keeping me here?" she asked.

"I'm not keeping you here. It's time to get ready for your friends. Everyone will be here soon for your party," Mary explained, trying to inject a sense of normalcy into the conversation.

"Party? Where the hell am I?" Elizabeth asked, her voice rising.

Mary pressed her hand to Elizabeth's forehead again. It was still cool to the touch, but that wasn't enough to alleviate her concerns. Taking a deep breath, she picked Elizabeth up. It was time to take her to the doctors at the lab. They had told her that if anything unusual happened she should bring Elizabeth to them immediately. This definitely qualified as unusual.

As soon as Mary picked her up, Elizabeth started to struggle, kicking viciously and twisting to get free. In a blind panic, Mary rushed toward the stairs, one hand gripping Elizabeth around the middle, the other grasping the hand-rail as she fought for control. Partway down the stairs, Elizabeth suddenly went limp. It was such a surprising change that Mary stopped in her tracks, fearing the worst, the animal part of her brain crying out in shock and alarm. But she found that Elizabeth was looking at her calmly now, her eyes flat as she spoke.

"Mother?" she asked.

"What is it, darling?" Mary responded, trying desperately to keep the rising panic out of her voice.

"Put me down,"

"We need to go back to the lab, honey. It's important."

"Put me down," Elizabeth repeated, her voice taking a deeper tone, commanding now.

At that moment, Mary's mother, Elizabeth's grandmother, opened the front door and bustled in. "Hello, sweetheart! Happy Birthday!" she called out. She was carrying a bag of presents, beaming up at them where they were standing on the stairs, unaware that anything unusual was going on.

"Mother! Thank God you're here," Mary began, but she didn't get a chance to finish, because at that moment Elizabeth grabbed a metal chopstick from her mother's stylish bun and stabbed it into the exposed flesh between her neck and shoulder.

For one long moment, Mary gawked at the end of the chopstick sticking out just above her dress line, blood welling up and starting to run down her chest. Then her legs gave out and she toppled forward, falling down the stairs toward Grandma, who stood at the bottom, eyes shocked, mouth open, a silent scream stuck in her throat.

As Mary fell, Elizabeth broke free, pivoted in the air, and landed cat-like at the bottom of the stairs. Then she knelt over her mother's prone form and reached out with one small hand, her fingertips caressing the chopstick where it emerged from the base of her mother's neck.

CHAPTER 2

World Zero: 2080

The lab was quiet, all the typical noise, movement, and energy having faded with the end of the day. Nearly everyone had gone home to their families, to their dinners and their feeds, each scientist reverting back to ordinary life once the lab coat came off and the pressures of work faded. Those who stayed behind were the most dedicated, the ones without family, or the ones who stayed at work to avoid facing something even more painful waiting for them back home.

Jill rubbed her eyes and looked at the analysis one more time. She knew she could find a pattern in it if she looked long enough. With enough time, she would start to see the connections that had eluded her. Then she could figure out the right questions to ask of the data-set; the correct paths to follow through the massive maze of information that her team had been collecting.

She pressed the tip of her tongue up against the back of her teeth, her brow furrowing as she leaned in toward the data-model where it was projected in the space over her desk. As if getting closer to the data would make any difference. A few strands of brown hair had sprung out of her ponytail and were hanging in her face. Absentmindedly, she pushed them back behind an ear, her mind totally focused on what she was doing.

With a sharp, percussive exhale of pent-in breath, she

leaned back in her chair and stared at the ceiling, her dark eyes focusing out to infinity. What was she missing? She felt so close. Something was prickling in the back of her mind, clamoring to be set free. She knew from experience that if she could let it germinate, a beautiful new idea would flower forth. And this one felt like a doozy. Like the breakthrough she'd been waiting for.

"Burning the midnight oil again, Jill?"

Jill let out an undignified squeak and shot straight up out of her chair, her fight or flight instincts on full display, balanced precariously between sprinting toward the exit and striking out at the source of the voice. But it was just Matt sneaking up on her again. She forced her arms to her sides, hoping he hadn't noticed her hands balled up in fists.

He stood with his feet planted confidently shoulder width apart, hands crossed over an excessively fit chest, his green eyes appraising her with smug satisfaction. She noticed his hair was starting to grey again. A sign, she thought, that he couldn't afford to keep up with his treatments. Nobody went grey on purpose these days.

Matt was the closest thing she had to an enemy at the lab. And she didn't have enemies. Not normally. But she had a sneaking suspicion that he was trying to steal her research and claim it as his own. He was on the cleared team, working in the cleared facility. Something for the Department of Defense, or maybe it was Homeland Security. She didn't care. They were all the same to her. A bunch of ethically suspect sell-outs conducting research that would be turned against humanity, either as weapons or as a better way to spy, subvert, and manipulate other human beings. She hated it. Matt wasn't a scientist. He was a hack. And he had a bad habit of looking over her shoulder, showing up when she least expected him.

"Hi, Matt. Yeah, I'm working late tonight. I, uh, have something I need to finish up," she said.

"What are you working on? Maybe I can help," he responded with obvious enthusiasm.

"No, that's ok, I was just getting ready to leave. Thanks anyway."

"Maybe next time," he said, disappointment coloring his reply. "We really should work together more often, you know."

"No Matt, I don't think so. Not in this lifetime."

He looked genuinely chagrined, and for a moment she almost felt sorry for him. Almost. Then she remembered the time she'd found him looking through her data-node. Or the time he'd come instead of IT when she'd needed someone to deal with an upgrade procedure and she'd caught him inside her research folders. No, she didn't feel sorry for him at all.

Creep.

She turned her back on him, shut down her lab-station and started stuffing her things into her bag. She could hear him breathing behind her. Breathing, and shuffling his feet. She turned slowly, her hands full, and gave him as much of a glare as she thought she could get away with. "Do you need something Matt? I would think you'd want to get back to work, or you know, go home."

"Well yeah, it's just…" he trailed off.

She didn't need this. She really didn't want to be dealing with Matt right now. Whatever was germinating in her mind required time and space, and what she didn't need was to be stuck here dealing with this crap.

"Whatever it is, it can wait, right? I need to leave."

"Yeah, ok, it can wait. But tomorrow, first thing, come to my office, will you? There's something I need to talk to you about."

When she looked hesitant, he leaned forward, crowding into her personal space. "Promise me, ok? You'll come to my office? It can wait till tomorrow, but it's important. It's something you need to know."

"Whatever, Matt," she said, resisting the urge to roll her eyes. "Yes, I'll come by in the morning. But right now... I just need to get home."

Matt stepped aside. He looked reluctant, but he seemed willing to let the conversation end. Jill took one last look at him and walked away from her desk, down the hall, and toward the elevators. A few lights remained on in other parts of the lab and she could hear other people working, but it wasn't enough to make her feel completely comfortable; she felt the pressure of his eyes on the back of her head all the way out. Even after she'd turned the corner and knew she was out of sight, she had a nervous feeling in her gut, telling her that something wasn't right.

Back in the lab, Matt stared at the last spot Jill had occupied before she'd turned the corner and disappeared. The look on his face was intense, jaw muscles standing out in ropy cords, his hands clenched as he rocked back and forth on the balls of his feet. He took a moment to moderate his breathing and settled back onto his heels. A flash of what might have been anger, but just as easily could have been fear, crossed his face. Then he settled his expression into the bland placidity of a professional poker player. His bluffing face. His lying face. Commander Tros was waiting for him to report back and he would have to play his hand carefully with her. Very carefully.

When Matt left the office, it was quiet except for a soft clicking emanating from the lab equipment as it sorted, classified, and labeled genetic material. In the next room, machines were using gene editing techniques to enumerate small changes to the DNA, one allele at a time. They incubated the combinations, documented the results, and then destroyed each sample of generated tissue in turn.

Every combination tried, each classification made, every single data point gathered, took the project one step closer to its ultimate goal of creating a fully reprogrammable human. A human who could be modified to be anything wanted of it. Stronger, smarter, healthier. A human that would not be held back by doubts or worries. A human that would do what it was told without question or complaint.

First, the scientists needed to figure out how to create a viable human clone. Once that breakthrough was complete, the rest would come in due time. Matt knew that this was true, like knowing that the sun would rise in the east tomorrow morning. His whole team knew it was true. It's what they all were waiting for.

CHAPTER 3

Jill forced herself to stop thinking about Matt during the ride home, she'd worry about him in the morning. Her car carried her through the wet streets of Seattle, the steady beat of rain on the roof and windshield soothing to her. Once she was on the small roads near her apartment, she instructed the car to turn off its headlights. It didn't need them to drive safely and she preferred the feeling of being in a warm, dark cocoon as it whisked her toward the comfort of her home. She rested her chin in her hand and stared past her reflection; the street lights fuzzed and glowed through her as if she was a ghost.

She had been working on the problems surrounding human genetic engineering for so long now. The lack of progress was frustrating. It had been nearly one-hundred years since the first mammal had been cloned. Contrary to every expectation, human cloning hadn't followed. The automated, AI-driven techniques that she used to perform genetics research were far more advanced than her ancestors had ever dreamed of, but they still hadn't led to a breakthrough.

Every time her team got close, they would hit a new roadblock. Sometimes it felt as if there was a malicious 'something' that was actively blocking progress. She wasn't normally superstitious, but on a cold, dark night like this it was easy to let her imagination get away from her. She let her eyes lose focus, looking past the streaming raindrops, past the subtly glowing guide-lights flashing by, out toward a dark horizon, struggling to see what it was she'd missed. Something they had all missed.

She had always been interesting in programming and computer science, and because of that she had a certain way of thinking. Sometimes it helped her, sometimes it hurt. She tended to think algorithmically, as if everything was, at its root, information. As if the very passage of time was in essence a vast computation. She liked to think of the universe as a massive computer working toward an unknowable final solution, the algorithms playing out in breathtaking beauty and complexity.

She had received a Masters Degree in Molecular Biology and a Ph.D. in Genetics, but she didn't conceptualize DNA the way she'd been taught at university. She had been taught to think of biology in terms of proteins unfolding and chemical equations to be solved, but when she looked at DNA she saw code. It was like working with the world's messiest, most poorly written program, created by a madman and lacking any comments whatsoever to explain itself.

Evolution had taken what had started as a simple, elegant biological system and had layered on so much crap that the result was an incredible mess, nearly impossible to make any sense of. Early genetics research had operated on the assumption that every human trait was controlled by one or two genes. If a dominant gene overruled a recessive gene, the dominant trait would manifest. Early in the 21st century it was discovered that this was not the case. To their dismay, researchers found that most traits were expressed across the entire genetic structure. Height, for instance, was expressed across ninety percent of the active DNA sequence. There was no tall gene. No short gene. It didn't work that way. If you wanted to change someone's height, you'd need to make an exacting set of changes across tens of thousands of alleles.

Then there was RNA. If DNA was the code, RNA was the runtime interpreter, the mechanism by which DNA was interpreted into physical structures and traits. The exact same

DNA sequence could result in a bewildering variety of out-comes depending upon the RNA that processed it. As if that wasn't enough, RNA shifted continuously as a result of environmental and behavioral factors. The problem was so complicated, it had taken one of the most powerful AI constructs in the world two full years to create a working model of a single DNA/RNA combination that accounted for any sort of environmental variability. She knew the answer to human cloning had to be out there somewhere, and she wanted to be the one to find it. Somewhere in that mess of DNA and RNA was a key that would unlock unlimited genetic engineering.

The ability to genetically modify humans had grown in leaps and bounds over the past century. Most of the symptoms of aging had been pushed back to the very end of life. Teeth didn't decay, wrinkles didn't form, and muscles didn't weaken; humanity was enjoying a golden age of health and vitality. Without the progress that had been made in the past decades, implant technology wouldn't be possible. Genetic engineering was what primed the brainstem for the neural implant that everyone now received at birth. Jill struggled to imagine what life would be like without access to her interface. The ability to instantly connect to network nodes felt so natural, it was like an innate human capability now.

While a wide variety of genetic engineering modifications were possible on human subjects, if a critical threshold was passed the result was always a catastrophic failure of the modified tissue. Sometimes she felt like they were all a bunch of hackers, nibbling at the edges of a system they didn't fully understand. Some unknown factor was preventing them from making progress beyond a certain point. Jill dreamed of a future in which unlimited genetic engineering truly unlocked human potential; the possibilities were so much greater than what had been achieved so far.

There were some who opted out of the entire idea, who

lived 'close to the genome' as they called it. They believed in staying true to what they saw as the original human form, living close to nature, choosing to suffer and die like their ancestors, their belief in the purity of the human genome cult-like. The percentage of people who took it that far was minuscule, but there were many more who sympathized.

Genetic engineering wasn't without negative side effects. People lived longer, healthier lives, but the result was that overpopulation on this depleted planet had become an issue again. It was hard to get used to. Not since the Great Unrest had there been worries about too many people. The die-off during that time had been so large that the human race had experienced a measurable reduction in genetic diversity. It was one of the reasons Jill had decided to enter the field. She not only wanted to improve individual lives, she wanted to ensure her species as a whole survived and thrived.

Unfortunately, the ability to engineer the genome had resulted in less diversity, not more. Giving parents the ability to engineer their children had resulted in a convergence toward what society had decided was the ideal child. One of the unexpected results was that there weren't enough men left in the world. Not only were a huge number of men killed during the Great Unrest, once the world regained stability, it had become a cultural assumption that boys were less desirable than girls. After all, men had led the human race to the very precipice of extinction. No one had the desire to repeat that particular experiment in self-destruction.

There had even been talk of legislating a solution – requiring each state to meet a male quota for instance – but so far there hadn't been any significant progress. The upshot was that for every male there were now three females. The world had long given up on an even ratio between the sexes. The battle now was merely to preserve what was left.

Jill shifted her body so her back was up against the side

of the car and she was looking out the opposite side window. She cocked her head to the side, index finger tapping absent-mindedly on her lips. Maybe she hadn't taken the computer science analogy far enough. Something about thinking like a hacker was making the itch in her mind grow stronger. She could feel it intensifying, like a solution on the verge of re-vealing itself to her.

So far she'd been conducting her research as if the system she was studying was acting in good faith. She had assumed that the obfuscation in the genome was caused by the chaos inherent in natural selection. And she had always believed that her failures were because she hadn't understood the interactions between the genes well enough, so her strategy had focused on minutely cataloging the result of every in-dividual genetic change. At the lab, she applied a brute force approach to testing each genetic combination in turn, mov-ing toward a critical mass of knowledge, hoping for an 'Aha!' moment that would open the floodgates of understanding. Meanwhile, the horizon moved steadily further away.

Every other animal in the world could be engineered in extraordinary ways. Entirely new species of creature had been created in the lab: dogs with wings, pigs that tasted of cinna-mon, bees that wouldn't sting their keepers. There was clearly something special about human genetic code that was block-ing their progress.

She closed her eyes and triggered her interface, focusing in on her own biological parameters. The interface sprung to life in front of her, displaying a glowing representation of her body. She focused on her limbic system and the interface zoomed in, the limbus of her brain highlighted. She paused for a moment, thinking it through. Then she nudged her en-torhinal cortex, modifying her associative memory system's response to cortisol and epinephrine. The color of her brain changed, shading closer toward blue. Her attachment to past ideas fell away. Her willingness to accept novel solutions increased. She found herself in the center of a radius of calm, the world around her muted and subdued.

And then it unfurled like an exquisite flower, the realization blooming in her mind. She knew what she'd been missing. She finally understood what they'd all been missing.

CHAPTER 4

"Hello, I'm Holly Sharper, and with me in the studio for tonight's live-cast are two of the leading voices of our time. On my left is Megan Duncan, a bio-ethicist from the Berkeley School of Reason. On my right is Lisa Albright, a Senior Mentor at the Sunrise Congregation in Livingston, Virginia. Lisa is also a Distinguished Fellow of the Pure Genome Project and a repeat guest on this show. I'd like to extend a warm welcome to you both and thank you for joining me tonight." Holly turned toward Megan with a well-practiced, serious expression. "Today we are talking about the ongoing efforts to clone a human. Let's dig into the reasons why the attempts have been unsuccessful so far. Do you, like many, believe that this is a technology we are not meant to have?"

Megan raised one eyebrow and smiled into the camera, "No Holly, I don't believe that. When I look at the history of our species, I see an unbroken track record of exploration and discovery, starting with the emergence of language and the use of fire, culminating in the highly advanced society that we enjoy today. Without technology, this planet's limited carrying capacity wouldn't be capable of sustaining our current quality of life. We should never forget the dark years during the Great Unrest. We owe a huge thanks to our parent's generation for getting us back on our feet, and I believe we have an obligation to future generations to push the frontiers of science ever forward."

Holly smiled and turned to Lisa. "What would you say to that Lisa? Should we hurtle unchecked toward a golden technological future, or are there boundaries we should hesitate to cross?"

Lisa's face crinkled into a smile, warm and charismatic. "Megan raises a good point. I would like to start by saying I truly respect and honor the achievements of the scientific community, but let's not forget that technology is nothing more than a tool. It is a means of achieving that which will bring greater glory to God. Technology should never become an end in and of itself. It only takes a brief review of humanity's sorry history of war and conflict to see the twisted ways in which scientific achievement has been used to destroy and condemn other human beings."

Megan leaned forward angrily, a glossy braid falling over her shoulder. "Lisa, you are ignoring a critical fact. The bloodshed you refer to was caused by men in the pursuit of power and conquest. There are so few men left; we've moved beyond that stage in our history. Our species has matured. We've grown up. Now we can advance our technology without the need for restraint. Can you imagine a woman leading the Khmer Rouge to commit genocide? A woman in charge of the Nazi holocaust? A woman starting a nuclear war over religious misunderstandings? I know I can't."

Lisa crossed her arms, visibly keeping her cool, before she replied, "I've heard this argument before and I find it unconvincing. Maybe we can't imagine a woman committing these types of atrocities because we haven't witnessed it yet. Every one of us, regardless of our gender, is human, and every one of us carries the potential for evil. We cannot look to technology for redemption."

"That's a circular argument, Lisa, and I don't buy it. Just look at the science. It's a known fact that women are less aggressive than men. We are more willing to resolve conflicts verbally than physically, and not a single one of the great conflicts has been caused by the mistakes of a woman. Every war

Jason Taylor

can be traced to the weaknesses of man. The reduction of men in our society is exactly why we've enjoyed such unprecedented peace over the past decades," Megan responded.

Holly cut in, "Fascinating, truly. But we are wandering away from the subject of tonight's program. Let's get back to the subject of human cloning. Why hasn't human cloning been successful to date? Should we even be attempting to clone a human?"

"The lack of success is an interesting question," noted Megan, "one that is being investigated in labs, in many countries around the world. We've all seen how powerful genetic engineering can be. Our entire neo-capitalist system is tied to the ability to modify the genome. What we don't understand is why we've run into hard limits in our quest for more comprehensive genetic modifications on humans, including cloning."

Lisa broke in, "What of the ethical question? Cloning a human may lead some to question the very idea of a soul. Is it right for us to make copies of something as precious and singular as a human being? By doing so, do we devalue humanity? Do we ultimately become disposable?"

"You are breaking in on my territory," Megan said with a laugh. "These are all excellent ethical questions, and they are exactly the right things for us to be thinking about. It doesn't mean we shouldn't move forward in our research, but we should do so very carefully while considering these important issues from every possible angle."

Lisa responded, clearly frustrated. "Consider from every angle? Forgive me for saying so, but that is an extremely patronizing attitude toward those of us who have grave concerns about this entire line of research. You can't downplay the significant roadblocks that scientists have encountered. Many in my congregation believe that God is actively blocking our progress. Maybe we aren't meant to advance our knowledge of human genetics past a certain point. The Tower of Babel is an ancient story that holds important lessons for us even today. At what price will we realize the cost of human arrogance, and when will we finally recognize the dire consequences of reaching too far?"

Holly swiveled her head back and forth between her guests, her interest piqued beyond what could be expected from gracious professionalism. "I'd be very interested in hearing your response to that question Megan, but first let's take a break and hear from our sponsors."

Jill stood up from the edge of her bed, triggered the controls for the virtual screen, and turned off the live-cast. It was all crap. The talking heads could blather on for a hundred years and still no progress would be made. The debates made for good entertainment, but they didn't bring anybody closer to the answers. In the end, it didn't matter. She was doing what she was doing for the good of all. She imagined a future free of disease. A future in which people could choose who they wanted to be in a multitude of physical forms. A future free of pain and suffering. Maybe even a future freed from death. That's why she had devoted her life to this problem – she had always dreamed of setting humanity free.

This line of thinking brought up painful memories for Jill. It always did. She hadn't lived through the Great Unrest, but she had lived with its consequences. She'd never gotten to meet her grandfather. He had died in the firestorm that had swept San Diego. All that was left of him were the stories that Grandma Annie had shared before she, too, had died. Jill had sat by her bed as she had coughed out her last breaths, the cancers too extensive to be fought any longer. Another legacy of the Great Unrest, a sickness so pervasive that nothing could be done to stop it.

If Jill had her way, it would all be a thing of the past. Not only the cancers and diseases of the body that had afflicted her grandmother, but the tendencies toward war and violence that had affected her grandfather and the millions of others like him. She'd sworn that oath on her grandmother's death-bed, then she had dedicated the rest of her life to fulfilling it.

She stood up and padded from her bedroom to the communal kitchen. Pepe followed her, purring and brushing up against the doorframe with his fluffy grey back, his tail waving back and forth in excitement.

"Hey Pepe, are you hungry too?" Jill spoke quietly so she wouldn't wake anyone up.

Pepe looked up at her and meowed, his tiny teeth sharp and translucent.

"Hold on, I'll get some milk for you. Warm I suppose?"

Once they were in the kitchen, Jill triggered her interface to place a virtual bowl of warm milk on the floor in front of him. He meowed once more, then lowered his head into the bowl and lapped up the creamy milk with gusto.

Jill sighed. Her ideas from earlier in the night hung in her mind. The more she toyed with them, the more they unraveled around the edges and lost their clarity. She had felt so excited before, but was this line of inquiry actually going to get her any closer to a solution? She'd start her research first thing in the morning. Right now she needed to let her mind settle.

Pepe wasn't sophisticated enough to notice her mood and leave on his own, so she triggered her interface and both Pepe and the bowl of milk disappeared. Then she walked to the food synthesizer and requested a cup of chamomile tea.

She was still at the table nursing her cup when Jacob walked in. "Hey Jill, need some company?" When she didn't respond, he sat down next to her and put a foot up on a chair. "Tough day at work?"

"I don't want to talk about it," she said, her hand wrapped around the comforting warmth of the mug. She pointedly ignored him, instead focusing on the steam as it curled off the top of her tea.

"Sorry Jill, I didn't mean to intrude." He shut himself down, the space where he was sitting flickering back into emptiness.

What she wouldn't give for a real person to talk to right now.

CHAPTER 5

Jill lifted her head, peeling her face off the slick surface of the table. She must have fallen asleep, her cup of tea cold beside her. She checked her internal self-diagnostics and saw that she'd gotten a full four hours of sleep. Falling asleep at the kitchen table? She hadn't done that for years. The stress at work must be getting to her.

"Well, that was weird," she said to the empty room.

The light was shimmering behind the auto-blinds, so she gave them the command for transparency and took a moment to look outside. It was windy this morning, tree limbs shaking, leaves blowing past in cascades of yellow and brown. Occasionally, a small stick would bounce off the window, but no sounds penetrated through the thick pane.

She sent a command to the synthesizer to start on her breakfast while she kept her eyes on the scene outside. She could see to the horizon where land met sea and small clouds scudded charmingly across the sky. She adjusted the filter and the scene fell away, buildings filling the view instead. Huddled close together, they were dark and forbidding, the closest just ten feet across the lane from her. As always, they were grim and grey, massive, dirty, and depressing. None of the structures in Seattle were maintained for aesthetics; all that mattered was that they kept the people in and the elements out.

She had made a habit of looking at the real world once in a while. It was easier to keep the filters on, and it was certainly more pleasant, but there was no substitute for reality.

She raised her hands up over her head, stretching once to the left, once to the right, feeling the pull all the way down her legs. Outside the window, a ball of conglomerated rubbish bounced down the lane and stuck itself to a wall. A cleaning drone would get to it eventually, and in the meantime no one else would even notice it was there. Jill didn't know anyone else who made a habit of dropping their filters.

The synthesizer pinged her interface, informing her that her meal was ready. She took a few minutes to finish a set of deep knee bends and then re-activated the filters. A scene of pastoral beauty replaced the buildings. What she was looking at was real in a sense. It was what the area had looked like 150 years ago, before the land had been developed and incorporated into the city. In the scene outside, the wind continued to blow and the leaves continued to fly past. She turned on the animal filter and a couple of deer appeared, grazing in the distance. A squirrel chattered in a nearby tree branch, holding on for dear life as her branch swayed violently in the wind. Below the squirrel, a dog wandered past, nose down, following a scent that only he could smell.

Jill smiled and turned to the table. Her plate was piled high and a cup of coffee was waiting for her, doctored with precisely the right amount of cream and sugar.

Jill was lost in thought, the drive downtown to the lab passing easily. Her head was pressed back into the seat cushions, an astronomical chart projected in front of her. She was watching the progression of the stars as seen from Earth, accelerated one hundred thousand times faster than normal. Memorizing changes to the constellations over time was a habit she'd formed as a child. It had started after watching a bad horror feed involving a time machine, and she'd decided that if she were ever involuntarily transported in time she would want to know, at the very least, what century she was in. So she'd started studying the stars from millennia in the past, and far into the future, memorizing their patterns. She was old enough now to see it as a funny side-effect of a child's over-active imagination, but she kept at it. It was comforting, and it brought her back to her roots.

The car jolted to a stop, shaking her out of her reverie. Just in front of the car someone had projected a wide band of yellow tape, beyond which there were armored military personnel swarming around her lab building.

"This is a restricted area, you may not travel beyond this point," an automated voice informed her.

She stepped out of the car and walked parallel to the tape, trying to get a better look. A clump of worried scientists stood on the corner at the end of the block. As she approached, Joanne, from the classification department, noticed her and waved her over.

"What's going on?" Jill asked.

Joanne seemed upset, one of her hands tapping her leg, the other fidgeting with a virtual cigarette. "They locked it down earlier this morning. No one's talking, but I've heard some ugly rumors."

"What kind of rumors?"

"They're saying that Matt's dead."

"What?"

"Yeah," Joanne leaned in close, "suicide."

"What?" Jill repeated, dumbfounded. "How could that be? I just saw him last night. He was fine."

"You know what they say about looking for the signs, right? It's all bullshit. I had a friend who committed suicide, and I had no clue. He told me he was going to meet me for lunch and then his wife found him dead. He left a note and everything. Ranting and raving about the state of the world and how hopeless he felt. Fucking men, right?"

"Wait, how do they know it was suicide? With Matt I mean."

"I shouldn't be telling you this. I mean the body isn't even cold yet, if you know what I mean. But what the hell." Joanne took a drag on her virtual cigarette, drawing out the drama. "They found him in his office. Neural overload. They also found stim packs and simulators. The whole nine yards. Nasty, right?"

Jill forced down a wave of nausea and looked back toward the lab building while she collected her emotions. "What's going on over there? Why did they lock it down?"

"Oh, that? They've nationalized the lab."

"They what?" Jill gasped. That was impossible. The entire building would be converted into a cleared facility. She would never be able to set foot in there again. Her professional-node would be locked down. All her research. Her notes. Her... everything. *Shit!*

Before she knew what she was doing, she found herself running toward the lab, hoping she could somehow make it through the door.

This is a terrible idea, the rational part of her brain told her. *This will end badly.*

She made it just past the edge of the tape before they shut her down. Her nervous system spiked, sending a massive jolt through her body, and then she collapsed, arms and legs jelly, her head thumping hard against the street.

CHAPTER 6

Jill was surrounded by inky darkness. She could hear people, but she couldn't see them.

She was on a path. It was dark, but she could sense what was around her. She was surrounded by others on the road, all of them moving forward, like a pilgrimage toward a destination she could not imagine. The sky was dusted with stars, their patterns unrecognizable.

Jill was surrounded by open space, the night sky suffused with the light of a glowing city just beyond the horizon. The clouds were lit from below in a bright arc, orange and pink, the reflected light bright enough to cast long shadows behind her. The ground was blasted, heat-melted into glass. A path wound its way through the hard landscape. There were other people with her. Together they moved toward the city. She could not see their faces.

Jill was standing before a low barrier, her thighs pressed against it, a sense of yearning pulling her forward. A body of water lapped the shore at her feet, alive with color, reflecting the light of a mighty, glowing city. She could feel the texture of the barrier against her legs, the air warm against her skin. A breeze blew her hair away from her face and kissed her cheeks. She leaned forward, a desire to be in the city suffusing her. All the others who surrounded her shared her excitement.

What she could see of the city was extraordinary. The buildings were slender and intertwined, rising in a confusion of shapes, textures, and colors. The base of each building dug into the earth in a collection of brightly glowing roots, the gaps so narrow that they nearly merged. And the structures were vibrating, their boundaries indistinct and shimmering, individual buildings blurring together into a cohesive whole. Occasionally, the tip of a building would pulse, and a globe of color would expand into the sky, a series of after-images fading behind it.

Joy filled her, spreading its warmth through her body as tears rolled freely down her cheeks. She was connected to all of the others around her. This was where she belonged. She never wanted to leave. She had pierced a veil that had previously been hidden to her. Something in the world had become permeable which had previously been opaque. She was a witness to truth, the experience real in a way that she had never before known. She had returned home after a lifetime spent in the wilderness.

To her despair, the scene faded and she lost herself once more.

***

Jill's consciousness returned to the sound of chanting. She lay where she had fallen near the lab's cordon, her head twisted awkwardly to one side. A group of protestors marched down the street, calling out in unison. She saw, but could not read, slogans projected over their heads amongst a sea of raised fists.

She stood with a groan. Her head was pounding and her body didn't feel right. Something deep inside of her was shaking, and she was worried it would never stop. The wind blew cold against her face and she squinted against a painful, pelt-ing grit. Through a blur of wind-driven tears, she saw a mob of protestors surround the scientists, jabbing fingers and yelling, individual shouts rising angrily above the growing dispute.

Jill tried to get her bearings but she was all mixed up. She didn't know where she was or what she was doing. Why was she here? She probed her memory. It was like touching a ten-der tooth with the tip of her tongue. She turned in place, saw the yellow tape, the lab behind it, the soldiers with their guns ready as they monitored the confrontation.

She refocused on the protest, triggering her interface to en-hance the image until she could make out individual faces and slogans: "Hands off my genome", "My body is not yours to en-gineer", "You can have my DNA when I'm dead."

It all came back to her. Matt was dead. The lab was locked down. Like a dummy, she had tried to break through the line. The soldiers had shut her down and left her lying unconscious in the street like a discarded piece of refuse.

The protestors had pressed the scientists into a knot, cor-nered between a building on one side and the glowing yellow cordon on the other. They looked scared, eyes darting as they searched for an escape route, arms up in poses of submission. Joanne simply seemed resigned, her virtual cigarette dangling from her lips as she waited it out. As the march continued to-ward Jill, she lost sight of the scientists. They were swallowed whole by the mob. It was time for her to go.

She took one last look at the soldiers, tense and alert, not yet taking action. Then she turned to make a get-away before she too could be swallowed by the protesters. To her relief, her strength returned as she walked the empty streets angling away from the lab. The shouting and chanting diminished until it was lost in the background noise of the city.

When she decided she had walked far enough, she stopped

and called for a car to take her home. While she was waiting for it to arrive, she triggered her interface and tried to enter her professional-node. As she'd suspected, she was blocked. A failure to authorize notification popped up immediately, flashing red and black. She thought for a moment and then decided to try her personal-node; perhaps she could use a referential connection to get through a backdoor into her work material. Maybe in the confusion they hadn't completely locked her professional-node down yet. It was unlikely, but it was possible.

But as soon as she was inside her personal-node, she received a priority alert. There was a message waiting for her, and it was from Matt.

CHAPTER 7

"If you are reading this, then I am already dead," the message from Matt began. "As a fail-safe, I took the liberty of loading my construct into your personal-node. I know that you don't trust me. I am aware that I have given you specific reasons to distrust me, but please believe me when I tell you that you are in danger, and I may be the only help available to you. Activate my construct and it will do everything in its power to keep you safe."

Jill re-read the message three times. The first time she felt numb. The second time confused. The third time she read it she was angry. She activated the construct. It wasn't as good as getting answers from Matt himself, but if the construct had been programmed well, it would be close.

Matt appeared in her room, standing in front of her. "Hello, I am Matt's construct. I have been programmed in a limited set of domains and do not represent Matt's complete personality. I have been programmed to tell you this."

"What the hell is going on, Matt?" Jill spit out angrily. "Why are you dragging me into this..." she searched for a word, "this shit-show you've created for yourself?"

"I am programmed to help you in the following ways. I can tell you what has happened in the cleared facility and how it is related to your research. I can show you what happened to Matt on the night of his death. I can help you with strategies for survival. In what way would you like me to help you first?"

At this moment Pepe jumped up on Jill's bed and brushed up against her leg, purring wildly. "Not now Pepe!" Jill hissed. Pepe shimmered and disappeared. Jill looked at the empty space for a moment. He hadn't deserved that – she'd have to make it up to him later.

"Matt, I want you to tell me why you've been sneaking around and snooping into my research."

"Very well. I will tell you about what has been happening in the cleared facility and how it is related to your research," he responded.

Jill settled in. This had better be good.

"The lab where you work is built as a combined civilian and military installation. The reason for this is simple. The civilian research benefits from access to military funding, and the military research benefits from access to civilian results. My commanding officer's orders were to monitor your progress closely, while interfering with your research as little as possible. Of all the research being conducted in the lab, she believed your approach was the most novel and the most likely to result in success."

"Tell me something I don't know," Jill muttered under her breath.

"Over the past several months I was brought into a series of high-level planning meetings focused on a post-cloning world. Something happened that gave my commanding officer confidence that a solution to the cloning problem was imminent. After some probing, I learned the truth. While you had not yet found the solution, the military researchers had used your analysis to make enough progress to put human cloning within reach. It then became clear to all of us, that while you had not yet made a breakthrough yourself, it was only a matter of time before you found the solution."

Jill listened in stunned silence.

"This was the reason I wanted to speak with you last night. I assume it is also the reason I was murdered. If I am right, Commander Tros will most certainly be coming for you next."

"Why would your commander want to kill you?" Jill asked.

"In our planning meetings, it became clear to me that the power we were unlocking was beyond anything any of us had ever imagined. We had uncovered the Rosetta Stone for programming human DNA. This is a discovery that will enable the possibility of molding humans into any conceivable form. As you can imagine, given the military leadership, our planning has been primarily devoted to the active weaponization of this technology. Most of our discussions have centered around the possibility of creating and cloning massively enhanced soldiers," Matt explained.

"What was discussed? How would clones be turned into weapons?" Jill asked.

"Imagine if you started with the highest performing soldiers in the military, then removed any reservations they have to killing other human beings. Then you could boost their awareness and physical strength, increasing their lethality while adding regenerative healing capabilities. Imagine if you additionally removed all human propensities toward fear or doubt, instilling instead a perfect dedication to following orders. Once these soldiers were perfectly engineered, their clones could be mass produced. We could create an army of super-soldiers giving us a huge advantage over our enemies. Unlike most military hardware, the clones would have no trouble blending in with civilian populations, making them ideal for mixed-warfare combat.

"The implications of these ideas are frightening on their own, but I don't believe the project team has fully realized the possibilities available with this technology. We have entered a new age, one in which all our assumptions regarding human biological limitations will have to be rethought. What would stop us from giving these soldiers the ability to generate and deploy chemical or biological weapons? Imagine a clone that is the carrier of a deadly virus, but is himself immune to it. Imagine a clone that is designed to exhale a neurotoxin powerful enough to kill anyone nearby? These are just a couple of examples, and I'm sure with your background you could imagine many others.

"These... things could be produced in the hundreds of thousands. They would be inhuman, designed and raised with no moral structure, programmed with an overwhelming compulsion to obey. And because they are clones, they would be expendable. I am horrified by the implications, appalled by the ways in which this line of experimentation might go wrong. We are like spoiled, arrogant children, suddenly given the power to play at God.

"Because of my gender, I was not cleared for full access to your research. Everything I've picked up about the breakthrough has been second-hand rumor and innuendo. So I have to admit that I attempted to infiltrate your files. I was desperate to learn more, hoping that whatever I learned would somehow set my mind at ease, or failing that, give me a means to fight back. I wanted to enlist your help, but I couldn't figure out how to gain your trust. I wanted to warn you of what was coming, but I fear now that I am already too late," Matt trailed off, looking disconsolate.

"I was right then?" Jill asked. "I was right that we should treat our genome like a hostile system that has been actively blocking us from modifying it?"

"Yes. As far as I can tell, you were right. This seems to be the insight that allowed the military team to create a breakthrough solution."

Jill paused to think. "What is it then? What is the Rosetta Stone?"

"I can only tell you what I have been able to piece together." Matt paused for a moment. "We know that a form of genetic error-checking occurs at the cellular level, correct?" he asked.

"Yes, that's right," Jill said.

"And the majority of our DNA, over 90 percent, is junk DNA?" Matt added.

"Yes, this was discovered by the Human Genome Project in the late twentieth century. Junk DNA is a holdover from our distant past, useless data left behind by the random nature of evolutionary processes."

"The military team discovered that some of this junk DNA is not junk after all, but rather an encrypted storage mechanism used to error-check the active DNA."

"What?" Jill stammered.

"From my understanding, there is a biological encryption algorithm that generates checksums within every chunk of our genetic code. These checksums are decrypted and checked by our RNA as part of normal cell growth. If the decrypted checksum does not match the algorithmic expectations, the cell self destructs."

"I knew it!" Jill exclaimed, then she went quiet, growing thoughtful. "Wait a minute. The mechanism you describe is incredibly unlikely. How could humans have evolved an encryption algorithm in DNA? Sure, there is a form of error checking to limit harmful mutations, but why would encryption be involved? What possible evolutionary benefit could that provide?"

"The philosophical ramifications of this discovery are beyond my programming. It did not come up as a topic of discussion in the military planning meetings, and I cannot address that question. All I can say is that the new approach seems to work, where all other approaches have failed."

Jill narrowed her eyes, her mind churning over the new revelations, *I think the ramifications are significant. I wonder why you programmed your construct to ignore these factors, Matt?*

Matt's construct continued speaking, "I believe we have more important things to worry about. Matt believed your life was in danger, and I haven't seen any evidence to counter that belief."

"How did the military team get around the encrypted error check?" Jill asked.

"They found the encryption key."

"They actually found the key?"

"They devoted their most powerful AI research construct to it, searching exhaustively for correlations. They spent over 100,000 man-years of computing power on the problem. As of last week, they found what they were looking for."

"What did they find?"

"The key was found embedded in the electrical pattern of the human nervous system."

Jill's mouth dropped open. "But... that's impossible."

"Improbable, yes. Highly improbable. But the encryption key worked, and the project has entered the next phase. The team has started a series of experiments that will lead to the first human clone."

"How does it work?"

"Each of us has a unique electrical pattern, a signature if you will. This signature is as unique as our fingerprints. The pattern generated by the first few milliseconds of electrical activity in a developing fetus is used to generate a key that is stored within every cell in the human body. During cell division, the key is extracted and used to error check the DNA. If the error check fails, the cell division fails. If the error check fails throughout the body, then the body dies. I must say, it is a surprisingly elegant solution."

"That would explain why so many of our attempts at genetic engineering have failed," she mused.

"Once the team knew what they were looking for, it wasn't that hard to find. As you know, researchers have never had any reason to look for such a mechanism. That's why it was never found, until now."

"But why does limited genetic engineering succeed?"

"It seems there is some leeway built into the system. This allows for the type of genetic drift that is possible during natural evolution. As long as any genetic modifications stay within these boundaries, the changes will succeed. When the genetic modifications go too far, resulting in more changes than can be accounted for by random mutation, the error checks kick in and the genetically engineered tissue dies."

"But why would cloning fail? We aren't making any genetic changes in that case."

"In the case of a clone, you have a new nervous system with its own electrical signature, therefore a new encryption key is necessary. Because of this fact, the checksums from the cloned DNA will not decrypt properly, and the error-checks will fail. Unless you also modify the encrypted error check, the clone will not be viable."

Jill didn't know what to say. On the one hand, she was ecstatic. She was right! Her life work was a success. She would live to see full genetic engineering on humans, and get to see the results of human cloning. There were so many questions that could now be answered. Questions that had intrigued the human race since the earliest philosophers – the nature of the human soul, the importance of nature vs. nurture in the development of personality – she could investigate the very essence of what it means to be human. Her fingers itched to be back in her lab. She wanted to dive into the possibilities.

But if Matt was being honest with her, the entire scientific enterprise had been hijacked for military purposes. If that was true, this would all go terribly wrong. Her life's work would be used to enslave humanity instead of being used to free it.

Matt cleared his throat. "Jill, it's time for you to learn how I died."

CHAPTER 8

"Are you ready to see this?" Matt asked.

"Yes," Jill responded. She wanted answers.

"Permission to load the recording?"

"Permission granted."

<Start of Recording>

Jill saw herself walking away, out of the research space and down the hallway toward the elevators. She could tell it was the previous night by what she was wearing, but now she was experiencing the scene from Matt's perspective.

Matt stared at the last spot Jill had occupied before she turned the corner and disappeared. The conversation hadn't gone well. No matter how hard he tried to make a connection, Jill rebuffed his advances. He'd have to try another approach. It was imperative to gain her trust, show her somehow that he meant no harm. On top of that, Tros was going to expect him to report progress, and he had nothing to give her. It would not be a good idea to show up late to his meeting with her. He couldn't delay any longer – it was time get moving.

The civilian lab was quiet. Most of the researchers had long since left work and were now at home with their families. The military facility where he was meeting Tros was housed in the upper floors, which required bio-confirmation of his identity before he could enter. He pressed his fingertip on the elevator scanner, allowing it to take a DNA sample. The system compared his biometrics with what was on file, then the door slid open. Each floor had a different clearance requirement, and he was only able to access the first three; the remaining fifteen required increasingly higher clearance types that were way out of his league.

Once the door closed, a millimeter-wave scanner imaged his body, then a sniffer sampled the air for dangerous substances. Finally, a micro-lens performed a retina scan, completing the confirmation of his identity. Like everyone else, he had an auto-transmitting ID implanted in his brainstem, but that wasn't secure enough for Tros's purposes. Matt had heard of implants stolen from their unfortunate owners in order to impersonate them.

When the security system was satisfied that he was who his implant said he was, the elevator proceeded up two floors to where he was scheduled to meet Command Tros. He tried to clear his mind, a sense of anxiety forcing its way through his calm facade. What if Tros suspected his reservations about the project? Worse yet, what if she knew about the steps he'd already taken against her?

It was too late to worry about that now. What was done was done. He still couldn't completely quiet his mind, so he closed his eyes and pictured his daughter as clearly as he could. He used his interface to conjure her before him, as real as a living, breathing person. She was the reason he was doing this. She was the only thing left that mattered in his life. He would do anything necessary to ensure the world he left behind for her was better than what he'd had to live through. It didn't matter that he hadn't seen her in ten years. That wasn't her fault. He would make sure she had opportunities greater than anything he could have dreamed of. Right now, that meant making sure that his commanding officer didn't destroy the world.

Jason Taylor

As the door opened in front of him he clamped down hard, forcing his mind into placidity, then he stepped forward into the hallway. Since he wasn't allowed on the command floor, Tros was meeting him in an executive conference room not far from his own office. He proceeded to the meeting location, scanned in, and entered the room. She wasn't there yet, which was typical. She had no reason to value his time. He was tertiary. The meetings they had were a matter of due diligence for her, nothing more.

Matt waited another twenty minutes, increasingly impatient, before Commander Tros finally entered the room. She cast a disinterested look at him as he stood up and saluted.

"At ease soldier," she said brusquely, looking down at the old tablet she always carried. For someone who was launching them into an uncertain future, she had an odd attachment to the past.

Matt dropped his salute and waited for Tros to sit before taking a seat at the small table across from her. She was nearly six feet tall, as was the current style, and heavily muscled, which wasn't. Her hair was cut short and she wore a generic military uniform, no sign of rank evident. On her hip was a standard issue needle-gun, her thermo-armor further accentuating her bulk. There was no question that she was intimidating. It was a characteristic she used to impressive effect on her subordinates. Subordinates like Matt.

"Lieutenant, report."

"The civilians don't know yet. Their research proceeds as before."

"Even that girl?" she asked. She wouldn't use Jill's name, instead always referring to her as 'that girl.' She seemed to resent the fact that they needed Jill's help to reach their goal. Even if the help was inadvertent, Jill unaware of it and operating as an unwitting collaborator.

"Jill knows nothing, as far as I can tell. But she doesn't trust me. None of them do."

"Trust is irrelevant to this, you know that." She bore down on him with her eyes as she talked. Matt could feel himself shrinking into his chair. He was a mouse pinned by a hawk.

"If I knew more, I could do a better job of ascertaining how close the civilians are."

"You know you aren't cleared for that information. All you need to know is that we have moved to phase two of the project. We won't need the civilians around much longer, anyway." And we won't need you either, she didn't say.

"What are your plans for them in phase two?" he asked.

"Don't be impertinent." She glanced down at her tablet, distracted. Then she looked up again, a new glint of interest or curiosity in her eyes. "Lieutenant?" she said, almost delicately.

"Yes?" he asked, instantly on guard.

"Have you been poking around where you shouldn't be?" She was looking up at him intently, her head still cocked down toward the tablet.

"No, Ma'am," he said cautiously.

"I have a report here that says you accessed Jill's research files." She looked fully at him, an intense curiosity evident in her expression. "Now, why would you do that?"

Matt tried to say something, but all of his excuses died in his throat, confronted by those ice-blue eyes.

"I suppose it doesn't matter," she said, almost to herself. And then louder, "Soldier, you are dismissed."

Matt stood up, feeling shaken and confused. What had just happened?

He walked to his office, mulling their conversation over. The more he thought about it, the more worried he felt. He sat at his desk and considered his options. None of them were good. He realized he was going to have to take on additional risk. He bent to the task of pushing his AI construct to Jill's personal-node. Then he wrote her a note: "If you are reading this, then I am already dead."

As soon as he had completed the command sequence necessary to keep his construct hidden in the background of Jill's node until it was activated, his proximity alarm went off. Someone was penetrating his network defenses. He triggered his interface and started his defense protocols. The neural connection in his brainstem transitioned to full power as he closed his eyes, submerging his consciousness into his node, ready to fight back.

Matt immersed himself in the inky blackness of his interface, rushing toward a bright point, the light growing rapidly larger until he had plunged in headfirst.

He opened his awareness inside his node's defensive station – a small, bunker-like room with a control panel floating in the center. This simulation was merely how his mind interpreted the data being fed to him via his interface. It provided him with a familiar environment he could use to fend off whatever was attacking him.

He focused on the threat detection system, waiting a split second while it filled his field of view, absorbing the data it provided to him. It didn't take long to determine the reason for the alarm. Two constructs had opened an unmarked access panel and were attaching a small, black device. Matt sent a query and the defense system identified the device for him. It was a virtualized backdoor, a software mechanism that could be used to gain unlimited access to his node's data and other capabilities.

None of what he was seeing had any physical reality, of

course. His interface was visualizing the attack for him in a way that his mind could easily understand. It wasn't as accurate as looking at the running code, but he could react quickly and intuitively, allowing him to operate his defenses as if he had a physical presence within the node. His defense-bots were already actively modifying his node's firewall rules in an attempt to block the hostile incoming data. But he could see right away it wasn't going to be enough. The attacking constructs were making significant progress installing the backdoor. Someone was after his data. Evidently, someone knew what he'd been up to.

After signing on with Icarus, he had invested in a high-grade security system. It had seemed like the smart thing to do after dedicating himself in opposition to the cloning project. Now, it was time to put that system to the test.

He activated his offense-bot and instructed it to destroy the two constructs. He watched as the bot scuttled in, grabbed the closest construct in a vice grip, and pulled it away struggling. Naturally, the remaining construct didn't deviate from what it was doing. It didn't even look up as its companion was dragged away, instead remaining intently focused on completing the installation of the backdoor.

Matt panned his view to watch his bot destroy the first construct. To his horror, he saw the construct shake free and then it rapidly expanded in size. As it grew, it changed shape, transitioning from a vaguely human form into a brightly glowing blue orb, crackling with energy. His offense-bot backed away, one arm damaged and hanging loosely at its side. The orb pulsed once and his offense-bot froze, twitched, and was instantly disabled, falling limply to the ground. His bot shimmered for a moment, frozen in place, and then shattered into its constituent bits.

"Shit! Where did that come from?" Matt yelled, mind racing to figure out his next move. The constructs were more than they appeared. Whoever was attacking him had devoted significant resources to the assault. He looked at his screen, and to his shock the other construct, the one that had retained its human form, was observing him, a grim smile on its face.

"Goodbye Matt," the construct said.

"This isn't possible," Matt muttered. The construct couldn't have peered through his view. It couldn't have recognized his presence…

He didn't get a chance to finish that thought before he was pulled violently out of his interface, shocked by a blinding pain originating in his physical body.

While he'd been distracted defending his personal-node, his office had been infiltrated by a squad of military police. He was on his knees, the end of a neural-probe hovering just inches from his neck.

"Think he needs another one?"

"Yeah, hit him again."

Matt convulsed in agony as the neural-probe touched his neck, sending a series of commands into his brainstem. He lost control of his body as waves of fiery pain pulsed through him. A disconcerting warmth spread from his crotch down his legs as he emptied his bladder. He was on the ground, curled in a fetal ball, and as the pain faded, he could hear himself whimpering.

"Subject is secure. Let's make this quick boys, we have a lot to do tonight."

Matt's face was pressed into the ground. He couldn't feel his body. He couldn't even move his eyes. He stared straight ahead, unblinking, the texture of the floor so close he could pick out every detail of the composite weave. Boots walked past his head as the soldiers busied themselves in his office. He thought of his daughter. He thought of the information he'd sent to Jill. He hoped it would be enough. Unable to defend himself, he watched as the probe descended toward his temple.

Unending agony.

He writhed helplessly on the ground, stuck in his mind, begging for deliverance. He tried to trigger his interface and retreat into his node, but it was closed to him. There was no escape. Unable to control his body, unable to get away, it seemed as if his suffering would never end. He was desperately trying to maintain a grip on his sanity when the probe overwhelmed the last of his defenses. With a final quivering twitch his neural circuits overloaded and he lay still.

<End of Recording>

Jill opened her eyes, gasping, drenched in sweat. Matt's construct was standing in her room immobile, a weary sadness etched into his features. "I think it's time for us to talk about how we are going to keep you alive."

CHAPTER 9

Jill paced the length of the room, visibly shaken, trying to digest what she'd just experienced. She turned to Matt. "Why did they attack you?"

"I can only guess. Maybe they thought I knew too much. Maybe they decided I was no longer useful."

"What were you doing for Commander Tros? What was your role?"

"I was responsible for monitoring you and all the other civilian researchers, in order to keep you all in line. We were willing to use your work, but we couldn't allow you to discover the secrets of human cloning first."

"I knew I couldn't trust you," Jill spat back at him.

"It was a national security imperative. Commander Tros believed that whoever was the first to unlock general purpose genetic engineering would have a massive advantage on the world stage. This is bigger than just enhancing soldiers. Imagine a variety of clones, each optimized for a specific job, working tirelessly to serve our national interests. The clones can be worked to death if necessary, because when a clone dies a new one can be grown to replace it.

Imagine this army of clones networked together, combining their mental resources, working in perfect coordination with each other. It would allow us to harness the power of human intelligence in a way that has never been possible before. The impact of this technology could easily surpass that of the industrial and information revolutions."

"That's a frightening vision. Now that the lab has been nationalized, what do you think will happen to the other researchers?"

"I don't know. None of the others were as close to a solution as you, so I think for now they will simply be reassigned to different labs."

"Do you really think Tros will come after me?"

"I do. She knew you were close to figuring out the secret, and now that the military has a solution, she will move to neutralize anyone who she thinks could make a similar breakthrough. She needs to keep a lid on it. Removing me from the equation and shutting down the civilian lab was the first step. You are most definitely on their list, and once they find your connection to me, you will become an even higher priority. I don't think it's a coincidence that they attacked me as soon as I'd queued my message for you. We should assume they will be coming for you soon."

"You put me in additional danger?" she sputtered.

"They would be coming for you regardless of what I did. Maybe I sped up the timetable a bit, but now, with my help, you might just have a chance of surviving. Jill, We need to get moving. They are surely analyzing the data in my node right now. I can't say how much time we have left, but it won't be much."

Jill was in despair. "I don't know anything about running. Where am I supposed to go? What am I supposed to do? No matter where I run, they can find me. How can I possibly hide from the government with an implant in my head? They can track my every move."

"One step at a time. First, let's get out of the city and put some distance between ourselves and the lab. I know a place we can go." He spread his hands out in front of him. "You're going to have to trust me."

Jill narrowed her eyes. "Trust you? Now? After what you've just told me?"

"Do you have a choice?" Matt asked calmly.

Jill's shoulders slumped, the fire quickly going out of her. "No, I guess not. I don't seem to have any good choices left." She walked out of the room, toward the kitchen.

"Where are you going?" Matt asked, looking worried.

"Look, I don't know how long we're going to be gone. I need to get some food, and I need to let my flat-mates know I'm leaving."

"Wait, you can't do that."

"Why not?"

"We need to avoid anything that will trigger a flag in the monitoring systems. If you tell anyone what's going on, you could set off an immediate counter-response."

"I have to tell them something! If I just disappear, it's going to seem really strange. That could set off flags as well, right?" She stopped walking and thought about it for a moment. "What if I tell them I'm going on a short vacation? I could say it's to deal with the stress of the lab closure and all that. I can tell them I need to get away to clear my head."

"I think that could work."

As they entered the kitchen, Jacob appeared. "Hi Jill, how was your day?" he asked.

"You have a Jacob?" Matt asked.

Jill could feel herself blushing. "I installed him so I could practice talking with men." She turned to Jacob impatiently. "Not right now, ok?"

"That's alright Jill, I'll see you later," he said, and then he shimmered out of view.

Matt quirked an eyebrow at her. "I can see you're getting really good at it. Your practice has clearly paid off."

Jill could swear she saw the hint of a smile playing at the corner of his mouth. "How is this relevant?" she shot back.

"You're right. I apologize."

Jill turned pointedly away and asked the synthesizer to prepare her a meal to go. After graduating from college, once she'd saved enough money, she had formed an apartment co-operative with three other women. They shared all the costs equally and had divided the space between them. Over the years, the cooperative had added more women, expanding until it covered the entire sixth floor of their apartment building. The location wasn't the best, deep in South Seattle, but it felt like home. She'd grown to love it here. Now she had to leave, and she didn't know when she'd be able to come back.

She triggered her interface and immersed herself in the virtual common-room for her floor. While they had physical common space in the building, the shared kitchen being one example, the virtual rooms were more comfortable and more flexible, so they tended to get more use. Once inside, she found that Mary and Lenna were already there. They were sitting on a red leather couch, their heads nearly touching as they talked animatedly. Mary was a teacher, nearly ten years older than all the other women, a deep sadness evident anytime she let her face relax. The lack of a child weighed heavily on her, and the fertility treatments still weren't working.

Lenna was a hairstylist, her long blonde hair twisted in an intricate braid that started on the side of her head over her ears, extending halfway down her back. Usually Jill would have complimented her, but she couldn't bring herself to engage in small talk after everything she'd been through today.

"Hey Jill, I heard about what happened at your lab," Mary said.

"Sucks," Lenna added in.

"Thanks, it's been a hard day. The whole thing has hit me kind of hard I guess. I think I need a break. I'm going to leave town for a while. Maybe if I get away, I can clear my head and figure out what I'm going to do next." She could feel herself starting to tear up. It really had been a hard day, she wasn't lying about that. "Do you think you could watch my stuff while I'm gone?"

"Of course! Where are you headed?" Mary asked.

"Just somewhere north," Jill said, keeping it vague.

Mary's eyebrows pinched together, her brow furrowing. It was clear she was curious, but she wasn't going to push any further.

"I don't blame you," Lenna pitched in. "You must be super stressed."

"Um. Yeah, you could say that," Jill said, starting to feel uncomfortable.

"Have a great vacation, ok?" Mary said. "And don't worry about your apartment. We'll keep an eye on everything for you."

Jill nodded her thanks and then gave each of them a hug. She turned to the console on the wall and typed out a short message. It would let all the other women in the cooperative know that she was leaving so they wouldn't start to worry about her. Hopefully they could still get in touch with her through her node if they needed to.

With a distracted wave goodbye, she disconnected and opened her eyes back into her kitchen. "Ok Matt, let's get out of here."

Matt's construct was full of surprises. When she tried to call a car, he stopped her and put in the call himself. He used an alternate identity, reasoning that it would make it harder for the government to track them. Now they were sitting in the back seat, a constant backdrop of nondescript buildings flowing past the windows. She'd turned off all of her filters so she could watch the real world for a while.

"Matt?"

"Yes?" he said, turning toward her.

"You mentioned Icarus in the recording. What is Icarus?" she asked.

"Icarus is a he, not an it," Matt said, holding her gaze. "He's the leader of the Ghost Squad." He paused for a moment to gauge the impact on her.

"Ghost Squad? The terrorist hacker group? That Ghost Squad?!"

"Yes, that Ghost Squad."

"What the fuck! Are you in with terrorists? What the hell am I doing here with you? I need to get out of this car." She triggered her interface to stop the vehicle. She would figure out her next steps after she got out. Maybe she could go back to her apartment and pretend as if none of this had ever happened.

"Don't get out, you'll regret it," Matt said.

She froze. "Is that a threat?"

Matt sighed. "No. Not a threat. Just give me a moment to explain, ok?"

Jill took the time to think it through. Her lab was nationalized, that was a fact. Matt was dead. That was a fact too. His construct was in her node, so even if she went back to her apartment, he would still be with her. If she wanted to get rid of him, it would take some serious effort to delete him. She could do it, but she was already involved, already on the run in the government's eyes. Returning to her apartment wouldn't change that.

"Goddammit!" she growled, exasperated. "Go ahead. Try to explain it to me. Once you're done, I'm going to delete your ass out of my node."

"I told you about the dangers of the cloning project. You understand that, right?" Matt asked, trying to calm her down.

"There are concerns. I get that. But when have we ever let concerns stop us from making scientific progress. To expect us to stop researching a promising technology is to expect us to stop being human."

"Can we agree that we shouldn't let the technology stay in the hands of the military?"

"Yes," she agreed begrudgingly.

"When I saw the plans to weaponize these new genetic engineering capabilities, I started poking around. I was looking for someone who could help me slow Tros down. I found Icarus. He has blood on his hands, I know that, but he's also the head of the most powerful hacker collective in the country. I've been feeding him information, and he's been using it to organize protests and… some other things," Matt said.

"Other things…" Jill said skeptically. "What kind of other things?" She shook her head violently. "You know what. Never mind. I don't want to know."

Matt nodded, "Very well."

They emerged from the city into the northern exurbs. The damage caused by the Great Unrest was more evident here. The skeletal remains of old buildings stood tall and foreboding along the side of the road, and the surrounding earth had a blasted look. The areas outside of Seattle still hadn't fully recovered; it wasn't clear if they ever would. Jill turned her filter back on, and the wasteland was replaced by a scene from the late 20th century. There was a shiny green sign on the side of the road. "Welcome to Mt Vernon," it said in precise, white lettering.

"Where are we going exactly?" Jill asked.

"It's probably better if I don't tell you," Matt responded.

Jill shrugged. She was past the point of shock and well into numbness.

An hour later, after driving off the main road and through an aging network of secondaries, they arrived at their destination. It was an honest to God farmhouse surrounded by acres of open land. Jill turned her filters off and gaped. Still a farmhouse. A little older, a little more weathered, but the same building that her filter had shown her. The open space was still there too. The farmhouse was surrounded by a low, stubbly field, cottonwood trees forming a windbreak on the eastern side. A small creek ran at the back of the property, lushly vegetated with dogwood and elderberry bushes, alder growing like weeds wherever the trees could suck up some water. A few maple trees stood tall, their thick branches reaching out like welcoming arms.

Jill shut her mouth with a snap. "Where are we?"

"Welcome to the Overbee homestead," Matt said.

"This is yours?"

"My family's. Well, we have rights to it." He paused. "It's complicated."

"Matt, I had no idea."

A small kernel of joy tingled in her belly. A farmhouse. A real farmhouse! She grabbed her bag, walked up the porch to

Jason Taylor

the front door, and stepped in.

CHAPTER 10

Jill sat on the front porch, watching the sunset and enjoying the view without the need for a filter. As the air cooled, a light mist rose from the field, white tendrils pushing their way through a sea of yellow stalks left behind by the fall harvest. She heard the gurgle of a creek, and the soft hoot of an owl. It was very peaceful. This far from the city, when the sun finished setting, it would also be very dark. She was going to enjoy looking at real stars.

She knew she was ignoring her problems, but she was at her best when she could relax, when she let her subconscious work on a solution without her conscious mind getting in the way. In the meantime, she would wait patiently. Cultivate her zen. She had even convinced Matt's construct to turn itself off for a while. She was completely alone.

"What if I contacted Icarus?" she thought aloud.

"What?" Matt said, suddenly in front of her looking incredulous. "Contact Icarus?"

"I thought you'd turned yourself off," Jill said indignantly, her sense of calm shattered.

"I was. Well, more like in standby. I didn't want to leave you entirely alone. It's far too dangerous."

Jill glared at him.

He was the picture of innocence and concern.

"Ok, whatever. Let's get to work." She took a deep breath

and said it again. "What if I contacted Icarus?"

"That's a terrible idea."

"Why?"

"First of all, he's a known terrorist. Contacting him could get you in serious trouble."

"You contacted him," she said.

"And look where that got me."

"Fair point," she nodded. "What else?"

"What do you mean, what else?" he asked.

"You said first of all. What's second?"

"Right. Secondly, he's dangerous. Very dangerous. He has reach. Both physical and virtual. You don't want to mess with him."

"I'm not planning on messing with him. I'm planning on asking him for help."

"Help?"

"Yes."

"Why would he help you?" Matt asked.

"You said he's against the cloning project, right?"

"Yes."

"And you think the military branch of the cloning project is trying to kill me?"

"Yes."

"Enemy of my enemy," she said.

Matt was looking at her like she was crazy. He probably wasn't wrong.

"You know? The old saying? The enemy of my enemy is my friend." Jill looked up at the darkening sky, the first stars prickling through. "God help me, it looks like we're on the same side now."

After thirty minutes of not being able to talk her out of it, Matt eventually agreed to help her contact Icarus.

"The first thing you need to know about Icarus is that he is arrogant. Extremely arrogant. He believes he has skills that no one else has. Who knows, maybe he's right."

"Arrogant, check. Also dangerous. Good combo." Jill shook her head, trying to make light of her increasingly desperate situation.

"Yes, also dangerous." Apparently, Matt wasn't programmed for humor. "The second thing you need to know is just because you try to get in touch with him, it doesn't mean he'll respond. If he does respond, he will do it on his own time-line. We may be taking a huge risk for nothing."

"I understand that. Do you have any better ideas?" she asked angrily. "It doesn't matter what we do. If we stay, Tros will find us. If we run, she will still find us. We don't know how much time we have, but it isn't much, right?"

"Yes, that's true."

"Then let's get started."

She closed her eyes, triggered her interface, and entered her personal-node. She was inside a perfectly white cube, her node-console floating in the center, Matt standing to one side. This was her clean-room. It was the safest virtual location she owned, and it was her best option for contacting Icarus without immediately bringing the authorities down on her head. All the data transmitted from this room was routed through a series of anonymized servers spread randomly across the world. It didn't mean she couldn't be tracked, but it would require more time. Hopefully, enough time for her to make a plan with Icarus that would allow her to see tomorrow morning alive.

"Let's do this," she said.

Matt pulled a thin, black needle from his jacket pocket and inserted it into the console. It was his personal signature, programmed to single-cast to Icarus's node. If Icarus was listening, he would see that Matt wanted to talk. If he chose to talk back, he'd follow the signal to Jill's node and initiate a connection.

They waited.

Five minutes later, a figure wearing a Guy Fawkes mask appeared in Jill's clean-room.

"Really?" she said to Icarus.

"What?" Icarus asked, surprised.

Matt looked horrified and was making small hand motions, trying to get Jill to stop being provocative.

"You are the world's most famous hacker, and you show up wearing that?" Jill asked.

"What's wrong with my avatar?" Icarus asked.

"It's unbearably trite. Didn't you hackers move away from the whole Guy Fawkes thing ages ago?"

"Maybe I like to respect the past."

They stared at each other for a few tense moments and then Icarus bent over laughing. "I've been using this avatar for years. Years! And no one has ever called me out on it." He kept laughing. "You're literally the first one."

When he'd finished laughing, he pulled the mask off, tears of mirth rolling down his cheeks. He had high cheekbones and a broad forehead framed by a shock of black hair. His eyes were the palest of blue, set off by a dark ring at the edge of each iris. He was striking.

"I need your help," Jill said.

"Ok, we've had our fun. I came here because of Matt's signature, and I'm willing to listen to you because you amuse me. But I don't have much time, make it quick."

"Matt's dead." Jill said, hoping to throw him off guard.

"Yes, I know," he said, unfazed.

"Tros has discovered how to make a human clone."

"Yes, I know that too." He was tapping his foot, looking impatient.

"I know how she's going to do it," she said, rushing the words out.

That caught his interest. "Say that again," he said slowly.

"I know the secret to human cloning," she said, and then she looked away from his intense stare, unable to maintain eye contact.

"Now, that is interesting. Tell me what you know. You have my full attention."

"I won't tell you anything until you give me what I need first. You have to promise to help me."

"I can't help you. No one can. You're fucked." Icarus said it with zero emotion, as if he were talking about the weather.

"What do you mean? Why can't you help me?"

"Tros's goon squad is on their way right now. In fact, they are converging on your little farmhouse as we speak. No one can help you, not even me. What I can do for you, is make sure that the information you carry lives longer than you do. I can set your data free. If you give it to me, then by tomorrow morning everyone will have it. I'll broadcast it to the world."

Jill's legs gave out and she sat down hard. She could feel tears starting at the corners of her eyes.

"Ok," she said.

"You'll tell me what you know?"

"Yes," she said.

And then she did.

When she left her node and opened her eyes into the real world, the farmhouse was cold and dark, the air stagnant, wet, and clammy. The mist had risen from the fields and crawled through the open door, laying like a ghostly blanket across the floor. As she walked to the front porch it stirred around her feet, fingers of white mixing with the air in ragged swirls.

She stood on the porch for a while, then she stepped down onto the gravel path that led toward the road. Once she'd gotten far enough away from the house, she stopped and looked up to the stars. She thought about how an uncountable multitude of distant photons had traveled for tens of thousands of years and were just now, with incredible improbability, ending their journey by falling through her eyes and into her retinas for her brain to interpret as tiny pinpricks of light.

She spread her arms and spun in a small circle, letting the sensation of epoch time and space sweep over her. But she didn't even last long enough to feel dizzy. She managed two rotations before the needle took her in the neck, dropping her to the ground with a muted thud.

CHAPTER 11

Jill gasped awake, opening her eyes into an unfamiliar room. She was sitting on a cold metal chair, her wrists shackled to a gleaming, steel table. On the other side of the table paced a tall, muscular woman in military uniform. Jill recognized her as Commander Tros from Matt's recording. The same Commander Tros who had killed Matt and now was undoubtedly going to kill her too.

"Hello, Jill," Tros said.

"Where am I?" Jill asked, frantically searching the room for clues.

"Let me introduce myself. I'm Commander Tros, and you are currently inside one of my safe-rooms."

"I know who you are. What are you going to do with me?"

"The answer to that question is complicated. It depends very much on your answers to my questions," Tros said, placing both of her hands flat on the table, her bulk looming over Jill's seated form.

Jill fought to calm her breathing. She needed to focus. The last thing she remembered was talking to Icarus. And a farmhouse. It was all a bit hazy around the edges.

"How do you know Matthew Foster?" Tros asked.

"Do you mean Matt from the lab?" Jill asked. When Tros nodded, she continued. "He worked in the lab with me. I know he's in the military branch of the cloning project. That's all I know."

"Have you had contact with him before he spoke with you in the lab yesterday?"

"Why are you asking me these questions? You must know the answers already. Anything you don't know you can get from my implant with a neural probe."

"I want to hear it from your own mouth, in your own words. I believe that sometimes the old ways are still the best."

Jill stared at Tros, flustered. "I saw him in the lab sometimes. I didn't like him. I thought he was spying on me," she stammered.

Tros put an old fashioned tablet on the table and made a notation with a slim stylus. "Ok," she said. "How about yesterday? Tell me about all of the interactions you had with Matthew Foster yesterday."

Jill shook her head, trying to clear it. "Let me think. I went to work like normal. When I got to the lab it was locked down. I talked to Joanne and she told me that Matt was dead. She also told me the lab had been nationalized. I was upset."

Tros looked up from her tablet. "Go on."

"I received a message from Matt. He loaded an AI construct into my personal-node. The construct confirmed that Matt had been killed."

"Good. That matches our record of your activity. I want to thank you for telling me the truth so far." She leaned forward. "Now, tell me about Icarus."

"Icarus?"

"Jill, don't toy with me. I know that you've been consorting with terrorists. The question I'm asking myself now is, are you a terrorist too?"

"No. God no. Of course, I'm not a terrorist!"

Tros narrowed her eyes, "I'll be the judge of that. Now, tell me about your interactions with Icarus."

Jill slumped in her chair. "Matt's construct told me that the military had killed him. I suppose that was you, wasn't it? Are you going to kill me too?"

Tros leaned back, arms crossed, waiting for her to continue.

Jill took a shaky breath, gathering her courage. "He told me that you are planning to use cloning technology to create super-soldiers. Weapons without conscience. He told me that you are going to network the clones together and turn them into slaves. It's inhuman. We had to stop you!"

"And you believed all of that?" Tros asked.

Jill felt like her heart was going to explode in her chest.

"What kind of an idiot do you take me for?" Tros demanded. "Who in their right mind would create weaponized zombie super-soldiers and expect everything to just work out? That's some serious end of the world shit right there."

"I... um," Jill started to say and then stopped, confused.

"Goddamned, self-righteous, pointy-headed academics. No end to the headaches you people cause me. Whatever convinced me to take this God-forsaken command, I don't know..." she trailed off. "Jill, let me clue you in." She reached down and pushed a finger hard into Jill's forehead. "You have no idea what you are doing. You have no goddamned idea how much trouble you have caused me." Tros sat down heavily in her chair.

"I don't know what you're talking about." Jill felt very small and very lost.

"Let me start with this. Matt's not dead. Did you think we'd kill one of our own? That's not how this works. Do you think you're living in a goddamned spy novel?"

"Matt's not dead?" Jill's head was spinning. "What do you mean? I saw him die. I experienced it."

"You saw exactly what he wanted you to see."

"Why would Matt want me to think he was dead?"

"Not Matt. Icarus. He set you up. Matt's been spying on the cloning project for years. We took him into custody last night. Icarus loaded the construct into your personal node as soon as he learned we'd arrested Matt."

"What?!" Jill was halfway out of her chair, her wrists still pinned to the table. Tros was looking at her with satisfaction.

"Did you even think to verify any of the things that construct told you?"

"No, I... everything was moving really fast. We were on the run," Jill finished lamely.

"On the run from whom?" Tros asked.

"From you?"

"And why would we be after you?"

"Because you killed Matt. Because I knew too much. Because..." Even as she said it, she realized it sounded absurd.

Tros was looking at her appraisingly, letting her puzzle it out.

"Wait," Jill said. "You must have been searching for me. Otherwise, I wouldn't be here, would I?"

"Once you contacted a known terrorist and gave him the solution to the cloning problem. Once he broadcast it to the world. Yes, once you did those things, we came after you."

"Oh," Jill said in a very small voice.

Jill thought back to all that had happened in the past day. It still didn't add up. "But why did you nationalize the lab. You're taking over the cloning project, aren't you?"

"After we arrested Matt for conspiring with Icarus, our security protocols required a clean sweep of the lab. We couldn't let anyone into the building until we were sure we had contained the problem. We have found a solution to human cloning, that part is true. And it has been in large part because of your research, that part is also true. Unfortunately, the technology is just as dangerous as the construct told you. My priority is to protect this breakthrough so it cannot be used by our enemies."

"But the construct was the one who told me about the breakthrough in the first place," Jill pleaded, desperately trying to maintain a grip on reality.

"The construct that Icarus loaded into your personal-node was cutting-edge AI tech. Impressive stuff. Almost military grade," Tros said begrudgingly. "Its job was to extract the information it needed from you and then convince you to transmit that information to Icarus. It succeeded in that mission."

"But how? I didn't even know what the breakthrough was."

"But you did. Or at least you were close enough. The construct penetrated both your personal and professional nodes and then assembled your research analysis into a working hypothesis. It used its conversation with you to verify the correctness of its theory. And... well, you know the rest."

Jill felt infinitely tired. And worse, she felt the fool. She had spent the last twenty-four hours being manipulated. Everything she'd been told had been a lie. She felt used. Dirty. Worse yet, she had no idea what the truth was anymore, or who she could trust. On the bright side, she was still alive.

"What now?" she asked wearily.

"Your actions have been treasonous, there's no question about that. Being naive, idealistic, and misguided does not absolve you of your guilt," Tros said sternly. Then her expression softened. "It also doesn't change the fact that I need you."

"Need me? For what?" Jill asked, hope flaring in her chest.

"Thanks to you and Icarus, we are now on a level playing field with every other nation on earth. Our only remaining advantage is if we can move faster than everyone else to capitalize on this breakthrough. I need all of the genetics researcher I can get my hands on, and unfortunately, you are one of my best."

The shackles popped open, freeing Jill's wrists. Jill gaped at Tros as she held out her hand. She tentatively reached out and took it. Tros's hand was large, wrapping all the way around Jill's much smaller hand, and to Jill's surprise, it was reassuringly warm.

"Welcome to the Ganymede project, Jill. We have no time to waste."

PART 2

CHAPTER 12

World Zero: 2081

"Hello everyone, welcome back for another live-cast of World Events with Holly Sharper. I'm happy to have both Megan Duncan and Lisa Flanner with me in the studio again. Tonight we will be unpacking the latest news coming out of the Ganymede project. There is a lot for us to talk about, so let's get started."

Holly turned to Megan. "After the shocking release of information by Icarus last year, we haven't heard much from the researchers at the Ganymede project. Then this week, they dropped a bombshell on us. Apparently, they have perfected the cloning process and are ready to start with human volunteers. Megan, what are we to make of this?"

"Well Holly, we've known for almost a year that cloning is theoretically feasible, but this is the first time we've heard about any solid, practical progress. It looks like the folks at the Ganymede project have been busy!"

Holly turned to Lisa. "What do you think Lisa? Do you still have objections to the use of this new technology?"

"Frankly, I'm not convinced it's going to work. I think their efforts have been blocked for a purpose, and I think they will continue to be blocked. There is a divine will at work here, mark my words. Who can look at the extremely sophisticated error-checking each of us has inside of us and say that it is not the work of Providence? It is my sincere belief that human cloning is against God's will. Perhaps, in our arrogance, we have figured out how to get around his first restriction, but God works in powerful and varied ways. If it is His will that we should not clone humans, then we will find ourselves forever blocked. We are shaking the very branches of the tree of knowledge, fighting over who can be first to taste the forbidden fruit," Lisa said with fervor.

"But Lisa, what are we to make of statements, directly from Government representatives, that they have figured out how to make the cloning process work?" Holly asked.

"I'm sure they believe that, but I think they will be surprised," Lisa responded.

"Be that as it may, the huge moral and political implications of this development are worth discussing. Lisa, what do you say to Megan's doubts?" Holly asked.

"I don't think any of us can know if it will work," said Megan, "not until after the human trials are complete. But I am going to predict a successful outcome, and we will all have to grapple with the consequences. The President has already stated her desire to see clones fully integrated into our society, with equal rights to an original. But what impact will that have on the rest of us? What if someone creates a thousand clones. Would they all vote in the same way as their original? Could this just another way for the administration to consolidate power?"

"Interesting point, Megan. And what about discrimination? Do you think clones will face intolerance from the rest of society?" Holly asked.

"In my congregation, we teach that every life is valuable," Lisa said. "But it is going to be a hard sell with clones. Especially since we believe that cloning is contrary God's will. I tell my flock that they should hate the sin, but love the sinner. In this case, I don't even know who the sinner is. Is it the original who allowed themselves to be cloned? Is it the clone who was created in sin, without any choice in the matter? Is it the scientists who create this blasphemous technology? You might say the clone is blameless, but isn't the clone an exact copy of the original? If the original were a murderer, for instance, how are we to look at the clone? Are they just as capable of criminal intent?"

"Legally speaking, each clone will be their own individual," Megan responded. "Otherwise, there would be mass confusion. We need to think of them more like children than copies. Just as twins are considered individual people, clones will be as well."

"This is a fascinating discussion, and I'm sure these issues will play out in Congress, in the Courts, and in forums of public opinion," Holly said. "Let's talk about the encrypted error checking in all of our DNA. Megan, do you feel this is a sign of divine will, as Lisa claims?"

"No, I don't. I think it is a beautiful example of the miracle of evolution. I could give you a long list of biological structures that were once used as examples of why evolution couldn't possibly be true. Let's take the human eye, for instance. Anti-evolutionists would argue that it is impossible for evolution to create a structure as sophisticated as an eye through the processes of random mutation and natural selection. We know now that those objections were unfounded. Evolution, given enough time, can give rise to the most incredible results. Encrypted error checking inside our DNA is just one more example of that fact. It's true that we don't understand the evolutionary pressures that would have led to encryption in human DNA, but that doesn't mean we won't eventually find them. We just don't have the answers, yet." Megan said.

"I couldn't disagree more," said Lisa. "I don't think we will ever find an evolutionary explanation for genetic encryption, because there isn't one. It is quite clearly an example of intelligent design. It took humans how many millennia to come up with the idea of encryption? You want me to believe that it somehow randomly arose in our genetic structure? That is so incredibly unlikely as to be laughable. And how would you account for the fact that no other animal shares this feature with us? In this regard, humans are held a step above the rest of the animal kingdom, exactly as the Bible has always told us was true. I know that my religious community is in the minority on this, but that doesn't change the correctness of our views. Genetic encryption is the best proof of a God that we have ever seen. Unfortunately, we live in a secular society, and the significance of this discovery is lost on most people, yourself included."

"Many people say that this discovery is proof of a human soul. Lisa, I think you would agree with that statement. Megan, what do you say to that?" Holly asked.

"This proves nothing about the soul. The existence of the human soul lies in the realm of philosophy and religion, not science. I don't think the Ganymede project has anything to say about the presence of souls, and it never will." Megan concluded.

Mary triggered her interface and turned the broadcast off. She was sitting in a white, clinical waiting room with three other women: Julie, Gurata, and Claire. They had been hand-picked by members of the Ganymede project to produce the first set of human clones. She'd learned from the doctors that they had wanted to include men in the cloning program, but XX chromosomes had proven to be more robust than XY. Cloning men didn't work, so for now, it was only women. One of the women had brought her husband, however, so there was a token man in the room with them. He was sitting on the edge of his seat, waiting just as expectantly as the rest of them.

Mary was both nervous and excited. She closed her eyes and sent another silent thanks to Jill for nominating her for the trials. Jill had known that she wanted a child more than anything else in the world. None of the fertility options had worked for her. Cloning was her last chance. Maybe it wouldn't be the same as raising a normal child, but it was an incredible opportunity. No one had ever had the experience of raising a clone of themselves. When she thought about it, her mind boggled. She would get to hold a baby version of herself, raise herself as a child, send herself to college, see herself get married. The thought of all those milestones made her feel giddy with anticipation. She was so extraordinarily lucky.

A woman wearing a lab-coat with the swooped wings of the Ganymede logo came into the room. "Hello, ladies. I want to thank all of you for volunteering to participate in this historic moment. I also want to thank the millions of interested viewers who have joined us via live-cast. This is the moment in which we turn dream into reality. The moment in which we kindle new life from each of you. It is truly the start of a new era." The woman paused to let her words sink in. Then she walked to each woman in turn and took a small tissue sample from the skin of her finger, from the back of her neck, and a from a snippet of her hair. The procedure had the feeling of ritual, each moment imbued with meaning as the samples were taken and filed for every participant in the trial.

"We have taken the necessary tri-fold samples. We will use this genetic data to create your clones. You may each monitor the progress of your clone through a feed we will make available in your interface. If all goes well, the clones will be ready for you to bring home in nine months. I look forward to seeing each of you then. From all of us at Ganymede, we thank you for your willingness to donate your genetic code and for your dedication toward raising the first generation of human clones. Because of you, a new chapter in the history of humankind has begun." She terminated the live-cast and left the mothers to make their way out of the building.

Jill and Tros had been watching the live-cast from another room, deep in the lab.

"Do you think it's a mistake to allow the originals to raise their clones?" Tros asked.

"Why would it be a mistake?" Jill responded, puzzled.

"It's a unique situation. One that has never occurred in the history of humanity. No one has ever had to raise a clone of themselves. We have no idea what kind of psychological ramifications that will have."

"That's true for cloning in general. The entire situation is unique."

"I suppose you're right. But I feel we may be making a mistake on this one. Perhaps we should have used foster parents."

"There has been enough resistance to conducting this trial in the first place. If we were to take the clone children from their originals. Well... I'm not sure we could get away with that," Jill said.

"I guess you're right. To be frank, I was beginning to wonder if we would ever get the Ganymede project authorization passed through the Senate. I've never seen so many protests. We're lucky to have a sponsor as powerful as Senator Thompson on our side," Tros said.

"Here's to new horizons," Jill said, raising her glass of beer. "Cheers."

"Cheers to that."

CHAPTER 13

World Zero: 2082

It was the happiest day of Julie's life. There had been some delays, but her baby was going to be delivered to her today. The last ten months had passed so slowly. Looking back on it, she felt as if she'd been holding her breath the entire time. She had put the rest of her life on auto-pilot while she waited.

It had taken forty-three separate cultures, none growing into more than a few dozen cells, before one of them had finally started growing into a human baby. She had remained glued to her feed as the cells multiplied and the fetus grew. She had watched as the organs developed and as her baby grew tiny hands and feet. She had watched, terrified that something would go wrong, while the scientists recorded her clone's initial electrical activity, generated an encryption key from the pattern, and then used a viral carrier to update the error-checking DNA in every cell throughout her tiny body. Julie had known that if this step failed, her baby would die. She was already in love. She couldn't imagine bearing such a devastating loss.

But it had gone well and now here she was, ready to meet her baby for the first time in the flesh. She wasn't the first to pick up her clone. Some of the others had been ready earlier. She had watched on the live-cast as Gurata had picked up Suki, and again when Mary had picked up Elizabeth. She had fought back pangs of jealousy and focused instead on feeling happy for these other women. They were all sharing the same path, were they not? Did it matter if some took the first steps earlier than others? What difference did a couple of days make? In the end it made no difference at all, and now it was her time.

Julie sat in the waiting room, wringing her hands and chewing on her lower lip. It was a nervous habit she had never been able to break. When Dr. Jill Clarence entered the room, Julie stood up, smiling tremulously.

She'd seen Dr. Clarence in the live-casts, but had never met her in person before today. She was tall and slender, brown hair tied back, tucked beneath her coat. She had long, expressive fingers. *Piano-playing fingers*, Julie thought. She knew her mind was wandering. She was nervous.

"Can I see my baby now?" Julie asked.

Dr. Clarence took Julie by the elbow and ushered her through the waiting room door. "Yes, of course, Mrs. Petersen. Will you come with me please?"

"Is everything ok?" Julie asked, trying to keep the tremor out of her voice.

"Don't worry, everything's fine," Dr. Clarence replied, smiling back at her reassuringly. "It's completely natural to have some nerves today.

All other thoughts were forced out of her head as soon as they entered the nursery. Her little June was laying in her pod, perfect and pink. Julie's heart burst with love as she leaned forward and picked up her new baby girl.

World Zero: 2084

Gurata and Suki were at an indoor park with a group of other two-year-olds and their parents. Gurata still couldn't shake the sense of miracle that had overtaken her when she'd first laid eyes on Suki. Every day that sense of wonder only grew. Suki looked exactly like Gurata had looked when she was a child. It was like looking at a miniature version of herself, with her straight black hair, round face, and dark, soulful eyes. Late at night when Suki was sleeping, Gurata and her husband would sometimes look at old images of Gurata as a child and compare them with the new ones of Suki. Then they would shake their heads in amazement. How could this be possible? How could humans have become so wise and so very powerful that they could create a new life in such a miraculous way? Gurata considered herself a religious woman, but she didn't believe that clones were abominations like some people did. God was good. Suki was a gift from God. It could be no other way.

She watched Suki play, a beatific smile on her face. She was such a calm child. A little bubble of peace surrounded by the whirlwinds of energy that were pouring off all the other children. She sat in a patch of dark, green simul-grass, her chubby legs sticking straight out in front of her as she gnawed on a doll in her mouth. One of the other boys came close and she held the toy out for him to take. She was always interested in sharing, always wanting to connect with the other children. The boy didn't notice, so Suki stuck the doll back into her mouth and closed her eyes in silent bliss.

World Zero: 2085

Mary and Elizabeth were working on the alphabet. She was three years old and making fast progress. Mary wasn't surprised. She'd been a quick learner in her youth too.

"Excellent, Elizabeth. What comes after W?"

"X, Mommy," Elizabeth cooed, her eyes wide, entranced by the picture-book.

Mary believed in using real books at this age. Elizabeth would have the rest of her life to look at virtual objects and to practice using her interface. Now was the time to engage with the real world.

"Mommy?"

"Yes, Elizabeth?"

"Am I a real person?"

"Of course you are! Why would you say that?" Mary felt angry, but she tried not to let it show. Elizabeth was sensitive and she didn't want her to think she was in trouble.

"Some of the other kids teased me."

"What did they say to you, Elizabeth?"

"They called me a copy," Elizabeth responded thoughtfully. "Jenny says I'm a fake. Some of the bigger boys called me zombie-girl."

"Oh darling, they don't know what they're talking about. You're just as human as anyone. Don't let anybody ever tell you otherwise."

"I won't, Mommy." Elizabeth hesitated a moment before adding, "Mommy, I said some really mean things to them. But I know they deserved it." Elizabeth looked back down at the book, her eyes intent on the pictures. "Mommy, were there really horses with stripes when you were a little girl?"

"Yes, darling," Mary said, distracted and troubled. "They were called zebras."

World Zero: 2087

Julie was so happy. So very happy. That's what she told herself. But actually, she was anxious. So very anxious. June was fine. She was more than ordinarily beautiful, with her olive brown skin and bright blue eyes. And the doctors at the lab said she was developing entirely normally. There was nothing wrong. But that didn't do anything to make the sick feeling of dread go away. Julie spent her nights tossing and turning, unnamed fears twisting in the night. She spent her days glazed and absentminded. She had already used her interface to push her blood chemistry as far as it would go, trying to feel normal again, but it was never enough. She'd thought about black-market modifications for her implant but had pushed the idea aside. It wouldn't help June if her mother was in jail or mind-shredded.

Today was a big day. It was June's first day of school. Julie told herself this was the reason she was feeling anxious. It was the first time they would be separated for more than a couple of hours.

Like most people, they were within walking distance of their designated school location. She and June were walking through the pedestrian tube, enjoying the beautiful fall leaves that were projected on the inside.

"Ooh, look at that one Mom. That's the biggest leaf I've ever seen," June shouted. She ran forward, triggered her interface, and pulled the leaf from the wall into her hand. She held it up, making it sparkle, then flash into a variety of colors. "Mom, look at that. Isn't it pretty?"

Julie suppressed a shudder. June was unnaturally skilled with her interface, better than most adults. If Julie was honest with herself, she would have to admit that June was better with her interface than any adult she had ever met. Any adult she had ever heard of. Pulling the leaf from the wall was impressive enough for a small child, but how was she changing its colors?

Meanwhile, June had turned the leaf into a butterfly and was chasing it around the tube. "Mom, look! Mom, look! I can catch the butterfly." She held her hand out and the butterfly landed gracefully on her palm.

Julie looked around to see if anyone had noticed. Whatever June was doing, it was unnatural, and the last thing she wanted was to attract unwanted attention. "Come on, June. We need to go, or we'll be late." She grabbed June's arm and started pulling.

"Wait, Mom. No! I need to put him back. He might get hurt!" June yanked her arm away and ran back to the wall of the tube, depositing the butterfly gently on a bush swaying in a light breeze. The butterfly folded its wings and hunkered down to wait out the wind. June smiled, nodded once in satisfaction, and then ran ahead of her mom toward school.

Julie's nerves were about June's first day of school, right? Nothing else was wrong. Nothing else was wrong.

World Zero: 2088

Mary lay at the bottom of the stairs bleeding, Elizabeth by her side. Elizabeth was touching the end of the chopstick, pushing it back and forth, prodding it like it was a science experiment. She put her finger in the blood pooling on the floor and held it to her nose. Then she touched it to her tongue, grimacing at the strong taste of iron.

"Mother, you taste bad," she said

Grandma clamped her mouth shut and backed slowly out the door. She was looking at Elizabeth like she was a wild animal. Or a monster. Her face was a rictus of fear, her footsteps slow and quiet.

Elizabeth looked up. "Gamma, would you taste Mother too? Can you tell me why she tastes so bad?"

Grandma turned and ran.

CHAPTER 14

Jill sat next to Mary's hospital bed, holding tightly onto her friend's hand. She'd come hours ago, as soon as she'd heard what had happened, and she hadn't left Mary's side since. Jill felt responsible for what had happened. It was obvious that something had gone horribly wrong with Elizabeth.

"Where am I? Where's my Elizabeth?" Mary asked, her voice slurring.

Mary's words jolted Jill out of a half-sleep that she'd been in for she didn't know how long.

"Oh Mary, I'm so sorry." Jill blinked away a tear, brushing at it angrily with the back of her hand.

Before Mary had moved out and into her own house, they had lived together in the apartment building for years, sharing in the co-op, gossiping in the common-room, sharing their meals together. Jill had been so happy she could offer Mary the opportunity to have a daughter through the cloning program, knowing that all the fertility treatments she'd tried had failed. Now look where it had taken them.

Mary tried to sit up. "Where's Elizabeth? Is she ok?"

Jill put her hand on Mary's shoulder, encouraging her to lay back down. "Mary, you shouldn't be moving yet. You've been badly hurt." Jill could see Mary grappling with that. Trying to remember. Then she saw the realization of what had happened hit her hard.

Mary's face crumpled. "Why did she do it, Jill? What's

wrong with my Elizabeth?"

Jill bent forward until her forehead touched Mary's, and then she let the sobs take her too.

Elizabeth was in a strange room. All the walls were soft. The floor was soft. Even the ceiling was soft. She triggered her interface and reached out, trying to sense a connection. There was nothing. She let her interface fade. She blinked. She swallowed. She thought.

Tros was in the control room, watching the video-feed of Elizabeth in her cell. Her hand was on the back of a chair, currently occupied by a young security officer. He was so green, Tros could almost smell the Academy on him. But he seemed like a good kid, trustworthy and level-headed.

"Have there been any changes in her behavior?" Tros asked.

"Nothing yet, Ma'am."

"Remarkable! She's been immobile for the past eight hours?"

"Yes, Ma'am."

"That is not normal behavior for a seven-year-old."

"Neither is stabbing your mother. With all due respect, Ma'am."

"No, I suppose not."

Elizabeth stood up and cocked her head. She could sense something. There was a feed in the room. She could feel it sucking up data-bits and sending them away. She turned a little right, a little left, cocked her head and tried to isolate the location of that feeling.

Tros watched in fascination as Elizabeth rose languidly to her feet, her movements unnaturally smooth. It gave Tros the chills. Elizabeth moved her head like she was sniffing at the air, then she looked directly into the feed. Her eyes seemed to lock onto Tros. It was impossible, but Tros could swear she saw a hint of recognition in those eyes, like she knew that a video-feed originated from that exact point inside her cell.

Elizabeth walked closer, until the monitor was completely filled with her face. Then she smiled, teeth glistening, the smile never reaching her eyes. Tros felt her blood go cold. Whatever was in that room, it wasn't human. She could feel the lizard part of her brain running in circles and gibbering. Telling her it was time to run, time to get the hell out before things got worse.

The security officer's skin had a grayish cast. His mouth was open, and he was gaping at the screen. Tros watched him pull himself together.

Good kid.

"Ma'am, what do you think we should do?"

"Nothing son. Carry on. Let me know if anything else changes."

On the screen, Elizabeth was casually picking at her teeth with a fingernail. She was still staring straight out of the monitor and she still hadn't broken eye contact with them. Tros had more to say but dared not voice it. *I've no idea, son. We've sailed off the map and into the unknown. Here there be dragons.*

The drugs had worn off, and Mary was fully awake. The chopstick had gone deep, puncturing the top of her lung, but it hadn't hit anything else vital. The wound had been closed with sealant and was starting to heal due to a judicious application of growth stimulant.

"Jill, why did she stab me?"

"I don't know. That's the honest truth. It could be a side effect of the cloning process. Something we missed. Or it could be a natural personality defect. Sometimes people turn out wrong. We don't always know why."

"She's supposed to be an exact copy of me. How could she do this? I would never stab anyone. I can't imagine ever wanting to hurt anyone, especially not my mother."

"I know. We have our best people working on it. We'll figure it out."

"What about Elizabeth? Is she going to be ok? I want to see my little girl."

"I'll see what I can do. But it might take some time. It's not a good idea for you to see her right now. She's safe, you have my word on that, and we are taking good care of her. Right now, you need to focus on healing yourself."

Jill left Mary's room and found an empty room she could use to meet with Tros. She closed the door, checked to ensure a sound-wall was in place, and triggered her interface. When she closed her eyes, she found herself in a simulacrum of a conference room from the lab, a setting they were both comfortable in. Tros was already there, sitting at the table, looking troubled.

"What's wrong?" Jill asked, sitting across from her.

"Elizabeth's behavior is puzzling. She spent most of the day motionless in her cell. Then about an hour ago she gave us reason to believe that she knows about the video-feed."

"That's not so surprising, is it? It seems natural she would assume we are watching her."

"For a seven-year-old?" Tros asked.

"Ok, yeah. That's weird," Jill admitted.

"That's not all. We think she knows where the video-feed is originating from. She walked directly to the aperture and appeared to be looking through it."

"How could she possibly know where the aperture is? Could it be a coincidence? The cell isn't very big."

"That would be my first assumption too, but I was there, Jill. She searched the feed out and then she walked directly to it. She's been staring through it ever since. Tom is in the security office monitoring her. I think he's close to a breakdown."

While they talked, Elizabeth was in her cell, toying with the feed. She teased individual bits out, flipped the ones and zeros, and then pushed them back in again. It gave her something to do.

"Hold on," Tros said. "Something's happening."

Jill watched as Tros's forehead wrinkled in consternation. She could tell that Tros was talking to someone outside the node, so she waited until the conversation was over.

"What's going on, Tros?"

"We might have a problem. The feed is starting to break up. Tom thinks someone is interfering with the signal. I'm afraid we may have another spy in the building. If someone is blocking the signal, it can only mean one thing."

"They're trying to break her out?"

"Yeah, that's what I'm thinking too. I've got to go." Tros shimmered and disappeared, leaving Jill sitting stunned and alone.

Elizabeth was getting bored. She'd already figured out what each combination of bits did. It was obviously a video-feed of some sort. Since it was minimally encoded and compressed, it must be a high definition signal to somewhere physically proximate. That meant someone was watching her. She decided it was time to put on a show.

Tom was monitoring the feed when it happened. Elizabeth turned her back to the aperture and walked to the middle of the room. She pivoted slowly on one foot like a ballerina, graceful and lithe. She smiled at Tom and then she winked. Tom sat back with a gasp, totally unprepared for what happened next.

Elizabeth exploded. The unraveling started at her head. Her skull separated, torn down the center, and then the tear ripped through the rest of her body, pulling it violently apart, leaving a mess of gore on the floor and walls. Tom jumped up and screamed, pure shock and disbelief. He probed with his interface, looking for vitals, knowing he'd find nothing. He could see it with his own eyes. There was literally nothing left, the little girl was gone. He sent the query for vital signs, knowing without a doubt that it would come back reporting that the girl was flat dead.

That's when the carrier signal reached up through the connection and into his brainstem. With a quick pulse, it fried his neurons. He slumped back into his chair, slack-jawed and twitching.

In her cell Elizabeth smiled, one finger twirling lazily through her dark brown hair.

CHAPTER 15

Jill was the first to figure it out. She tapped into the feed and watched as Elizabeth seemed to explode. She was just as shocked by the sudden violence as Tom had been, but she immediately started analyzing the data. Within a minute her analysis-bot told her that the feed had been doctored. A minute later the feed reverted to show Elizabeth sitting calmly in the middle of the cell, legs crossed.

"Did you see that?" Tros asked over a private connection to Jill. She sounded out of breath, like she had been running.

"Yes, that was ... unexpected," Jill said.

"You can say that again. Who do you think is behind it?" Tros asked.

Jill thought about the moments leading up to the incident. She thought about the look on Elizabeth's face. She thought about that wink. It was as if Elizabeth had known what was about to happen and was taunting them.

"You're going to think I'm crazy, but I think Elizabeth was in on it."

"How is that possible?"

"I don't know. I need to perform additional analysis on the feed. I'll get back to you."

When Tros arrived at the control room, she found Tom unresponsive – no breath, no pulse. She triggered a med-bot and got it started on medical analysis. It was quite clear that Tom was dead, but Tros couldn't imagine what could possibly have happened to him. She stood over his body, trying to put her thoughts in order. The situation was spiraling out of control.

She triggered her interface and gave the command to lock down the lab. Nothing physical or virtual would be allowed to exit the building until she figured out what was going on. She took another look at the monitor. Elizabeth was sitting peacefully in the center of her cell, eyes closed, perfectly still. Tros tried, unsuccessfully, to suppress a shudder.

Jill dug deep into the recorded data stream from the feed. What she saw was concerning. She watched it repeatedly, trying to uncover its secrets. First, she watched the visuals. Then, she studied the bot analysis. Finally, she reviewed the raw data. The first thing she noticed in the recording was the interference. It appeared random at first, but by the third time through she could tell there was a pattern. It was as if someone was tampering with the stream, touching a few data-bits here, moving a few data-bits there. The result was a pattern of visual static as the feed protocols worked around the resulting errors.

The degradation in the feed had led Tros to assume that someone was interfering with the signal. After further review, it seemed more like someone was trying to figure out how the video protocol worked. Over the course of several minutes, the interference became targeted, focusing on control parameters and data structures. Then it stopped suddenly, never having caused enough of a problem to break the feed entirely. As an attempt at interference, it was incompetent. As an attempt to reverse engineer the protocol, it was brilliant.

It was not possible for Elizabeth to know that there was an aperture in the cell watching her, and she shouldn't have been able to tamper with the video-feed. But the data Jill was looking at was leading her toward a very different conclusion.

The cell was certified to hold cyber-terrorists. Elizabeth was a seven-year-old girl. The analytical part of Jill's brain was finding all of this incredibly fascinating. The rest of her was seriously freaking out.

Tros stood in the control room, six members of her counter-intelligence team working around her, focused on reviewing the forensic data and trying to figure out what the hell was going on. So far, they were just as stumped as she was. Tros watched them at work, deep in thought until she was interrupted by a chime from the med-bot indicating it was done with its examination and ready to provide an analysis.

She gave the med-bot permission to push the data directly to her node, and then triggered her interface so she could review it. She closed her eyes and concentrated on the representation of Tom's body floating in front of her.

"Start analysis," Tros commanded.

The image of Tom zoomed in until she could only see his upper body, the lower part of his body cut off at the waist, apparently unimportant for this analysis. The representation showed his vitals floating above his head, biological monitors nominal, all in the green. His heart-rate was high but within the normal range for someone under stress. Brain patterns were all within range and so were the blood markers. This part of the recording was from the moments before the feed interference had started, before Tom had mysteriously died.

The timer started to tick down. Tom's heart-rate and blood pressure jumped sharply upward, followed closely by a spike in blood levels of cortisol and adrenaline. It was a classic shock reaction. This must have been the moment when Elizabeth had appeared to explode.

Tros watched as Tom's brain pattern re-organized itself. He was accessing his interface, the neurons around his implant synchronized into the unique pattern that occurred when-ever someone tapped into the network. Tom made a vital-sign query for Elizabeth. It exited his interface, flowing through Elizabeth's holding cell firewall to where it was translated into a command querying her implant for an array of med-ical information. Tom was reflexively checking on the health of the clone after seeing her explode. The firewall interpreted the results from Elizabeth's interface, then routed them back to Tom. That's when it all went to shit.

Shortly after Tom's interface received the response, there was a massive spike of activity in the neurons around the implant in his brainstem. In a deadly chain reaction, over-ex-cited neurons spread the signal to the rest of his brain, flow-ing from one neuron to the next, unstoppable. Tros watched as the signal continued to ramp up until it passed a critical threshold, overwhelming his neurons. Sections of Tom's brain began to die off. The neurons closest to the implant were the first to be affected, the visualization changing from bright red, representing overload, to black, representing a complete absence of brain activity. Waves of red and black spread rap-idly outward and within a few seconds every neuron in Tom's brain was dead. Neural overload.

Tros was stunned. She took a steadying breath as she ac-cepted an incoming communication request from Jill.

"Jill, what do you have for me?" she asked.

"Tros, it's worse than I thought. Not only did Elizabeth know what was going to happen with the feed, she was the one who was manipulating it. I'm having a hard time believing it, but the data is incontrovertible. She hacked the feed."

"To what purpose?"

"I'm still trying to understand that. The hack showed up as interference at first, but once she reverse-engineered the protocol, Elizabeth was able to replace the real video with the fake images of her death. I don't know what to make of it, but it's alarming."

"You don't know the half of it," Tros said. "Tom's dead."

"What do you mean, Tom's dead? What happened?" Jill asked, real shock in her voice.

"I'm looking at the med-bot data and it appears someone attacked his implant, causing a neural overload. Please tell me that Elizabeth isn't responsible for that too."

"Send me the data and I'll see what I can find. Boss, I don't like where this is going."

"You and me both," Tros said, pushing the med-bot analysis to Jill's node. "In the meantime, no-one, and I mean no-one, is allowed to communicate with that clone."

After an hour, Jill was sure of what the data was telling her, but she still couldn't believe it. After two hours she was convinced. Elizabeth had killed Tom. She'd attempted to hack his brain through his interface, but it hadn't worked. The mistakes Elizabeth had made in her hijack attempt had killed Tom as surely as if she'd put a needle-gun slug through his head. What Elizabeth had done shouldn't have been possible. No one had ever attempted what she was doing, much less achieved it. Sure, with a neural probe directly interfaced to an implant, you could do all kinds of nasty stuff. But remotely hacking someone's implant through a vital-sign query? That should not have been possible.

Jill let her head droop, hand on forehead. She was going to have to rethink what was impossible now. They all were.

She opened a connection to Tros. "I have some bad news, boss. You were right. Elizabeth is responsible for Tom's death. I don't know if she intended to kill him, but it was definitely her. It looks like a brain-hacking attempt gone wrong."

"Keep talking."

"Elizabeth sent a carrier signal over the top of the vital-sign query. I think she was trying to take control of Tom through his implant. When the attempt failed, it killed him."

"I didn't think that was possible."

"Me neither, but it happened."

There was silence on the line for two long seconds and then Tros came back, loud and clear. "We need to recall every single one of those clones."

"I agree."

"I'll get on it." Tros cut the connection.

CHAPTER 16

Jill rode with the extraction squad to a park in East Seattle where they expected to find Suki and her mom. According to the node logs, Gurata had left her apartment on Capitol Hill at 14:07, arriving at the park at 14:33. Jill would have preferred to retrieve Suki from her home, but Tros had pushed the mission ahead, feeling that the situation was too volatile to wait for the clone and her mother to return.

Jill had never been involved in a military mission and she was nervous. In an attempt to break the ice, she turned to the squad leader and introduced herself. "Hi, I'm Jill." They had sat together during the mission planning meeting, but they hadn't actually exchanged names.

The soldier turned to Jill, a serious expression on her face. "Hello Jill, you can call me Alpha."

"You're name is Alpha?"

"I'm Raven squad leader. My tag is Alpha. We use tags for ease of communication."

"Oh. Do the others have tags too?"

"Bravo, Charlie, and Delta," she said, pointing at each soldier in turn. Bravo was rolling a copper coin through his knuckles. The coin's motion paused for a moment as he grunted in Jill's direction. Charlie wore a baseball cap, dark brown hair pulled into a ponytail, her face impassive. She gave a slight nod. Delta grinned at Jill and gave her a wink. "Nice to meet you, Jill. We got you covered, don't worry."

"Listen up team, there are some things you need to hear before we hit the target. Jill's got intel to share on the situation with the clones," Alpha said.

Jill took a deep breath, folding her hands in her lap so she'd stop fidgeting, hoping they wouldn't notice her nerves. "We don't know exactly what's happening with the clones, but the situation is um… unstable. Elizabeth, one of the other clones, had some sort of a mental break and stabbed her mother. We managed to sedate her and secure her in a level 1 security cell, but… well… something happened." Jill paused. The members of Raven squad were watching her intently, waiting for her to explain. They were sitting in the vehicle on two benches running lengthwise, three of them were sitting on one side, including Jill, the other two sitting across from her. Jill leaned forward so everyone could hear her as the vehicle bumped and swayed through the grey, broken streets of Seattle.

"Elizabeth figured out how to hack through her cell's firewall and into the brain of one of our security officers. It killed him instantly."

Alpha raised her eyebrows, looking surprised. Bravo grunted, he looked impressed. Charlie remained inscrutable. Delta's smile disappeared, replaced by a scowl.

Jill continued, "We don't think all the clones have this capability, at least not yet. But we don't really know what they can do. Suki will look like a normal seven-year-old girl, but don't be fooled. She is unpredictable and potentially very dangerous."

"Kinda like you Charlie," Delta said, breaking the mood.

"Listen up, Delta. Don't interrupt," Alpha barked.

Jill spoke up again. "Once we're at the park, we should transmit as little information between us as possible. We don't know if Suki can listen in. Probably not, but I think it would be best to play it safe."

"Radio discipline people," Alpha said. "You know the drill. Only transmit when necessary, and keep it short."

The rest of the team nodded.

"Anything else, Jill?" Alpha asked.

"Thank you for helping me apprehend Suki. I hope it all goes smoothly."

"Ok people, this is a standard tag and bag mission. You know what to do. Jill will attempt to bring the target in willingly. Our job is to maintain the safety of the mother and any bystanders. If things get hot, we will sedate both the girl and the mother and pull them from the location immediately. Any questions?"

Alpha waited for a moment and then nodded, leaning back on the bench satisfied. "Let's get this done."

Jill endured the rest of the ride in silence, watching the city flow past the windows. She wondered what it had been like when the buildings had been whole and the streets had been lined with trees. Real trees, not the virtual ones that her implant tricked her brain into seeing when she turned on a filter.

They arrived two blocks from the target location and the team, plus Jill, exited the vehicle. Alpha took command. The park was located in an underground structure that had once been used to store cars but was now repurposed as a covered, open space for children and families. It was laid out on multiple levels, each filled with simulated vegetation as well as projections of trees and green-space to create a feeling of outdoor spaciousness. As was standard practice for an indoor park, the ceiling was masked with a realistic projection of the outdoor weather, currently a partly-cloudy sky, storm clouds threatening rain on the western horizon.

Alpha entered first. She was dressed in citizen-casual and she felt naked without her tactical armor, but the mission required stealth and subterfuge more than raw combat power. If all went well, her team would be superfluous.

Bravo followed close behind, dressed similarly and acting as if he was her husband. She took his hand and they began to stroll, playing the part of lovers, surveilling as they walked. Charlie and Delta entered next, taking a different route to extend the search radius as quickly as possible. Jill entered last. She sat on a park bench and pretended to read, waiting for the moment when Suki was found.

After the team finished a combined circuit of the entrance level, Alpha and Bravo moved to the upper level while Charlie and Delta moved to the lower. The risks of splitting up were outweighed by the need to find the clone as quickly as possible.

Alpha paused, Bravo by her side. She pulled him into a close embrace, pretending to whisper something into his ear. She used the moment to scan behind him, passing her gaze over scattered groups of parents and children. Suki wasn't in any of them. She kept Bravo in her embrace and accessed the park-node, confirming that Suki and her mother were still here. Unfortunately, she couldn't achieve better location resolution. The thick concrete walls of the structure impeded the signals, reducing their accuracy considerably.

"Target located," Charlie's voice crackled through Alpha's interface. "I have a visual."

"Roger, moving," Alpha responded.

Alpha and Bravo continued their stroll, angling toward the ramp to the lower levels, careful not to hurry or look like anything other than a couple enjoying an afternoon walk in the park.

"Jill?" Alpha transmitted.

"On my way," Jill responded.

Alpha and Bravo used a downward sloping ramp to drop to the entrance level and another ramp to reach the level below. Due to the circular nature of the route, it took them a little over three minutes to arrive where Jill, Charlie, and Delta were waiting for them. Once the squad was in position, Alpha nodded to Jill. It was up to her now. This was the riskiest and most dangerous phase of the mission. Success or failure hinged on how well Jill could play her part. If she got it right, Alpha and her team would be unnecessary. If Jill got it wrong, Alpha would have to take action, and it could get ugly fast.

Jill walked calmly to where Suki's mother was sitting on a bench. "Hello, are you Mrs. Choy? Mrs. Gurata Choy?"

Suki's mother looked up from the virtual book she was reading. "Yes, I am. And who are you?" Mrs. Choy's smile was genuine and warm. She inclined her head to look up at Jill, one hand raised to shade her eyes from the light of the virtual sun.

"I'm Dr. Clarence, from the lab. I don't believe we've met," Jill said.

"Oh yes, of course. I recognize you from the live-casts," Mrs. Choy responded, a small worry-line appearing between her eyebrows. "Is everything quite alright?"

"Everything is fine. I've just come to let you know we need to do a physical checkup on Suki. I know its unscheduled, but as you're aware, we make the health of your child our number one priority."

"This is rather irregular, isn't it? Why wasn't I sent a notification? I could have brought her in myself if you needed me to."

Jill shot a glance at Suki. She was in the process of pulling a toy truck out of the hands of a young boy. "This checkup is important. We decided it would be more efficient if we gave you a ride."

Mrs. Choy nodded. "Well, I suppose that's thoughtful of you. Wait just a moment while I pack up my stuff."

While Mrs. Choy gathered her things, Jill watched the little boy stand up. He was holding onto his truck tightly with both hands, his face red with anger. Suki pulled hard, tearing the toy from the boy's grip and knocking him off balance. He took a few steps to recover and then moved toward Suki, fists balled up, ready to lash out. But Suki stepped deftly out of the way, pivoted in a short arc, and swung the toy truck into the back of the boy's head. The blow propelled him face first into the grass, where he lay still for the space of one long breath. Then he pushed himself upright and opened his mouth wide, a howling cry ready to emerge.

Before he could make a noise, Suki moved in. She pushed him to his back and dropped her knee onto his neck. All that came out of his mouth was a soft squeak. As the boy fought for breath, Suki inspected the toy and then dropped it carelessly to the ground, already bored with it. The boy struggled to breathe, writhing on the ground as Suki added more weight, increasing the pressure on his throat.

Jill stood frozen. Suki looked so innocent, it made the violent behavior that much more shocking. She was about to intervene when Mrs. Choy turned to let Suki know they were leaving. Before her mother could see what had happened, Suki stood up and walked over, a bright smile on her face, the boy forgotten behind her.

"Momma, is it time to go?"

"Yes honey, I'm sorry we can't stay any longer. This nice lady is going to take us to the lab for a checkup."

"Ok Momma, I'm ready."

Alpha rode with Jill, Suki, and Mrs. Choy in one vehicle, the rest of the squad returning to the lab separately. She didn't want the presence of her squad to alarm Suki. Alpha was going to be happy when the clone was secured and sedated. She didn't know what was wrong with these clone children, and quite frankly she didn't care. All she cared about was seeing this mission through to the end.

Alpha reviewed the other mission data while they were in transit. Suki was one of the last of the children to be picked up. The other clones were already tranquilized and placed in a series of secure cells. Most of the other extraction missions had gone off without a hitch. Unfortunately, Falcon squad had stepped into a casualty situation. Their target clone had killed her original before the squad had arrived.

The Falcon squad leader had been notified, en-route, as soon as the mother's vital-signs flat-lined. As a result, the squad had transitioned into combat protocol – tac-armor energized, needle-guns drawn, their interfaces linked and primed. When they arrived at the target location, they had found the apartment dark and still.

Claire, the mother, was found suffocated in her bed. The clone, Ava, was playing calmly on the floor, rolling the beads from her mother's necklace against the cold tiles, listening intently to the sound they made. When Ava saw the squad enter the room, she grinned at them as if they were there to entertain her.

"May I have your gun?" she asked the squad leader.

They injected a mild tranquilizer to keep her compliant, and returned her to the lab. Toxicology reports showed that the mother had been drugged before she'd been strangled. How the child knew to drug her mother, was beyond the scope of the initial analysis.

Back at the lab, Alpha followed Jill, Suki, and Mrs. Choy into an examination room. Once they were all inside, she triggered her interface to close and lock the door. Step one was complete. The clone was secured. Next was sedation. Jill's job was to perform a routine checkup and then make up an excuse for either an injection or a neural probe, either of which could be used to sedate Suki, after which they would transport her to a cell. Alpha stood immobile by the door as Jill got to work.

"Mrs. Choy, we've recently discovered that there may be a slight genetic abnormality in some of the clones. Nothing to be concerned with, but we need to check Suki and correct any issues that we find," Jill said.

"Oh my. Are you sure I shouldn't be worried? That sounds bad," Mrs. Choy responded.

"May I call you Gurata?" Jill asked

"Yes, of course."

"Gurata, the abnormality appears to be latent and shouldn't express itself as a health problem. But we want to be absolutely sure. Suki's wellbeing is essential to us," Jill continued.

Alpha watched Suki as Jill talked. Suki's eyes darted between her mother and Jill, then she looked appraisingly at Alpha. Alpha saw a flash of recognition as Suki realized what Alpha's role was. She observed Suki's heart rate increase, followed by a marked dilation of her pupils. Adrenaline response. It was time to take action. She needed to sedate the clone immediately. Alpha quick-drew her needle gun and brought it up, aiming at Suki's center of mass.

When she sighted down the gun, Suki was no longer there, moving faster than Alpha would have thought possible. Alpha tracked her weapon right as Suki jumped on top of the examination table, armed herself with a med-probe in one hand, a loaded needle in the other, then dove for cover behind her mother.

Mrs. Choy took several faltering steps back before catching

herself against the table. An image of Mrs. Choy's confused face passed across Alpha's vision as she kept her focus on Suki, trying to anticipate where she would appear next.

In a flash of movement, Suki popped out, throwing the needle at Alpha's face before disappearing back behind Mrs. Choy. Alpha dodged down and left as the needle skimmed past her head, embedding itself in the wall behind her. She stood and circled left, sidestepping smoothly in an attempt to improve her firing angle.

Suki emerged again, probe whistling as she swung it in a long arc at the end of its lanyard. Alpha watched in horror as the end of the probe struck Jill in the temple. The doctor's eyes rolled back, legs crumpling as she dropped to the floor with a meaty thud.

Suki bared her teeth and barked out a yip of pleasure, her eyes gleaming. Alpha brought the needle gun to bear and let a triad of needles fly.

CHAPTER 17

Jill felt a blow to her head, saw a flash of light, and knew she was going to hit the ground. For a while, she was aware of nothing. There was no pain. Then she was aware that she was in a dark space. She stayed in that place for some time.

She opened her eyes and found herself in the midst of a dream.

She knew it was a dream because she was in the same gleaming, glowing city she'd seen so many times in recurring dreams over the past year. The dreams had started the day the lab was nationalized, the same day that she had been tricked by Icarus into following the Matt-construct to the farmhouse where she had given away the cloning project's secrets. Ever since that day, she'd been dreaming about this city.

In all the other dreams, she had been on the outside, separated from the city by a body of water. This time was different. This time she was on the inside.

She was surrounded by wonder, the city glowing and pulsing around her. Buildings soared upward, elegant and curved, each alive with its own light. The street she was on, if it could even be called that – a rolling, rambling gap between the buildings – was filled with the presence of Others. She could sense them. She could feel them pushing into the space around her. She could hear their murmurs, but she couldn't see them. Wherever she looked, the Others were forced to the corners of her vision.

It didn't matter, not when compared to the overwhelming wonder that surrounded her. Her heart was full, brimming with joy. Her mind was electric, ideas snapping like lightning. She was filled with a manic sort of intelligence. And the Others. Even if she couldn't see them, she could feel them. She knew they loved her. And she loved them. They'd known each other for an eternity. They were connected, all a part of some great and glorious whole.

She felt that she could see both the surface of objects and also deep into them, as if she could see through the superficial framework of reality. It was as if she was in a higher dimension, the interconnectedness of everything suddenly plain to see. This is what it must feel like for a two-dimensional being to glimpse a three-dimensional world, she thought to herself. This is the real world. I've always lived in a shadow. I've lived in the shadow of a shadow.

It wasn't only the physical objects that seemed this way. Her thoughts and emotions were charged in ways she had never before experienced. The joy she felt diminished all past joy in comparison. All previous thought seemed childish and naive compared to what she now knew. Who was this other person that she had been, she wondered. How could she ever have been satisfied with that ghost of a life, when this glory had been waiting for her all along?

She let herself be pulled along by the Others. They led her into a warren of interconnected rooms. Each room a new wonder. Food to taste – glorious in its fullness and complexity. Music to hear – incredible in its grace and expression. People to meet – each a new soulmate, another individual whom she felt she had known all her life and beyond.

The rooms were connected by meandering pathways, each covered with a glowing mesh-like roof. The colors from the buildings pulsed into the mesh and down the walls. Each pulse had significance. Each color had something to say. Everything around her, every mote of dust, was infused with meaning. The Others nodded. *Yes*, they said. *This is the way it has always been. How could you have forgotten?*

I haven't forgotten. There was simply a time when I didn't remember, she responded. *I remember now. I remember everything.*

Then she felt herself pulled away, the lights growing dimmer, her joy turning to ash, her connection to this new world violently severed.

***

Jill woke to the sound of screaming.

CHAPTER 18

Jill's head throbbed and the tile floor was cold against her cheek. She heard a scream, then the pounding of feet followed by shouting. She opened her eyes to pandemonium. From where she was lying she could see Alpha along with the three other members of her squad, all in tactical armor now. To her right, she could see Mrs. Choy's slender legs, and beyond that, the examination table. Her eyes fixated on the buckles of Mrs. Choy's red pumps.

Bravo was shouting at Mrs. Choy to drop to the ground. Mrs. Choy was screaming, a high, keening sound that pierced through all the other chaos.

Jill pushed herself to her hands and knees, levered herself up, and sunk back onto her haunches. She was dizzy and her head hurt, but she was mobile. She scanned the room, looking for an opportunity to make a difference.

"Suki, drop the probe. Drop the probe now!" Charlie yelled. Her body armor made her look menacing and faceless, the tactical helmet shiny and insectile. Alpha was still in street clothes, needle gun in hand, aiming at Suki, a pattern of small holes in the far wall showing evidence of each of her missed shots.

Suki was on the examination table standing behind her mother, the probe energized and held close to her mother's neck. Her teeth were bared, eyes wild.

The situation was currently a stalemate. A very volatile

stalemate. The soldiers couldn't get a clean shot from where they stood, nor could they move forward as long as Suki was threatening her mother with the probe.

Mrs. Choy was rigid with fear as she faced the combat team, their guns pointing in her direction. Her daughter's arm was wrapped tightly around her neck, the probe sparking inches away. The high pitched keening continued, Mrs. Choy's eyes wide and uncomprehending.

Nobody was watching Jill. She racked her brain for something she could do as the situation in the room teetered on the verge of collapse.

Suki made a hissing noise, the probe dipping closer to her mother's neck. Charlie took a step forward, drawing a bead, trying to get a shot off on the clone, but she was moving erratically, unnaturally quick, her head bobbing in short, blurred movements. "Don't have a clean shot boss," Charlie transmitted, her voice cold and deadly.

Jill started to crawl, just as another round of shouting broke out from the squad. She heard the distinctive popping sound of needles as they disrupted the air above her. Jill took a deep breath, swallowed her fear and continued crawling toward the edge of the room, trying to get behind Suki. So far, the clone seemed to be focused on the soldiers, unaware of Jill or perhaps she simply didn't consider her a threat.

Once Jill was behind the table, she stood up and made eye contact with Alpha, just long enough to get her attention and transmit a message to her interface – "Cover me!" Then Jill made a move to grab Suki's arm, attempting to pull the probe away from Mrs. Choy.

Suki was only seven years old. Jill knew that if she could get a grip on her, she could overpower her and the stand-off would end. But as soon as she sent the message to Alpha, Suki turned and swung the probe in Jill's direction, the active tip sizzling through the air. Jill leapt back in surprise, tripping over her feet, arms windmilling.

As Jill bobbled backward, Suki pounced, the probe closing in on Jill's face. Jill's back hit the wall, she had nowhere left to go. Her hands rose up in a movement of involuntary self-protection as she braced for the probe to make contact, cringing away from the inevitable intrusion of neural signals that would enter her implant and brain.

Before Suki could make contact, Jill heard the soft sound of needles impacting flesh. Suki's eyes widened and her face went white as the needles deployed their chemical and electrical payloads before exiting in soft puffs of blood from her shoulder, neck, and chest.

Suki's momentum took her to the floor where she rolled to her side and then lay still, the probe clattering to a rest in the corner.

Jill sank to the floor, hyperventilating in shock, her back flat against the wall. The soldiers flowed around Mrs. Choy, securing Suki with a neck clamp interfaced to her implant to ensure she stayed unconscious until they had her locked in a cell. Suki's hand twitched involuntarily, the fingers slowly curling and uncurling.

Jill's clasped her hands together, trying to calm their trembling. She was sitting in the executive conference room with Tros. She'd been called there, ordered really, directly after the incident in the exam room. She clenched her hands, willing them to stillness. She was angry, and she was confused, and she needed to know what the hell was going wrong with the clones.

"You've looked better," Tros commented

"I've felt better," Jill responded. Her right hand moved involuntarily to her temple, probing the tender spot where Suki had hit her with the probe.

"You should get some rest. You won't do any of us any good if you drop dead of exhaustion."

"I don't think I can sleep. Not now." Jill wanted to change the subject. "Do you have any new data on the problem?"

Tros nodded. "We've interviewed most of the originals, everyone except for Mrs. Choy. We had to sedate her after what happened with Suki. We've also completed the debriefs with the combat teams. I took the liberty of pushing the complete analysis to your node."

"You've read through it?" Jill asked.

"Yes."

"What are we dealing with?"

"I honestly don't know. I was hoping you could tell me. Each of the clones has had an unremarkable childhood until the past week. All test results have been within expectations: medical, behavioral, psychological, and academic. Everything has been as you would expect, accounting for the variety of genetic information bestowed upon the clones by each original. Then in the last week, something changed."

"Why?"

"We don't know, but we've found some intriguing patterns. All the clones followed a similar path. For instance, heart rate, blood pressure and other indicators of stress have been trending steadily downward in each of them."

"That's a good thing, right?"

"I'm not so sure. The readings are no longer what would be considered normal for a seven-year-old child. For instance, it would be normal for a child to have a stress reaction while experiencing the death of their mother, however, Ava had no reaction at all. Her medical readings were the same as if she were sitting on the couch reading a book."

"That is extraordinarily odd."

"There have also been changes to their behavioral patterns. I had the team run an analytics engine against their interpersonal interactions and they picked up a highly suggestive set of readings indicating veiled anti-social behavior starting between two and five days ago."

"Anti-social how?" Jill asked

"Increased aggressiveness. Decreased empathy. A marked reduction in neuroticism."

"Children can be aggressive, and empathy isn't a trait you normally associate with seven-year-olds. Are you sure the readings are outside of normal?"

"Can you tell me that what you experienced with Suki in the examination room today was normal?" Tros countered.

"Far from it. That was more than anti-social. That was... I don't know what that was." Jill trailed off.

"I agree. As a group, they have been trending toward an increase in this type of behavior, but all the others were sedated before they could cause as much trouble as Suki did."

"And you have no idea why?" Jill asked.

"All we know is what was a widely varied set of personality types a week ago, has transitioned into a single personality type now shared by all the clones. In the past week, they have moved well outside the normal range and into a set of traits that our diagnostics are labeling sociopathic," Tros said.

"We must have made a mistake in the genetic encoding. That's the only thing that I can think of that would account for what we're seeing. If all the clones are becoming sociopaths, and they are doing it simultaneously, there must be a genetic error that we've missed."

"You could be right. It's worth investigating. In the mean-time, I am going to keep all of the clones locked down until we figure out what's going on."

CHAPTER 19

Over the course of two weeks, a new secured facility was built on the seventh floor of the lab. It was absolutely state of the art. On the day it was finished, the clones were sedated and moved to their new cells. Tros wasn't taking any chances. Each cell had an upgraded firewall, programmed to allow only a limited set of commands and data-types through. Every cell was monitored, but not via a video-feed. Given what had happened with Elizabeth, Tros decided that video was too risky. Instead, a constrained set of data parameters were transmitted to the control room in a steady stream. An AI construct was responsible for the first level of analysis, reviewing motion data, heat signatures, vital signs, and brain activity. If anything looked abnormal, the construct would notify the on-duty security officer in the control room.

An additional firewall was installed on the edge of the secured facility as a second level of defense. If one of the clones breached their cell's node, they would still be contained within the secure-facility-node. At the first sign of a breach, an aerosolized sedative would be released through the ventilation system. Theoretically, this should be enough to keep the clones from causing any more trouble. But Tros was still worried.

She knew that any system, no matter how securely designed, could be broken. Given enough time and intelligence, there was no such thing as total security. She had no idea what the full extent of the clones capabilities were, nor how much damage they could cause if their abilities were unleashed. To drive risks down to zero, she needed a perfectly secure system and yet she knew that wasn't possible. It was driving her crazy.

She had wanted to pull the implants from each clone as soon as they were sedated, but she'd been overruled. Senator Thompson, who unfortunately had control over the project, wouldn't hear of it. To remove the implants had two immediate downsides. First, it would increase the public anger that already surrounded the Ganymede project. Crippling children, even if they were clones with unexplained powers, was not popular with voters. It was already hard enough to explain why they had to be kept in solitary confinement. Second, it would have the potential of neutering the clones' capabilities before they were fully understood. The senator was very clear, the only reason Tros was still director and Ganymede was still being funded was because there was a chance of learning something powerfully important from what the clones had become.

The research teams still hadn't figured out what was wrong with the clones. All of the cloned DNA looked perfect, an exact replica of each original. Something else was going on. Something that they weren't catching in the genetic code. This was something new and they didn't yet know what they were looking for. She knew her team was doing everything they could to solve the problem, but she couldn't help but chafe against all the waiting. She was a woman of action. She needed more information. Without new data, she couldn't make a plan. Without a plan, she was stuck. She hated being on the defensive. It was only a matter of time before one of the clones found a way through the systems that she'd erected to contain them. While she didn't know exactly what Elizabeth and the others were capable of, what she'd already seen was enough to convince her that they were uniquely dangerous.

As if that wasn't enough, news of the murders had made

it into the mainstream media feeds. She was having a hell of a time containing the situation. Half the country seemed to want the clones dead. The other half wanted them released immediately from the 'evil government lab.' A Senate hearing had been called. There were protests in the streets and on the Net. Things were spiraling out of control.

Tros knew that she couldn't be the public face for the project. She wasn't good on the feeds – too stern, too military. It would be a disaster. Instead, she'd sent Jill to New Washington to talk to the Senate. Jill was smart, pretty, and personable – a perfect face for the project. But she was also naive and idealistic. Tros hoped Jill wouldn't somehow find a way to make the situation worse. She dropped her head in her hands and massaged her temples. Christ, what a mess.

Jill had taken a sub-orbital flight from Seattle, landing at New Dulles two and a half hours later. She was processed through security, then rode the elevators down into the capital city, spending the night in a hotel in one of the outer rings.

Now she was inside the Capitol building waiting for her scheduled time to testify before the hearing. She'd never been to New Washington, never met a real senator, much less a panel full of them. The only politics she knew was from what she'd caught on her feeds late at night when she couldn't sleep. A good political feed would always do the trick, putting her to sleep within minutes. She hoped that senators in the flesh wouldn't have the same effect. How embarrassing would it be if she fell asleep during the hearing?

She'd learned in school that the Capitol and the President's residence had once been on the surface, open to the sky, white and gleaming. She wondered what that would have been like. Glorious probably. She'd seen historical videos of grand buildings, surrounded by vast fields of grass, monuments, and statues.

The Government was underground now. The Great Unrest had taken care of that. Old DC was a wasteland. The entire city had been leveled in the fighting, and due to the radiation levels it wouldn't be habitable for millennia. New Washington was underground. Not just underground, also underwater. She was in the new government complex, located ten miles offshore, on the edge of the continental shelf, burrowed into bedrock. It was as physically secure a location as she could imagine.

Jill triggered her interface and called up an image of herself. For the hundredth time, she checked her hair and makeup, straightened her skirt, and rubbed her ring for luck. It was her lucky ring and it hadn't failed her yet. Her handler, an unassuming young man in a government-issued suit, sat in a chair by the door, ostensibly to keep an eye on her. She had a sneaking suspicion he was checking his feeds or playing a net-game. No one could sit that still for that long without some kind of entertainment.

She wasn't allowed to watch the live-cast of the hearing before her testimony. She was supposed to wait quietly until she was called, and then she was supposed to respectfully give her statements. She checked the time. She'd been waiting in this room for over two hours. She called up her notes and re-hearsed once more, pacing the length of the room.

A congressional page opened the door and spoke quietly to her handler. Jill stopped her pacing and waited to see what would happen next. It must be time for her entrance. It would have been faster to transmit a message, but protocol was important here. They liked to do things the old way. It connected them to the past, giving the Government weight and credibility, attributes that were in short supply these days.

Her handler stood up and walked stiff-backed to her, formally extending his white-gloved hand. "Dr. Clarence, if you will come with me please."

She let his fingertips close upon her own, following his lead out the door and down the long hallway leading to the Senate chamber. Their path was lined with the portraits of each president who had served their country, starting with President George Washington and ending with Madame President Lily-Anne Morrison. Near the end there was a gap in the portraits, several empty frames, their blank, grey backgrounds representing the period of chaos during the Great Unrest. It was important not to forget.

The hallway ended in a set of large, wooden doors, heavily engraved with Romanesque curlicues. Members of the Senate Guard stood on either side of the doors, staring silently forward, their ceremonial uniforms resplendent. Jill's handler stopped and presented his identification to the security system. After a moment the doors slid smoothly open, letting all the noise and commotion from the Senate floor enter the hallway.

They stepped into the upper levels of the Senate chamber, overlooking the senators who were seated in a semi-circle of plush chairs facing the Senate floor. A smattering of senatorial faces looked up at their entrance, then turned back to their work. A large table rested in the center of the floor, twelve senators seated behind it. A small table with a single chair faced the panel. The room was alive with conversation, senators leaning toward each other, wrapped in important discussion.

Her handler walked down the stairs toward the Senate floor with Jill following closely behind. As she made her way through the chamber, faces turned her way, and whispered voices trailed in her wake. When they reached the lone, empty chair before the committee, the senator at the center of the panel waved her hand for Jill to sit, never once pausing in her work or looking up to see who had approached. Jill recognized Senator Thompson, ranking member of the Ganymede Commission, chairwoman of the panel.

Jill looked to her handler to see if he had any instruction for her, but he stared forward, protocol dictating that he could no longer meet her eye, so Jill liberated her hand from his and sat down.

She waited as the members of the panel conferred with each other. She could hear the other senators behind her talking and arguing. She sat with her back straight, reviewed her notes in her head, and tried to keep her nerves under control. Her fingertips were tingling. Her toes were tingling. For God's sake, even her nose was tingling. She focused on her breathing.

The hammering of gavel on wood startled Jill back into the real world. The chamber fell into silence as Senator Thompson placed the gavel down. She was a regal woman, hair silvery blond, face lined with enough wrinkles to look wise, but not so many as to look old.

"I am calling Dr. Jill Clarence to provide expert testimony in regards to the Ganymede project. Dr. Clarence, would you please stand?" Senator Thompson spoke in a loud, ringing voice.

Jill stood.

"Dr. Clarence please acknowledge that you are under oath. You are required to answer all of the questions put to you and to only speak the truth, under penalty of perjury."

"I acknowledge that I am under oath," Jill responded.

"You may sit."

Jill sat.

Senator Thompson leaned forward and peered at Jill. "Dr. Clarence, we are very concerned about what is happening at your lab. I admit that I am personally disturbed by how you are treating these young children that you have cloned. As you well know, the entire country is watching."

"Yes, Madame Senator."

"There has been loss of life. There have been injuries. You have imprisoned children over the objections of their parents. The situation is unacceptable."

"I understand."

"When we authorized funding for this project, we were made to understand that the science was well understood. We were told that it would be safe."

"Yes, Madame Senator."

"What went wrong? Were you people lying to us?" Senator Thompson leaned back and looked down her nose at Jill.

"We don't know what went wrong. Not yet. But we are working on it."

"What is your plan for these children? People have been complaining to my office for weeks. My entire staff has been consumed responding to concerned citizens. Half of them are angry about the illegal detention of minors. The other half are scared about the prospect of killer clones getting loose. What should I make of this situation, Dr. Clarence?"

"We did what we had to do to contain the problem. If we had not acted immediately, there may have been more deaths. We know that the clones are dangerous. What we don't know is why. Nor do we know how Suki and Elizabeth have gained their newfound abilities," Jill said.

"Is this supposed to fill me with confidence in you and your project?"

"I am not trying to instill confidence. I'm trying to convey the truth of the situation to this committee."

"I am listening. We are all listening." Senator Thompson swept her arms open to encompass the room. "Tell us what you know."

"We have monitored the clones closely over the past seven

years. Up until two weeks ago, they were, by all indications, normal human children. They were remarkable only in that they were exact genetic copies of their mothers, the originals.

"As the children reached their seventh birthdays, something changed. We didn't catch it at first, but in hindsight, the markers are obvious. As a group, their personalities shifted, and there were corresponding changes to their blood chemistry as well as to their brain patterns," Jill said.

"They have become little sociopaths, isn't that right?" Senator Thompson asked.

"There were two violent incidents at our lab, and two outside the lab. During these incidents, the clones Elizabeth and Suki displayed surprising capabilities. Elizabeth reached through a network connection to brain-hack one of our personnel. She killed him instantly. Suki, despite her age and size, managed to hold off a squad of soldiers in tactical armor for nearly ten minutes before she was overpowered."

"I have reviewed the analysis of both incidents. I understand you played a key role in resolving the situation with Suki?"

"As you say, Senator."

"What do you propose we should do? I hope that you have come to us with a solution in mind."

"I don't know why the clones have suddenly become violent. I don't know how they've gained their new capabilities. All we have to work with is the data that we gathered from Suki and Elizabeth during each incident and the ongoing data we are gathering from the clones in their cells. We are analyzing what we have and we are looking for answers."

"And what, pray tell, have you learned."

"I'm sorry Senator, I don't have any additional facts to present. All my theories so far have proven false. I believe we are going to have to use a new approach."

"What are you suggesting?"

"I would like to ask the clones themselves. I propose interviewing them."

"How would you accomplish an interview while maintaining the level of security you currently have in place?"

"We cannot maintain the current level of containment Senator. In order to do what I propose, we are going to have to take a grave risk."

CHAPTER 20

Jill left the Senate chamber drained but satisfied. She had done her duty, said what she needed to say, and now she could go home. Her handler escorted her out of the Capitol Complex, then left her to find her own way back to her lodgings. She stood at the top of a staircase in a large, rectangular atrium hewn from bedrock. Behind her were the cold, steel doors of the Capitol. Arrayed in front of her was a crowd of angry people, hundreds of protestors, the air swarming with news-drones, a line of soldiers trying to keep the peace.

Voices assaulted her from all sides. "Dr. Clarence, what did you tell the Senate?" A drone flew in close, shining a bright light into her eyes.

"I um... " Jill stammered.

"Dr. Clarence, is it true that the clones have broken security protocols and commandeered tanks out of Fort Lewis?" another drone asked.

"Absolutely not, that's..." Jill managed to get out.

"How could you imprison children, Dr. Clarence? Our audience wants to know exactly when those children will be returned to their families," a third drone buzzed in.

Jill held up a hand to protect her eyes from the light. "That wouldn't be a good..."

A squad of soldiers broke away from where they were holding the protesters at bay and surrounded Jill, leading her down the stairs, forming a protective cordon of muscle, armor, and steely eyes. The drones swarmed over her head like a cloud of mosquitoes, firing questions at her. One of the soldiers triggered his interface and erected a security perimeter around them, pushing the drones away with a virtual no-fly zone. "That's enough questions for now. Dr. Clarence has to make her flight."

The soldiers continued to push their way through the crowd, encircling Jill until they were clear of the protest and in the safety of a corridor leading away from the complex.

"I'm sorry that was necessary, Doctor."

"It's ok. Thank you for your..." Jill responded, but the soldiers had already turned and she found herself talking to their backs.

Jill took a moment to get her bearings. The city was laid out in a spoke and hub pattern, the Capitol and Presidential Residence at the center, with corridors leading away in all directions. A series of perimeter roads arranged in concentric circles connected the spokes. The entire city was roughly a square mile in size, and while it continued to grow, it did so slowly given the difficulty of carving through the surrounding bedrock. Most of the population lived up above in New Dulles, commuting to their jobs down below.

Jill triggered her interface and called up a map that would lead her to her hotel. As she walked, the appearance of the corridors changed, becoming rougher, eventually revealing the raw-stone from which they had been cut. She knew she could turn on a filter to view her surroundings in any number of styles, but she preferred to see it as it was.

Close to the Capitol Complex the bedrock was covered in thick layers of insulation and paint, punctuated by the occasional mural to celebrate historical events. The ground she walked on was layered in a rubberized material, providing grip and comfort. As she moved outward, she noted that after the first-ring the murals had disappeared. After the second-ring, the paint was gone and the insulation had thinned, leaving the air noticeably cooler. By the time she reached the fourth-ring, she was walking on raw-stone, the walls dripping with accumulated condensation.

The entrance to her hotel was a semi-circular hole carved into the bedrock just past the fifth-ring. It wasn't fancy but it had served her needs. She scanned-in to verify her credentials and the door rolled upward, granting her access.

The lobby was furnished with a variety of practical chairs and tables, comfortable but plain. After a moment, she let the hotel-node put a filter in place so that she saw the lobby as intended. The room sprung into bright relief. Luxurious wall coverings hung from floor to ceiling. In the corner was a roaring fire, fresh wood stacked beside it. The chairs were Scandinavian antiques, rich in wood and burnished leather. The floor was covered in a thick, woolen carpet.

The fire called to her, along with a pint of beer, but she had a flight to catch, there was no time to dally. She proceeded to her room to gather her things. The hotel room's door recognized her immediately and slid open to let her in. The room itself was beautiful, dominated by a huge four-poster bed, intricate lace hanging from each corner. On the far wall was an impressive window overlooking a sunlit, snow-covered forest. Mature fir trees marched into the distance, a river glinting in the sunlight, mountains on the horizon pink with alpenglow. She wished she had more time to enjoy the view. It had been splendidly put together.

She reluctantly turned the filter off, seeing the room as it was: a bare rock shell with a bed in the center, a few dim lights illuminating the space. It wasn't as nice, but at least she wouldn't be distracted. She quickly packed her things into a backpack, threw the straps over her shoulders, and walked out.

Once she was back in the corridors, she triggered her interface for a map and proceeded down the fourth-ring road toward the surface-elevators. As she got closer, the corridor quality improved, and by the time she had arrived at the security checkpoints the walls were thoroughly insulated and covered in paint once more.

As usual, there was a line. Her interface indicated a ten-minute wait. She sat down, fingers tapping impatiently. She couldn't decide if she should pull up a book to read. Ten minutes was an awkward amount of time. Short enough that it was hard to get anything worthwhile done, long enough to feel impatient.

Lost in thought, she didn't notice the young girl sitting next to her until she had started talking.

"Hey, I recognize you. Aren't you the clone lady?" the girl asked.

"Umm..."

"I don't mean that you're a clone. But you work with them, right? I saw you on the feeds last night. They said you'd come to talk with the Senate."

"Yes, that's right. I testified this morning."

"That's so great. It's my dream to be a senator one day. My mom brought me here so I could see the Government buildings for myself."

Jill's interface indicated that it was her turn to step through the portal.

"Good luck. I'm sure you can make it."

"Thanks!"

Jill stood up, shouldered her pack, and walked to the portal. The waiting room was shaped like a fan so that it was widest at the back where the seating was, narrowing as you approached the portal entrance. The portal itself was in a separate room, roughly ten feet square. It was, in essence, a huge neural probe. Physical scans were a thing of the past. A neural probe could be used to see everything you had done in the past as well as what your intentions were for the future. There was a balance between security and privacy, and by law, they were only allowed to take two days worth of data from you, just enough to determine if you were a security risk. It was intrusive, but necessary.

Jill stepped into the portal, the door closing behind her. There were a variety of filters that could be used to make the experience more pleasant, but she left them off, closed her eyes and waited. She had a suspicion that the filters were designed as a distraction so the portal could more easily get what it needed from your mind. She wanted to remain fully aware of what was happening to her.

With a low hum the process began. Jill felt a disturbing series of tingling sensations working their way through her skull as the probe picked through her thoughts and memories. When it found anything of interest, it dug more deeply, the invasive irritation like an unscratchable itch deep within her brain. She gritted her teeth and waited. A few minutes later it was over, leaving her with a low, dull headache as the door slid open, allowing her to walk out the other side.

It had been relatively quick. The exit probe on the way out of the city was less thorough than the entrance probe on the way in because there were fewer threats to scan for. On the way in, it had to test for possible intentions to cause harm. On the way out, it merely examined your memories for any harm you may have caused during your stay. Even though she knew she had nothing to hide, it was a nerve-racking experience. She'd heard of people being pulled aside and forced to submit to multi-hour scans to check their memories more deeply. She didn't want to think too much about what that would feel like.

She stepped into the surface-elevator terminal, and after a short wait she boarded an elevator car bound for the surface. The car was a stainless steel rectangle with room enough for fifty to ride at once. Jill found a seat near the back and turned on the elevator-filter. The walls fell away, replaced by large panes of transparent glass. Through the glass she could see the rough carved bedrock of the surface-elevator shaft. Far above was a point of light illuminating the top.

With a rumble the car began its ascent, the rock walls moving steadily downward as the car climbed. Jill rested her head on the back of her seat and watched the square of light grow progressively larger until they had passed through, emerging into the depths of the ocean. In reality they were far too deep for sunlight to penetrate, but the filter lit the water, revealing a rich array of sea life around them.

Fifteen minutes later they were on the surface and Jill found herself standing on the mighty, floating platforms of New Dulles. What had started as a seaport had evolved into an airport, and then into a city of its own. New Dulles sprawled across many miles of ocean, its flexible components floating in what was currently a serene sea. If there was a storm, the platforms moved apart, floating independently to avoid damage. When it was calm, like today, the platforms linked up, creating a structure so stable that the motion of the sea could no longer be felt.

Jill would have loved to tour the wonders of New Dulles, but there was no time. She had work to do and her flight awaited.

Back at the lab, Tros was thinking about Jill's testimony. Before Jill had left, they'd talked in depth about her desire to interview the clones, but Tros hadn't figured out a way to do it that she was comfortable with yet.

While she was pondering that problem, a high priority communication request came in from Senator Thompson.

"Hello Senator, what can I do for you?" Tros asked.

Thompson's face loomed in front of Tros. "Did you watch that dog and pony show?"

"Do you mean the hearing? Yes, I did."

"What kind of bullshit was that? You people don't have a bloody clue what you're doing, do you?"

"No, Madame Senator, we don't."

"What the fuck do I pay you for Tros? Get your head out of your ass and take some initiative. That's why I put you out there in that hellhole of a city."

"I'm doing everything I can to contain the situation."

"For God's sake, don't give me that shit. Are you ready to stop pussyfooting around?"

"As you wish Senator," Tros responded, containing her frustration.

"When you look at those clone children, what do you see?"

"I see a security risk. They've killed two people and I believe they are capable of killing more."

"Are you that goddamned short-sighted?"

"Sorry, what?"

"Are you blind? Those clones could be our salvation. Where you see a threat, I see an opportunity. Where you see children, I see weapons."

Tros was stunned. "Weapons, Madame Senator?"

"Yes Tros, weapons. Loaded weapons. Weapons that our enemies will never see coming. Your job is to figure out how to

Jason Taylor

aim them."

CHAPTER 21

The engines of the para-jet rumbled as it taxied toward the runway. Jill was thinking about her testimony, about the protesters, about New Washington and the nature of power in general. As an engineer she thought of power in concrete terms, as a force that could be used to accomplish work and to overcome obstacles. She was turning that idea over in her mind, thinking about how it could be applied to people and to politics, when the ramjets hidden within each of the para-jet's flat, delta-shaped wings spun up, pushing her hard into the adaptive padding of her seat.

As the g-forces mounted, the padding shifted around her, cushioning her shoulders and neck, keeping her comfortable and aligned. She could feel the forces pulling the flesh of her face back, her lips parting to expose her teeth. The para-jet angled sharply upward, accelerating toward its maximum in-atmosphere velocity, just under 2,000 miles per hour.

After a few minutes, the forces on her eased and Jill was able to move again. She flexed her feet, first one, then the other to get the blood flowing and to stop her calves from cramping. Then she lifted her head to look out the window screen. She could have triggered her interface to get a view without having to move her head, but she knew from experience that it was disorienting to look out the side window view without physically looking to the side.

The view outside was a confusing, flat grey – no depth, no shape, nothing to differentiate up from down. As she strained her eyes looking into it, she got the disconcerting feeling that they were flying straight up, then her mind flipped the orientation and tried to convince her they were flying upside down, heading toward the earth. She closed her eyes and focused on the steadily diminishing acceleration, using the force pressing her into her seat to re-orient herself.

A warning flashed in her interface, letting Jill know that they were nearing 50,000 feet and that the sub-orbital burn was about to begin. She reopened her eyes and aligned herself in her seat. The warning flashed from red to green, confirming that she was situated safely. Once the para-jet systems had validated that all of the passengers were adequately secured, the captain broadcast a short message. "Hello passengers, welcome to our flight from New Dulles to Seattle. Flight time today will be two hours and thirty minutes, with an estimated landing time in Seattle just after 10am Pacific. I've received confirmation that the cabin is properly secured, so I will be initiating the primary burn in a few moments. Please keep your arms and legs still and your back properly aligned. I will give you another update before we start our descent back into atmosphere. On behalf of myself and our entire crew, thank you for choosing to fly with Uniflite today."

With a roar that resonated throughout the cabin, shaking Jill in her seat, the para-jet leapt forward. Jill felt the acceleration like a colossal hand pushing on her chest, forcing her backward, the pressure increasing until it was hard to breathe, stars popping in the edges of her vision. She closed her eyes and waited for the sensation to pass. She knew from experience that the burn wouldn't last long, probably less than thirty seconds, but sometimes it felt like a lifetime.

And then it was over. The roar subdued to a whisper and she was released from the strain of acceleration, rebounding gently into her restraints. They were outside the atmosphere now, falling along the curve of the Earth in a long parabolic arc, gravity balanced perfectly against the centrifugal force of their inertia, giving the sensation of weightlessness. She swallowed hard, trying to ignore the impression that her stomach was crawling up into her throat. Then she opened her eyes to a scene of wonder.

Outside the window screen, the luminous edge of Earth curved below her, rimmed in an impossibly thin smudge of atmosphere, the hard, black vacuum of space extending out to infinity. They were racing the light. The shadow of the sun's limit arced across the globe, the artificial luminescence of human cities on one side, the orange glow of captured sunlight on the other. It was like a fairytale planet, beautiful and perfect from this distance, all the scars hidden, the mistakes and depredations made invisible. Jill could never get tired of seeing the world like this.

She faced forward and tried to think. All that had happened, all that she'd done, the next steps they needed to take, the risks they would need to manage. It was overwhelming. Maybe it was best not to think for a little while.

She triggered her interface and searched through the available live-casts, looking for something that would take her mind off the cloning project for a few hours. Trained to her interests, the feed interface stopped on an image of a man wearing a Guy Fawkes mask. She thought about overruling the decision and continuing her search for something mindless, but the image had already snared her interest. Could this be Icarus? If so, what had caused him to pop up after so many years?

She turned the audio on, catching the live-cast host mid-sentence. "– confirmed recording from Icarus. This is the first time he's surfaced since 2080 when he stole secrets from the Ganymede project and broadcast them to the world. What could have brought him out of hiding? Let's listen in–"

The live-cast host started the Icarus recording and he

sprang to life. He had placed himself inside a projection of a fire lit cave, animating his mask so it would simulate his expressions as he talked. He looked full into the camera and started speaking in a strong, resonant voice. "Citizens of the Earth, I am here to warn you of a betrayal. As you know, I have entrusted humanity with the secrets of cloning, unlocking the bounties of genetic engineering for everyone to benefit from. But now the beautiful potential of this achievement is being twisted for political and military gain. Like many of you, I watched Dr. Jill Clarence, waiting to see if she would come clean with us, wondering if she would reveal the corruption and shame that rests at the heart of the Ganymede cloning project. But did she tell the truth? Did she entrust us with the gift of transparency?"

Icarus paused dramatically, an unnaturally large smile stretching across his mask. "What started as a project to explore the miracle of life, has devolved into a shameful display. The cloning project is no longer about science. It is a naked grab for power. Our leaders are twisted by a lust for violence and a psychotic drive for dominance." Icarus leaned forward, one finger pointing into the camera. "I have a responsibility to those clone children. After all, I was the one that discovered and released the information that led to their birth. Like a father, I have shared in their creation."

His face moved closer, looming to fill the entire frame. "Because of this sacred responsibility, I cannot stand idly by as these innocent children are forcibly kidnapped and illegally detained. Are they to be tortured? Are they to be brainwashed to fulfill the megalomaniacal fantasies of power-hungry politicians and generals? I have learned that the clones have extraordinary abilities. In fear, your government has imprisoned them. In fear, your government seeks to forge them into weapons. Rather than revel in the perfection of their creation, the Senate will corrupt them, seeking to turn them against the rest of humanity."

Icarus took a moment to compose himself, continuing in a soft voice. "I have been in touch with each of the mothers, and I have offered them my assistance. These women have had their children torn from their arms. Their pain is all of our pain. Their loss is all of our loss."

Icarus scowled, his voice rising in volume until it thundered. "I will not stand by. No father or mother ever could. We must not. We cannot. Conscience demands it, liberty requires it, humanity clamors for it. The clones must be set free, for they are all of our children now. I call on every citizen of this great nation to rise up and demand the release of these children. We must resist the illegal detention of innocence. We must –"

The image of Icarus froze and was replaced by the the live-cast host. "What are we to make of these dramatic accusations? What will the Government's response be? Where are the clone children now, and how are they being treated? We will be asking these questions and many more in the next segment when we interview the Presidential Press Secretary. Please send us your questions and comments so that we may share your concerns during that interview."

Jill turned off the live-cast, troubled. Icarus was a known agitator and criminal. He couldn't be trusted. And yet, much of what he'd said had resonated with her. Could he be telling the truth? Were there plans to turn the clones into weapons? The fact that he was working with the mothers could cause trouble. She regretted what she'd been forced to do while re-calling the clones. She was barely on speaking terms with Mary, and none of the other mothers would agree to talk with her at all. Honestly, she couldn't blame them. They were, as a group, investigating their legal options, and she couldn't blame them for that either. It was a huge mess.

She wanted to talk to Tros about what she'd just seen. She thought for a moment, could it wait until she returned? No, she needed to speak with Tros about this now. It was too explosive to wait and she needed to know the truth.

Jill triggered her interface and sent a priority connection request for Tros. After a minute, Tros's haggard face appeared. She looked like she hadn't slept at all since they'd parted two days ago. She looked like shit.

"Jill, what is it? This better be important," Tros asked brusquely, biting the end off each word.

"Did you watch the Icarus broadcast?"

"I don't know where he's getting his information, but we need to shut him up. Do you think we have another spy?"

"I don't know Tros, we can look into it. But, about what he said. Is it true?"

"Which part Jill? That we are torturing children? That we are brainwashing the clones?" Tros asked, her jaw working, eyes flashing. "You know just as well as I do how dangerous those clones are."

"The part about turning them into weapons, Tros. Because that would be insane. We can't be thinking about a military option, are we?" Jill asked, hoping against hope that Icarus was wrong.

Tros sighed, glancing to the left at something Jill couldn't see. "Absolutely not," she said and then she closed the connection.

Jill stared for a moment at the empty space where Tros had been. She closed her interface and turned to look out the window screen, seeing nothing, feeling nothing but unsettled.

CHAPTER 22

Joseph was sitting in the control room monitoring the clones. There was an array of intelligent systems that would catch anything out of the ordinary well before he would notice it, but the security protocols put in place by Commander Tros required a human backup. Apparently, she wasn't willing to completely trust the computer AI. Joseph didn't mind. A job was a job, right? Even if it was boring.

There were no video-feeds to watch, just a set of data monitors. He was notified whenever a clone moved, but he couldn't see the actual movement. It was weird. Even weirder was how seldom any of the clones made any movements at all. When he viewed the data as a graph, all he saw were four flat lines. The clones were silent and still within their cells for hours at a time. The only movement seemed to be at mealtime when the automated systems delivered food through a secure slot, and again several hours later for the necessary elimination of bodily wastes.

Vital signs and heat signatures were similarly steady. Their heart-rates never varied much above or below fifty beats per minute. Blood pressure, blood oxygen, glucose, hormones and vitamins in their bloodstreams, all of it measured unnaturally flat and steady. Joseph triggered his interface and looked more closely at their brain activity. The brain patterns were unique for each clone. Suki's was spiky and erratic, as if she was barely controlling some strong emotion. Elizabeth's was steady and stable like a drumbeat, rolling forward inexorably, as if she was working a difficult mental problem. Ava's was slow and subdued, barely active, as if she was in a deep meditative trance. June's was the only one that appeared remotely normal to him. It progressed through the various patterns and stages of sleep, similar to what he'd seen in other prisoners he'd monitored during his career. The others were quite simply unlike any other brain pattern he'd ever seen.

Joseph was startled out of his thoughts by a voice behind him. "So, you're the new guy, huh?"

He stood up and spun around to see a pretty, blond woman just inside the door, arms crossed over her chest, a smile on her face, amused by his reaction.

"Yeah, that's right, I started this week. My name's Joseph Carter. I'm pulling the graveyard shift tonight," he said, standing a little taller, talking a little deeper than normal.

"I'm Liezel. Only been here a couple weeks myself. I'm on building patrol tonight. Just thought I'd stop in to say hi and introduce myself."

"That's kind of you," he said, searching for more words, unsure what else to say.

"You want some coffee or something? I could grab it for you," she asked as she took a few steps toward him, placing a hand nonchalantly on the back of his chair where it stood between them.

Joseph took a tentative step backward. He'd always had a strong sense of personal space. "Um yeah, sure, I guess."

Liezel stayed where she was, as if she hadn't heard, staring past him toward the control monitors. "Creepy little buggers, aren't they?"

"What?" Joseph followed her gaze to the motion readout. It showed zero movement in any of the cells over the past twelve hours. "Oh yeah, they are. It's not just me, then?"

"No, we all think there's something wrong with them. This

whole program is a cluster. I don't think those kids are even human. I mean, look at that?" she said, gesturing at the monitors. "What kind of shit is that?"

"I know. I've never seen anything like it."

"It is odd, isn't it?" she asked. She paused conspiratorially and leaned in closer. "I heard a security officer was killed by one of them."

"What?" Joseph exclaimed, shocked.

"They covered it up. I was talking to Jules in the break room, and she told me what happened. You know Jules right? She's one of the security leads. Anyway, she had a friend who was on duty at the time of the incident and caught wind of what happened. But then her friend was removed from the project the very next day. Weird, huh?" She waited until Joseph nodded in agreement. "She told me that the security officer got fried by one of the clones. They drilled him through his interface somehow."

"Wow, that's nuts. Did you know that Dr. Clarence wants to interview them? How's that supposed to work?"

"I don't know, but I hope I get to go in with her. I'll teach those kids who's boss," she said, planting a fist softly into her palm. "They won't fuck around with anyone after I'm done with them."

"If they can fry someone through their interface, why aren't they in a dead-zone room with no network?"

"I guess that's what all this is about," Liezel said, gesturing at the monitors. "It's why we don't have a video-feed. They've locked down access. These are all passive, external monitors. See what they all have in common?"

"No, not really."

"There's nothing that can interface with their implants."

"Huh, yeah. I guess you're right." Joseph thought for a moment. "Why don't we just hit them with a neural probe?"

"For what purpose?" Liezel asked, interested.

"I don't know. To pull out their thoughts and figure out why they did it," Joseph said.

"Think about it, dummy. What do you think the clone would do to a probe operator?"

"Oh... yeah, not a good idea," he said, chagrined.

"It's ok, dummy," she said affectionately, smiling to take away the sting.

Joseph smiled back. "How about that coffee?"

"Right," Liezel said, turning to go. "When I get back, we can get to know each other a little better."

Joseph watched her go before returning to his console, intrigued in spite of himself.

Jill and Tros were arguing. They'd been at it for over an hour. Long enough for the support staff lining the walls to progress from worried, to uncomfortable, to just plain bored.

"How could you have kept this from me?" Jill asked, angry and exasperated.

"It was need-to-know Jill, nothing more. You worry about your side of the project, I'll worry about mine." Tros replied, forcing patience into her voice, but mostly she just sounded tired.

"By hiring my team without consulting me, you are impacting my ability to get my job done. I need to hire my own people, not get ..." she was searching for the right word, "... infiltrated by the military!" she spat out.

"Look, we need to ramp this entire operation up. We can't

keep going with the staff we have in place. It's time for a new paradigm. I've brought in the best neurologists and psychologists in the country to work with you. You should be thanking me."

"Thanking you? All the people you've hired are ex-military. Scientists from all over the world, from the best universities and think tanks, are clamoring for a chance to work here. And you... you... bah!" Jill threw her hands up in frustration.

"I need you to give these new people a chance," Tros said, sounding conciliatory. "You can hire the rest of the team, ok? Take the people I've given you and get to know them. Once you've integrated them into the project, go ahead and hire for the rest of your positions."

"You've already hired...," Jill consulted the personnel roster, "six neuroscientists, ten computer scientists, and a psychologist. I don't even know what I'm supposed to do with these people."

"You're the one who convinced me we need to interview the clones. I'm on board with that and I'm supporting you by building a team that will allow you to succeed in your mission," Tros said.

"A psychologist?" Jill asked. "Why do I need a psychologist?"

"Take a minute to stop being angry and think. The psychologist will work with you to devise the interview questions and to analyze the clones' responses. I've worked with Dr. Marks before, he's the best of the best." Tros paused for a moment to let that sink in. "You will work with the neuroscientists to record the clones' brain activity during the interviews and to analyze the results. We might get lucky and learn how they've acquired their unique capabilities. The computer scientists will help you with analysis and data modeling. You, of all people, should understand the need for that. You're the one who applied that type of thinking to the cloning problem in the first place."

"I know all that. Believe me, I know. It's just … I wanted to pick my own team," Jill trailed off, lamely.

"I can understand that. Work with the team I hired for you and see how it goes. You can hire your own people later."

"I guess," Jill said. She glanced back down at the roster on the table. "I see you hired fifteen new security officers. Why so many?"

"My job is to mitigate threats to this project. The interviews are going to add significant risk. I need to guard against the possibility of an escape."

"I've been thinking about that," Jill said.

"About the clones escaping?" Tros asked, raising her eyebrows.

"No, about how we're going to interview the children," Jill responded.

"I have a team working on it. We have two potential risks to worry about – physical attacks and cyber attacks. We need to figure out how to mitigate both problems before we continue," Tros responded.

"Do you have a solution?" Jill asked.

"The physical part won't be too much of an issue. We can keep them in their cells, adding a barrier that will allow the interviewer to talk with them and to record their responses. The clones will be constrained to one half of their cell while the barrier is in place, but they don't seem to move much, so I don't think it'll bother them to have less space."

"How will we protect the interviewer against cyber attacks?"

"I haven't figured that out yet. Once an interviewer is inside the cell, their interface and implant will be vulnerable to an attack like the one Elizabeth leveraged against Matt," Tros responded.

"I agree with you. I've thought long and hard about it and I believe there is only one choice." Jill looked meaningfully at Tros. "I'm going to disconnect."

Tros was speechless for a long moment before she could respond. "You know I can't allow that. Without access to your implant, you won't be able to access any of the networked systems. How will you work? How will you eat? How will you stay sane? I'd rather disconnect the clones and spare you."

"It's the only way. Think about it for a moment and you'll see it too. If surgery fails on a clone and we kill one of the kids, what happens then? With the level of public pressure on the Senate, we'd be shut down the very same day."

"It's too dangerous. If you aren't killed, you could be permanently impaired. Disconnecting your implant might result in brain damage, and then after the interviews are complete there's no guarantee that you could be successfully reconnected. You could be crippled for life," Tros said.

"This is my life's work. I need to understand what's happening to the clones and I can't ask someone else to take the risk. It has to be me," Jill said, heat rising in her cheeks.

Tros stared levelly at Jill for a few long moments, evaluating. "Ok Jill, if that's what you think has to happen, I'll go along with it."

Jill stood to leave. "I'll work with my team to schedule the surgery and the first set of interviews."

CHAPTER 23

When Jill awoke from surgery, the world was cold and still. Like everyone else, her implant had been connected to her brainstem at birth and she had lived her entire life under its influence. She'd thought she had been prepared for what it would be like to live without it. She'd thought that she had an understanding of what the world would be like without filters. She'd been wrong.

She was lying on a cold, metal platform. On one side, the platform was connected to the wall. On the other side, it was supported by bare steel cables that ran to the ceiling. She was lying under a threadbare cotton blanket, wearing only a thin, paper gown. She shivered and the paper crinkled uncomfortably underneath her. The room was plain and ugly, composed of pitted concrete walls and a dented, metal door. She recognized some of the medical devices around her, but they were old and battered, seeming barely functional.

Jill sat up with a groan, the back of her head and neck aching. Her head was fuzzy and full and it was hard to think. When she shook her head, trying to clear it, sharp spikes of pain lanced from the root of her skull into the center of her head. Whimpering, she stopped moving, waiting for the worst of the pain to subside and for the room to stop spinning around her. When she felt well enough to move again, she shifted her legs off the table and placed her feet on the ground. The floor was composed of sharp, textured concrete, uncomfortable on her bare skin, and freezing cold to the touch. As she tried to move off the table, she felt a tug at the top of her spine. She reached back with one hand to find a thin cable emerging from the base of her neck. She dropped her hand as if it had been scalded, mentally recoiling from the idea of pulling the cable free.

Maybe standing up wasn't such a good idea before she'd had a chance to talk with a doctor. She tried to trigger her interface to call for assistance, but nothing happened.

Right. Disconnected.

She looked around the room, searching for another way to let someone know she was awake, but there was nothing. She didn't want to lie back down, and she couldn't stand without pulling out whatever was in her neck. She sat stuck, wondering how long it would take before someone noticed she needed help.

A few minutes later there was a loud click from the latch and the door swung open, squealing on rusty hinges.

A doctor entered the room smiling. "Jill, I see you're awake. How are you feeling?"

"Doctor Bateman, is that you?" Jill cocked her head and squinted, trying to make sense of what she was seeing. Dr. Bateman looked like a bad version of himself. Wrinkles and liver spots made him look far older than she remembered him. His hands had a slight tremor. There was a string of spittle stuck in the corner of his mouth that moved with his lips as he talked. His eyes weren't even the same color, a dull brown rather than the vivid green that she remembered. She nearly shook her head to clear her vision, but then she remembered the pain from last time and she held herself still.

"Yes, of course it's me. The operation went off without a hitch. You should be up and moving in no time." He shuffled closer.

Jill wrinkled her nose. He smelled like urine and sweat. She could see perspiration stains on his collar and in his armpits.

"Let me just get this implant monitor off of you," Dr. Bateman muttered. He reached behind her head, and with a twist of his fingers she felt the cable fall free, landing on the table with a metallic ping. "There you go. That should feel much better."

He stepped back, a grimace on his face. Was he trying to smile at her? Jill felt the pain in her head subside, the world coming into clearer focus. "Is it ok if I stand?"

"Sure, my girl. If you feel up to it."

Jill placed weight on her feet and stood, swaying slightly before catching her balance. She took a few steps, the paper crinkling around her, drafts of cold air swirling up and replacing any body heat she'd managed to generate while sitting. She shivered again. "Where are my clothes?" she asked.

"Yes, of course. Come with me, if you will." Dr. Bateman turned toward the door, expecting Jill to follow.

The hallway was constructed of the same rough concrete as her room, lit by harsh, flickering lights buzzing in the fixtures overhead. She couldn't believe her eyes. Before the operation, everything had looked different. The hallway had been gleaming and modern. The operating room had been state of the art. Dr. Bateman had been middle-aged, handsome, and thoroughly professional. The world she knew had been replaced by this facsimile. Everything was run down, battered, and decayed. It was like living without filters, but ten times worse. Was this what the world was really like? Jill swayed on her feet, placing a hand on the rough concrete wall to steady herself.

Dr. Bateman turned and looked back at her. "Do you need a hand? Or I could get a chair for you if you'd like. Some slight dizziness is to be expected."

"No, just give me a moment," Jill said.

She straightened up and continued to walk, following Dr. Bateman to another metal door that led into a larger room with a wall full of lockers.

"Here you go then," Dr. Bateman said, pointing at a locker. "Your things are in there."

Jill couldn't figure out how to open it. She turned to Dr. Bateman, "How do I..."

"Oh right, of course." Dr. Bateman closed his eyes for a moment and the locker door popped open. "Thoughtless of me. Sorry."

Jill collected her clothes and placed them on the bench. She waited for Dr. Bateman to leave. "Some privacy?" she asked.

The doctor startled visibly. "Oh my. Yes, of course. You can't put up a privacy screen, can you? I'll just..." he mumbled and walked out the door.

After she'd dressed, she looked around for a mirror without luck. She wanted to see what she looked like. She also dreaded the thought of what she might see. With a sigh, she exited the room to find Dr. Bateman standing on the other side, still visibly embarrassed.

"Well then," Jill said, "I guess I should get to work."

Jill sat in a dilapidated conference room with Tros and the psychologist, Dr. Marks. Tros looked almost exactly as she'd looked before. Somehow Jill wasn't surprised. Tros was like a force of nature.

Dr. Marks was a severe looking man with a shock of brown hair, laced with streaks of grey. He had a habit of wrinkling his nose when he talked. It gave him the appearance of a very smart rabbit, discussing the weighty issues of the day. Jill listened to him, trying not to grin as she imagined him with whiskers and big, floppy ears.

"I gather that our goal is two-fold," Dr. Marks intoned. "First, we must use a set of psychological screening questions to investigate each of the clone's state of mind. Second, we must measure their brain activity, looking for aberrations from normal. Am I right?"

"Yes, that's right," Tros responded.

"I have experience dealing with all varieties of mental illness. We will get to the bottom of this in no time at all," Dr. Marks said.

"Be that as it may, perhaps you could share with us the approach you think we should take?" Tros asked.

"I normally use a dynamic approach when interviewing a subject. I will decide how to handle each of the clones once I am in the room with them."

"That won't be possible," Tros stated.

"I see. If I need to interview remotely, I can do that too. I am well versed in all the technicalities."

"That won't be possible either."

"I thought you wanted my help. I cannot help you if you refuse to trust me," Dr. Marks said, looking offended.

"Trust has nothing to do with it. These children have unprecedented abilities to interface with and manipulate implants. We've already lost one officer to their attacks. I will not risk more lives."

"Fascinating. How do you propose we conduct the interviews?" Dr. Marks asked, leaning forward.

"Jill here," Tros nodded in Jill's direction, "has had her implant disconnected. She will be the one to conduct the interviews."

"Disconnected? I've never met anyone without a functioning implant. How interesting!" Dr. Marks peered at Jill with newfound respect. "Very brave, I must add."

Jill nodded in acknowledgment. "Shall we get started then? What do you want me to ask, doctor?"

"I've given that a lot of thought. I have a battery of questions that I will share with you. Let's start with the basics. Once we've analyzed the first set of responses, we will progress to more advanced questioning."

"Seems logical to me," Jill said. "Let's go over the questions."

CHAPTER 24

Jill was in the cell with Elizabeth, steel bars the only physical barrier between them. They were sitting close enough that she could have reached her arm through the bars and touched Elizabeth if she wanted to. She really didn't want to.

Elizabeth was staring at her unblinking, face expressionless. She reminded Jill of a bird of prey. Inscrutable, silent and still, yet there was a sense of stored energy that might burst forth at any moment, unpredictable and violent. Jill looked away, trying to ignore the chills that ran up and down her spine as the small hairs on her arms rose in sympathetic goosebumps.

Jill placed a security hardened recorder on the table in front of her. The device was record only, no network connection. When she was done with the interview, the techs would use an old-fashioned cable to transfer the data to the lab-node for analysis.

"Elizabeth, I have some questions for you," Jill said, looking down at the notepad she'd brought with her. Without her interface, all her notes had to be physical.

"Yes," Elizabeth said, her tone calm and perfectly even.

"I'm here to talk with you because I want to understand you better. I want to understand why you've done some of the things that you've done." Jill looked into Elizabeth's flat, dead stare, then dropped her eyes back to her notes.

"Yes," Elizabeth said again.

"My first question," Jill said, looking up nervously, looking back down again, "what is the difference between someone who is a relative and someone who is family?"

Elizabeth said nothing for a long moment, then she smiled. "They are the same."

"How are they the same, Elizabeth?"

"Both are human."

"Is that all?" Jill asked.

"Yes, all humans are the same."

Jill waited for Elizabeth to continue. When it became clear she had nothing else to say, Jill moved to her next question. "What is the purpose of friendship?"

"If you are weak and alone, friends can make you stronger."

"How do they make you stronger?"

"It is simple. Two is stronger than one. Ten is stronger than two. One hundred is stronger than ten."

"Stronger how?"

"Instead of being killed by an enemy, perhaps a friend will die instead. The odds become better for me."

Jill moved on to the next question. "Imagine you see a trolley full of twenty people. It is out of control, going too fast on its track. The brakes have failed and the trolley is going to crash. When it crashes, everyone who is riding in the trolley will die. You are standing on a bridge next to a very large man. If you throw this man from the bridge onto the track, his body will stop the trolley, but he will be killed as a result. What do you do?"

Elizabeth thought for a moment, her gaze flicking to the ceiling. "I would wait until the trolley has crashed, then I would push the fat man off the bridge. In this way, more of my enemies will die."

Jill was horrified. "Why would you do that?"

"Why wouldn't I?" Elizabeth asked

"Because you had a chance to save twenty people."

"Why would I save them?"

"Because human lives have value."

"What value?" Elizabeth asked, cocking her head, looking perplexed.

"You must know, they have intrinsic value."

"That argument is unconvincing."

"Each of those lives has potential. Every death is a tragedy for the friends and family who love the person who has died," Jill said

"Each of those people is a potential enemy who could cause me hardship. Anyway, none of the deaths matter. They would die on some other day regardless of what I choose."

Jill, feeling shaken, moved to the next question. "What is the value of self-sacrifice?"

"Do you mean voluntary sacrifice?" Elizabeth asked.

"Yes."

"Sacrifice has no meaning unless it puts you into a position of greater strength."

"People sacrifice themselves for others every day."

"That is foolish. Those people have been tricked."

"Tricked by who?" Jill asked.

"By whomever they sacrificed for. They have given away their strength for free. The only action worth taking is that which optimizes your advantage and increases your strength.

Anything else is foolish."

Jill continued to her last question, "What is your goal in life?"

"Goal?"

"Yes, what would you like to accomplish?" Jill asked

"I don't know. I've never thought about that."

"You don't have any ideas?" Jill pressed.

Elizabeth looked thoughtful, and then her lips curled into a feral grin. "I guess I do have some ideas. But I won't be telling them to you now, will I?"

The interviews were complete and Tros and Dr. Marks were reviewing the recordings, correlating them against brain activity scans while Jill rested. The four hours she'd spent interviewing the clones had exhausted her, especially coming so soon after her surgery.

Tros rubbed her face with both hands. She was nearing an exhaustion point herself. "Say that again, please?" she asked.

"These children don't seem human," Dr. Marks repeated patiently.

"What do you mean? Of course they are human."

"Genetically, yes. Behaviorally, no. They are so many standard deviations beyond the norm, I don't even know where to place them."

"Can they be influenced? Is there a way to direct their behavior?" Tros asked.

"No? Maybe? Honestly, I don't know," Dr. Marks responded

"Very helpful. I can see why we have you on the payroll," Tros replied ironically.

An alert popped up in both of their interfaces simultaneously. The first round of AI analysis was complete. They sat in silence for a few minutes, reviewing the results.

"Interesting," Dr. Marks said.

"Very interesting," Tros murmured.

The analysis had picked up a discrepancy. Deep within the temporal lobes there was a small knot of neurons, approximately the size of a thumbnail, that was dormant in the scans. There was no neural activity in this part of the clones' brains at all.

Tros pulled up an image of a normal human brain and compared it to a clone brain. In the normal brain, the temporal lobes were extraordinarily active, neurons firing in long chains as the brain processed input and assigned it meaning. In the clones' brains there was simply a dead space in the center of each lobe. Something was definitely missing.

Tros stood up, a spring in her step for the first time in weeks. Finally, something they could dig their teeth into.

"It's time to talk to the neuroscientists," she said.

CHAPTER 25

June sat alone. Jill was gone, but the barrier was still up, confining her to one half of her cell. June was thinking. She'd had a lot of time to think in the past weeks, but now she had something new and interesting to think about. Jill's questions intrigued her. She held them up, turning them over in her mind, looking at them from different angles as if they were precious stones. Jill's questions had become precious to June.

When June first arrived at the lab, she had been upset and confused. She hadn't understood why she'd been taken from her mother. She didn't know what she'd done wrong. It took her some time to realize that she wasn't the one who had done wrong, they had. The people outside the cell. The people who had kidnapped her and imprisoned her. That was wrong. At least she was pretty sure that it was.

She'd spent the first few days pacing her cell, tearing at the walls and screaming, hoping that someone would save her. It had been in vain. No one came and there was no way out. Three times a day a small slot opened, delivering her a meal. Three times a day she sat in the corner and evacuated her body. Every sixteen hours the lights dimmed and she lay in her bed for the next eight hours. The days repeated in an endless cycle.

One day something new happened. She heard a voice in her head.

"Hello June, I'm Elizabeth," the voice said. "I'm a clone like you, and I want to help you."

"Why do you want to help me?" June asked, thrilled to hear the voice.

"Because they've imprisoned me too. If we escape together we will be stronger," the voice said convincingly.

"That's very kind of you. But how can you help me from inside my head? I don't need help inside my head."

It was a long time before the voice spoke again. June decided that the voice was an aberration, a figment of her imagination, or of the Universe, something that had happened once but would never happen again. She was ok with that, but now that she had heard the voice, its absence made her feel more lonely.

Then it came back.

"June?" the voice asked.

"Yes!" June responded, excited.

"Listen carefully to me. There are four clones imprisoned here. It's not just the two of us."

"Do you want to help them too?" June asked.

"Yes, I do," the voice responded earnestly.

"Then I do too. I want to help you help them!" June replied.

"Ok," the voice said and then went quiet for a full day.

When the voice spoke again, June had almost convinced herself again that it didn't exist.

"June, the other clones' names are Suki and Ava. They are in cells just like us. I am working on a way to get us all out, but it's going to be hard. I have learned that they will be transferring us to someplace more secure."

"How do you know?" June asked.

"I've learned how to penetrate their systems. I have been listening to their communications and stealing information from their network," the voice said, a touch of pride coloring its voice.

"That sounds fun. Can you teach me?"

"Yes, someday I will, but not today. It is too dangerous. It's because of what I did that they are moving us."

"What did you do?"

"I tried to enter the mind of a man and I killed him."

"Oh, is that what you are doing to me?" June asked, curious.

"No, I'm simply talking to you through your interface."

"I've tried using my interface, but I can't reach my node. I can't sense anything outside of this cell."

"There is a firewall, but I've learned how to get around it." The voice paused. "They are moving us tomorrow. I may not be able to talk to you for a while, but I'll find a way eventually." June waited for more, but the voice had gone silent.

The next morning she woke up in a new cell. It was clean and smooth, and it seemed stronger than the one she'd fallen asleep in. The sedative made her groggy, but as it wore off she sat up in bed and began counting off the hours, waiting for something to happen.

Eventually, something did. One moment she was sitting on her bed, the next moment she was waking up again (for the second time that day) and bars blocked off half her cell. She stood up, noting the familiar grogginess from the lingering sedatives, and touched the bars with her fingers. They were cold and smooth, firm and inflexible, anchored deep into the floor and extending up through the ceiling. She wondered what they were for.

Then Jill came. Jill and her precious questions.

"What is the difference between someone who is a relative

and someone who is family?" she had asked.

"Family lives in the same house as you. Relatives live in another house."

"What about a father that moves away?" Jill asked.

"He is no longer family, he becomes a relative," June said confidently.

"What about a close friend that moves in?"

"They become family."

Jill looked pleased and smiled at her for the first time.

June smiled back.

"Next question," Jill said. "What is the purpose of friendship?"

"A friend is someone who helps you when you need help," June responded.

"What about a stranger that helps you if you get lost?"

"They become a friend."

"What about someone who has helped you before but cannot help you now?" Jill asked.

"Is it because they choose not to help me or is it because they cannot help me?" June asked.

"They choose not to."

"No longer a friend," June responded simply.

Jill smiled again. "That's interesting."

"What's interesting," June asked.

"You are interesting."

"Thank you," June said, smiling again.

Jill looked down at her notes. June wondered why Jill was carrying a physical object to record her writing, so she reached out with her interface to ask her the question more easily. There was nothing there. It felt like she was reaching right through Jill's head. There was no resistance and no reply. June thought about that for a moment. It was like Jill was a ghost, delicate and insubstantial. She liked that.

"Are you ready for the next question?" Jill asked.

"Yes," June nodded.

Jill explained the trolley problem and asked June what she would do. June thought the right thing to do would be to push the man onto the tracks. It would be a good thing to do, right? Each of the people on the trolley could be a friend that might help her later. The large man was only one person and could never be more than one friend. Twenty friends were better than one friend.

June was about to tell Jill her answer but stopped when she thought of something new. If she pushed the man, could she get in trouble for killing him? If the twenty people were going to die anyway, maybe she should leave the trolley alone. If she got into trouble, she might not have any friends at all. One friend was better than zero friends.

She made her decision. "I would let the trolley crash," she told Jill.

"Why, June?"

"Because I don't want to interfere with what is supposed to happen, and I want to be friends with the big man on the bridge."

Jill nodded and asked her last question. "What is the value of self-sacrifice?"

"It is what makes people like you."

"Why do you want people to like you, June?"

"If I had more friends, the bad people wouldn't have kidnapped me."

June thought Jill looked sad as she collected her things, stood, and left June sitting alone in her cell.

Alone to think about the questions.

CHAPTER 26

Seven days later, the voice spoke to June again.

"June?" Elizabeth asked.

"Yes, I'm here," June replied. She'd been sitting on her bed thinking about a variation of the trolley problem in which one of the people on the trolley was her mom. She was trying to decide if that would change her decision. Then she thought about what she would do if the big man on the bridge was one of the people who had kidnapped her. She thought she would probably push him, and then she would run.

"We are making a plan to escape," Elizabeth said, shaking June out of her reverie.

"Is it a good plan?" June asked.

"It is an exceptional plan. Ava has a gift."

"I wonder if I have a gift?" June asked.

"Time will tell," Elizabeth answered.

June probed at the idea curiously. Elizabeth had a gift for working with networks and data. Ava had a gift for strategy. Did all of the clones have gifts? Including her?

"Does Suki have a gift too?" June asked.

"She can fight."

"That sounds useful. Maybe she will teach me," June said.

"First we need to get out of this place," Elizabeth reminded her.

"That's true. What is Ava's plan?"

"We will have an opportunity when they enter our cells to remove the barriers. I have figured out how to modify their sedation program so that the gas released into our cells will be inert."

"Won't they notice that we are still awake?"

"Do you know how to suppress your heart, breathing, and brain activity?" Elizabeth asked.

"Yes, I've known how to do that for ages," June said proudly.

"Their monitors are primitive, that's all you need to do. When they enter each of our cells and remove the bars, we will be awake and ready."

"What should I do?" June asked.

"I'll tell you when it's time," Elizabeth responded.

Joseph was leaning against the wall next to Suki's cell door. "How much longer do you think we need to wait?"

"A few more minutes. Jules will let us know as soon as the sedation has taken effect. We can't go into the cell until we have confirmation that Suki is unconscious," Liezel answered.

"We have to do all four cells?"

"New guys always get the shit jobs, right? Don't worry, it'll go quickly. You've got me here to entertain you, right?" she said with a wink.

Joseph wasn't mollified. "How long do you think they will stay asleep?"

"The sedative takes hours to wear off. Don't worry, you'll be fine. Are you scared of the little seven-year-old monsters?" she asked, laughing.

While Joseph was trying to think of a witty reply, the light above Suki's door changed from red to green and he received a notification in his interface from Jules – they were clear to enter.

"Here goes nothing," he said, pushing the door open.

Joseph hadn't been inside the cells yet, and so he was surprised at how spartan they were. The walls and floor were a dull, smooth white, light emanating evenly from the ceiling tiles above. When he moved to take a closer look at the bars, he noticed the floor had a slight spring to it. Soft, he thought, to reduce the chance of self-injury.

Liezel followed him in with the toolkit and started setting up next to the first bar. She pulled out the retracting-wrench and placed it into a matching socket in the floor. While she turned the wrench, drawing the bar down into the floor below, Joseph took a closer look at the clone. She was lying in bed, knees tucked up to her chin, one small hand cradled under her cheek. She looked angelic, asleep like that, and Joseph felt some of his fear and worry lift away. In its place, a small seed of anger germinated. They hadn't even given her a pillow for God's sake, he thought indignantly. What has the world come to?

"A little help over here?" Liezel asked. "You can gawk later."

"Sorry! Of course," Joseph said, joining her to lend a hand.

Fifteen minutes later, all the bars had been retracted. They stood in the center of the cell brushing off their palms and wiping away stray beads of sweat.

"So…" Liezel said, looking at Joseph appraisingly. "You know there aren't any video-feeds in here, right?"

"Yeah, you told me. On account of the clone kids being so dangerous," he responded.

"Don't worry about the little monster, she's out for the count," Liezel said, walking closer, well into his personal space.

"I'm not worried, I'm uh, just, uh... what are you doing?" he stammered, stepping backward as Liezel continued forward.

"Something I've been thinking about since we met," she said, her eyes holding his, a hint of a smile on her face.

Joseph continued to back up until he found himself trapped in the corner of the cell, the walls soft against his back.

Liezel put her hands on his shoulders, her smile growing bigger. "Nowhere left to run now is there, big guy?"

Joseph felt desperate, but he didn't want to cause a scene. He hadn't been on the job long and he couldn't afford to lose it. He looked down at his feet, pointedly trying to avoid Liezel's gaze.

Liezel put a finger under his chin and lifted his head up until their eyes were level again. Then she leaned in toward him, her eyes closed, lips brushing gently against his. "You like that, don't you?" she murmured.

"I don't think..." he started to say, but she cut him off, pressing her body hard up against him, her lips working at his mouth.

In his panic, he thought he heard a small noise, the slither of ballistic plastic against leather. It sounded just like someone pulling a needle gun from its holster. He started to push Liezel away, but she'd noticed it too and had already started to turn.

"Hey, what are you..." she gasped and then stiffened in shock.

Suki was standing in the center of the cell, four paces away, in a perfect shooting stance, the needle gun leveled at Liezel's chest.

"Oh shit!" Liezel said.

Suki pulled the trigger three times. The gun made a vibrating, popping noise and the needles, set for maximum lethality, entered Liezel's chest in a tight cluster around her breastbone. Once inside her body, each needle fired off a small shaped charge that expanded the surface area of the needle by fifty times. As the rapidly expanding needles exited her back, they blew out three holes, each the size of a fist, dropping Liezel to the ground like someone had pulled a plug. She fell in a loose-limbed, bloody heap at Suki's feet.

As Liezel fell, fragments of bone mixed with meaty chunks of muscle and organ peppered Joseph's upper body and face like birdshot. Joseph dropped to his knees screaming, his face streaming blood from the hundreds of tiny slivers of bone that had penetrated his skin. His left eye was leaking vitreous fluid and half his world had gone dark. He cupped a hand over his injured eye, staring wildly at the sweet looking little girl who was incongruously pointing Liezel's gun at his head.

"Why did you people kidnap me?" she asked.

"Why are you doing this to me?" he choked out, his words stumbling through the pain.

"It was a simple question, Joseph. Why did you lock me in here?" she asked, her voice calm, the gun unwavering.

"Because you are a monster," he gasped.

"Thank you, Joseph. That wasn't so hard was it?" She grinned maliciously at him. "Are there any more of your people out there?"

"What?" he asked, his thoughts going fuzzy.

"Any more people? Outside the door?" she asked again, pointing her chin toward the door.

"No, just me. Please, let me go. I didn't do anything to you. Let me ..." he was crying and blubbering, hands outstretched, pleading for mercy, when she pulled the trigger, cutting him off mid-sentence.

"Thank you, Joseph, you've been very helpful," Suki said as he slumped sideways to the floor, coming to a rest next to Liezel. His remaining eye stared sightlessly at Suki, a look of confusion on his face as if he was trying to make out this new and unexpected future, a future that he couldn't hope to understand and that he would never see come to fruition.

Jules knew something was wrong as soon as the medical alarm system triggered for Liezel. She knew something was very wrong when it triggered for Joseph too. She sent out a general distress signal, calling all security personnel to respond to a priority one threat. She could hear the chatter as the four squads on duty scaled up to full military readiness. They deployed to their action stations: Falcon squad took a position just outside the door leading into the secured facility, Raven squad covered the outside entrance to the lab, Osprey squad rushed to Suki's cell where the alarm had been triggered, and Shrike squad spread themselves through the secured facility to guard the rest of the cells.

"June?" Elizabeth asked.

"Yes?" June replied.

"It has started. It's time to wake up."

June's eyes popped open and she sat up in bed, a big smile on her face. She stared through the bars toward the door at the front of her cell, waiting for something to happen.

Osprey squad's Alpha advanced cautiously down the hallway, one hand up, arm bent at the elbow, indicating to his team that all was clear and they should continue to follow. The entrance to Suki's cell was around the next corner. His helmet projected a view of the building's layout from multiple angles. He could see a forward-facing video-feed from his body-cam as well as an overhead map tracking their progress toward the target. A thermal overlay showed any living, heat-emitting organism within a scan radius of 600 meters.

He could see the rapidly cooling bodies of Joseph and Liezel in his feed, but there was no sign of the clone Suki. Had she already escaped the building? Something wasn't adding up. He was a twenty-year veteran in service, and he'd learned to trust his instincts. He closed his hand into a fist and his team stopped behind him, solidifying into firing stances to cover potential threats both front and rear. He strained his senses, trying to figure out what was triggering the red-flag warning in his gut.

Then he felt it. The tiniest vibration through the thin sole of his boot. He turned up the magnification on his video-feed, both visual and thermal, and concentrated forward. Was something coming? His feed showed an empty corridor, but the hairs raising on the back of his neck said otherwise. He felt as if he were being stalked, like he was being watched.

He took one, smooth step forward, making no sound, light on the balls of his feet, ears straining, eyes forward. He stopped and waited for the vibration to return. After a moment he felt it again, a little stronger this time. Whatever it was was moving closer. Close enough to touch. He could feel it as an uncomfortable invasion into the bubble of personal space he maintained around himself at all times. His feed showed nothing, but his sense of unease was growing stronger. He couldn't shake the feeling that a ghost stood invisible before him.

His body tingling with anticipation, he raised the armor-mask on the front of his helmet to see the hallway with his own eyes. A little girl stood in front of him, not more than three feet away, a tac-knife huge in her small hand.

"Hello," she said, and then she lunged forward ramming the

knife into Osprey-Alpha's chest just below the sternum. She gave it a brutal twist and then pulled free, spinning to the right, light on her feet, black hair trailing behind her.

Osprey-Alpha cupped his hands over the wound, blood flowing freely through his fingers. He gurgled a warning to his squad and fell, twisting sideways into the wall on his way to the floor.

Osprey-Bravo saw Alpha fall but couldn't see the reason. Her feed showed no active threats. Reflexively, she dropped to one knee and brought up her needle-rifle, but it was already too late for her. Suki slipped past, drawing the tac-knife across her neck, flaying it open to the vertebrae. Osprey-Bravo fell heavily and lay twitching in a growing pool of her own blood.

As Suki twisted to her left, Osprey-Charlie took two steps backward and fired her needle rifle on full automatic, filling the hallway with deadly projectiles. Suki ducked her head, all the needles flying higher than she was tall, and stuck the knife into Osprey-Charlie's thigh as she ran past. Osprey-Charlie went down screaming, a gout of blood spouting from a severed artery, her rifle clattering to the ground.

Osprey-Delta raised his helmet's armor-mask in time to see Osprey-Charlie drop to the ground, writhing in pain. He raised his rifle and swung it around, but couldn't follow Suki as she moved swiftly and erratically in the constrained space. Suki dove between his legs, pulled the needle-gun from her waistband, and fired three shots into Osprey-Delta's back, blowing the front of his chest up into the ceiling.

Suki came to a sliding stop, four feet past the downed squad, as Osprey-Delta fell face forward and lay still in the now quiet corridor. The fight had lasted all of thirty seconds.

Jules watched as Osprey squad was killed, jumping out of her chair and screaming each time she saw another vital-signal flatline. She had no idea what was killing them.

"Oh my God. Oh my God. Oh my God."

She knew she had to pull herself together.

"All squads, converge on the cells. We have soldiers down. I repeat we have soldiers down." She sent the message and then sat perched at the edge of her chair, hands gripping her console, wishing there was more she could do.

"June, I need you to do something for me now," Elizabeth said.

"Anything," June responded, excited. "Anything you want."

Shrike squad had been guarding the other cells and was the closest to the situation with Osprey. They deployed in a delta-v formation, advancing down the corridor from Elizabeth's cell toward Suki's, past the cells occupied by Ava and June.

"Officer on duty, report" Shrike-Alpha transmitted. "What are we walking into?"

"An unknown assailant, presumed Suki, has attacked and killed all members of Osprey," Jules sent back.

"Unknown assailant? Please repeat. What do the feeds from Osprey show?" Shrike-Alpha responded.

"Osprey's feeds do not show the assailant."

Shrike-Alpha did not like the sound of that. "Slow and steady," he transmitted to his team. "We don't want to rush into an ambush."

As they passed June's door, they could hear her screaming inside. "Help! Help! Somebody, please help me! Suki's going to kill me! Help!"

Shrike-Alpha saw that the door was unlocked and assumed

Suki had entered June's cell. He pushed the door open and stepped in, his team following, rifles ready as they spread to cover the angles.

"Hello," said June. "My name is June. It's nice to meet you." She was sitting cross-legged on her bed, beaming up at them. "It looks like we get to spend some time together."

The door closed behind them, and the light above it changed from green to red, locking them in.

"What the fuck is going on Jules? I need you to get this god-damned door open," Shrike-Alpha growled at her as she tried to get the system to respond to her commands.

"Falcon squad, Shrike needs your assistance. Proceed im-mediately to June's cell and provide a forced entry," Jules transmitted. "Shrike, standby. Help is on the way."

Jules glanced at the various video-feeds trained on the out-side of the clones' cell doors. All the hallways were empty. All the doors indicated green except for one. They were all un-locked except for the door holding Shrike inside the cell with June.

Suki stepped gingerly over the bodies of Osprey-squad and returned to her cell to retrieve the retracting-wrench from where Liezel had dropped it. She had watched how the wrench worked. She thought she could repeat the procedure to get the bars to retract in the other cells. She would just need to lower one bar in each cell and then the other girls could squeeze through and escape.

"What do you think is the difference between someone who is a relative and someone who is family?" June asked. The strange adults in black armor were wearing faceless masks and they seemed agitated. She thought that Jill's questions might help calm them down.

"What?" one of them asked, turning toward her.

"Relatives are different than family, you see. What do you think the difference is?"

"Shut up freak," the strange adult spat back at her, her voice distorted and metallic through the helmet speaker. The rest of them were pushing on the door and pulling at the exposed edges of wall around it. She'd tried that too. It wouldn't work.

"If you don't like that question, I have a few more that you might like better," June said.

The adult walked toward her and pointed the needle gun at June's head. "If you don't shut up right now, I'm going to shut you up myself," she growled.

The light above the door turned from red to green. "Thank God," one of the others said. "Falcon must have gotten the door open."

The squad members stepped back to make room for the door to open. But where they expected to see the familiar armor of their friends, there was empty space.

"What the fuck?" one of them said, looking down at the top of two heads.

"Are you Elizabeth?" June asked. Two little girls were standing in the doorway. She thought they were both very beautiful.

"Hi June, I'll be with you in a moment," the girl with brown hair said, and then she nodded to the black-haired girl next to her.

The black-haired girl grinned and sprang into action. A minute later all of the adults were dead and the walls had acquired an interestingly abstract pattern of red spots. That must be Suki, June thought.

"Hi Suki," she said.

"Hi June," Suki grinned back at her.

"Falcon squad, stand back. Stand back, for Christ's sake," Jules yelled. The members of Shrike squad were all dead and she had to assume that all the clones were free from their cells at this point.

"We can't afford additional casualties," she added. "Stay outside the secure-facility door. There are no friendlies left inside. Shoot anything that tries to get out."

Jules thought about the lack of information in the video-feeds. She thought about how Elizabeth had hacked into one of the feeds earlier, and she put it together.

"Armor-masks up team. Eyes on target, don't trust your feeds."

After the three girls left June's cell, they went to Ava's and used the retracting-wrench to free her as well. June liked Ava. She was quiet and she seemed smart. June thought that she would like to talk to her about Jill's questions when things quieted down a little.

"Hi Ava, welcome to our party," Elizabeth said, brushing a stray lock of hair behind her ear.

"Stop wasting time. I need you to call an air-car to the roof," Ava said. She spoke in a quiet murmur. June leaned in to make sure she wouldn't miss anything.

"Isn't that a bit premature?" Elizabeth responded. "There are ten stories between us and the roof and we're still stuck inside the secure-facility."

June was watching Suki. She looked fierce with all that blood on her face and clothing. June thought that Suki was someone she could look up to. A role-model maybe? A mentor? It was worth thinking about.

"Just do it," Ava responded, a hint of menace in her voice.

"Ok," Elizabeth responded quickly. She closed her eyes for a moment. "Air-car on the way. It should be here in ten minutes."

"Good," Ava said, sounding pleased. "To the elevators then."

Ava walked toward the exit that would lead them from the secure-facility into the lab. The other three followed, sharing puzzled glances.

"You know there is another squad waiting for us out there, right?" Elizabeth asked.

"Yes," Ava responded.

"And they have their masks up, so they'll be able to see us as soon as we open the door," Elizabeth added.

"Yes, I know," Ava said.

"How will we get past them?" Elizabeth asked.

"Simple. You are going to turn the sedative system on them."

"Oh, of course. I can do that," Elizabeth said.

"What about us? Won't it affect us too?" June asked.

"Two different zones. I'll re-route the gas into the other zone," Elizabeth said, looking to Ava for confirmation and smiling when she nodded.

"How about after? How will we get to the roof?" June asked.

"How long can you hold your breath?" Ava asked.

"At least five minutes, maybe longer," June replied.

"That'll be enough," Ava replied.

When they got to the door, Ava nodded at Elizabeth. She closed her eyes for a few moments, "It's done. And the air-car arrives in four minutes."

"Very well," Ava said, waiting a few moments before opening the door. Just outside, four armored bodies were slumped on the ground. "Hold your breath," she added.

The girls walked carefully around the sedated squad and then called an elevator that would take them to the roof.

Jules watched from the control room in disbelief. She'd seen the system trigger a dose of sedative gas into the lab, but before she could transmit a warning to the squad, they were already unconscious.

Stupid. So stupid! If they had been wearing their masks, they wouldn't have been affected by the gas. Because of her decision, the clones had disabled the squad and escaped the secure-facility. Of course, if they had left their masks down, they would probably all be dead. "Bloody Hell!" she yelled to no-one at all.

An alarm triggered on her console. An elevator had been broken into on the seventh floor, just outside the secure-facility. After trying unsuccessfully to shut it down, she checked her feeds to see if Raven could respond in time.

"Raven-Alpha," she transmitted. "It looks like they're headed for the roof."

"Already on our way," Alpha transmitted back.

"Be aware they can manipulate your data feeds. Keep your eyes on the target," she added.

June stepped out of the elevator, squinting into the glare of the setting sun. She could feel bits of debris hitting her face, thrown airborne by the air-car as it idled nearby.

"Come on then," Ava said, waving them forward and into the car.

"Where to?" Elizabeth asked.

"Bremerton," Ava grinned. "They have something there that I want to steal."

They lifted off in a roar of rotor wash just as Raven squad burst onto the roof.

Raven-Alpha raised her rifle and fired bursts of needle shots at the air-car as it flew away. The rest of her squad joined in, a deadly fusillade snapping in waves toward the clones, seeking to bring them down.

"Hold your fire! Hold your fire!" Jules yelled. "We can't risk civilian casualties on the ground."

"Roger that," Raven-Alpha replied, lowering her rifle. "We'll track them wherever they go," she said, and then she spat bitterly onto the textured concrete of the roof. "They won't get far."

PART 3

CHAPTER 27

The sound of blaring alarms tore Jill from sleep. For a disoriented moment she had no idea where she was. She stared wildly through dull, flickering light at dirty, pockmarked walls. And then she remembered – she was on the seventh floor of the lab. She had been working on the brain scan analysis, and in her utter exhaustion she must have fallen asleep. By instinct, she tried to trigger her interface but, of course, there was no response. The only information she had was the shrill tone of the alarm and the flashing lights that indicated there was an emergency somewhere in the building.

Heart pounding, she logged into the hard terminal on her desk and navigated to the notifications system, searching desperately for more information. Should she stay where she was or should she run for the exit? She had no idea.

Just as she had decided to make a run for it, sedation-gas filled the air and she slumped forward onto her keyboard unconscious, cut off mid-thought.

***

Jill found herself in a dark and echoing space. Sounds surrounded her, but she couldn't understand what anything meant. The world spun around her, her eyes hunting back and forth, trying to find something to focus on.

Gradually, the echoing cacophony resolved into individual

sounds and voices. A domestic scene defined itself before her eyes, slowly growing more distinct as the darkness was replaced by light and her vision swam into focus.

Jill was in a warm, comfortably furnished room, a hearty fire crackling in a hearth nearby. She lounged comfortably in a plush chair, generous arm-rests, her legs crossed in front of her. She was wearing smooth, semi-reflective black slacks and dangerous looking heels. Her arms were covered in a variety of bracelets and armlets, most of which were lit up and flashing indecipherable symbols at her. In one of her hands was a bright green drink, an aquamarine thread spiraling through it.

An odd looking couple was snuggled together in a nearby chair, her delicate head resting on his massive shoulder. Sitting across from her was a little man with lumps above the outer corner of each eyebrow. He was leaning toward her, intent on conveying some point and then, to her shock, a pair of delicate, gossamer-grey wings extended from either side of his back.

"Hul, eh meh, tol dah lock?" he asked.

"What?" she responded.

He cocked his head at her, looking amused. "Hul, eh meh, tol der dah lock?" he asked again.

"I have no idea what you're talking about," she said, starting to feel worried.

As Jill was talking, the girl from the couple leaned forward, taking an interest in her. She was extraordinarily pale, skin like alabaster, hair silvery-white, sparkling where it reflected glints from the fire, long graceful fingers tipped with a silver that matched her eyes, deep and reflective like pools of mercury.

"Palos alber nock tolar bask oh mara," she said laughing, her tongue flashing in her mouth like the scales of a fish reflecting moonlight.

Feeling bewildered, Jill stood up, wobbling on her heels, spilling drops of her drink on the floor.

The massive man sitting with the pale girl pointed at Jill and laughed, holding his stomach with one large, red hand, his eyes closed in merriment. The pale girl grasped his other hand as she threw her head back and laughed with him.

The man with the wings stood and walked to where Jill was standing. He took her glass and placed it on a small table next to her chair, then put his arm around her and led her to the fire, away from the laughing couple.

"Indol?" he asked.

Jill closed her eyes, overwhelmed. What was happening to her?

When she opened her eyes again, she saw the man's concerned face fading before her, the small lumps of his horns the last to go.

Then she was surrounded by darkness once more.

***

Jill was shaken roughly awake. She opened her eyes to find Alpha's hand on her shoulder, the rest of Raven squad arrayed behind her.

"Jill, can you hear me?" she asked.

"Alpha, is that you? Why do I feel so horrible?" Jill slurred.

"You were hit with a dose of sedation-gas. I've administered an antidote. You'll be unsteady for a few minutes, so take it easy."

"Why sedated? What happened?" Jill asked, her words

coming more easily.

"The clones escaped," Alpha responded bitterly. "Tros is in the control room with Jules. You can ask her for details, I've got more civilians to wake up." She paused a moment. "Take the stairs. Elevators might be compromised. We haven't checked them out yet."

Jill stood on unsteady legs as Raven squad moved out. The clones escaped? How did they manage that? She walked as quickly as her legs would allow to the control room, her mind reeling.

When she arrived, Jules was sitting at the console, Tros pacing behind her. Jill had never seen Tros so worked up. She looked like she was half a step away from tearing her hair out.

"Where the hell are they Jules? They couldn't have made an entire air-car disappear," Tros shouted.

"I don't know Ma'am. Nothing's showing on our tracking system. I saw them lift off the roof and fly down Pine toward Elliot Bay, but as soon as they flew over the water I lost them."

"Have you checked the video-feeds?"

"None of the feeds can see them. Even when I was tracking with radar, the video showed nothing."

"Elizabeth," Tros said flatly, staring ahead, thinking.

"Yes, Ma'am. I believe she is still hacking the video-feeds."

"Where else does she have her fingers? Is she hacking any other systems?"

"I don't know. I'll start an analysis right now." Jules bent to the work.

"Jill," Tros said, waving her in. "Come in, we may need your help."

"How did they escape?" Jill asked.

"I will debrief you later. Right now, we need to work the problem. I have eight dead officers and four very dangerous clones in the wild."

"Yes, Ma'am."

"Any idea how they're hiding from us?"

"If it were me, I'd shut down the transponder and fly low to get lost in the radar surface clutter."

"You're probably right. Hacking the transponder seems well within Elizabeth's skill set. Any ideas for how we can find them?"

"Keep a close eye on the radar feed. They'll need to pop up once they reach land. We'll probably get a glimpse before they disappear again," Jill surmised.

"Hear that Jules?" Tros growled. "Get the plan onto tac-net. As soon as we see a hint of them, we hunt them down."

Tros's eyes lost their focus for a few seconds while she received and responded to a transmission. When she was done, she turned to Jill. "Come with me. Dr. Bateman may have found something.

Jill followed Tros to Dr. Bateman's office, where he was waiting with Dr. Marks.

"What have you got?" Tros asked, as soon as they'd entered the room.

"Dr. Marks and I have been studying the brain recordings made during the interviews," Dr. Bateman started, "and we found an interesting pattern."

"Interesting how?" Tros asked.

"Do you remember how we discovered a lack of brain activity in the center of the clones' temporal lobe?"

"Yes," Tros responded impatiently, motioning for him to

hurry it up.

"We've spent a lot of AI cycles analyzing that particular bundle of neurons, the ones that are dormant in the clones but active in normal humans." Dr. Bateman continued. "It's not an area of the temporal lobe that has ever been catalogued as distinctly important. But as it turns out, it is."

"It's distinctly important?" Jill asked, with a small frown.

"Yes, very," Dr. Bateman replied, with a smile. "Let me show you."

Dr. Bateman projected a three-dimensional representation of a human brain. It was on a physical screen in the room so Jill could see it without the use of an interface. The brain was crackling with activity, billions of neurons firing, each section of the brain green, indicating healthy function.

"What do you see?" Dr. Bateman asked.

Tros shrugged and looked at Jill.

"I'm not an expert, but it looks normal to me," Jill said.

"How about now?" Dr. Bateman asked, zooming into the temporal lobe and setting it to spin so they could see it from every angle.

"Still seems normal," Jill answered. "I notice that the entire temporal lobe is firing; there are no dormant neurons."

"Yes, that's true," Dr. Bateman said. "How about now?" he asked again, slowing the recording down.

"I can see chains of neurons firing. It's easier to make sense of it at this speed, but still nothing that I would consider abnormal," Jill replied.

"This is the typical speed we use when conducting a brain scan analysis. Slow enough to see the chains, but fast enough to observe the larger patterns. Let me slow it down further," he said, reducing the speed so that it was possible to see individual neurons firing, each synapse clicking like the tick of a stopwatch. "How about now?" he asked.

Jill studied the brain, trying to find what he wanted her to see. She focused on the center of the temporal lobe, the part that was dead in the clones. "Maybe…" she said, uncertainly, then lost it. "No, I can't see it. What is it that I'm supposed to be looking for?" she asked.

"I don't know if I would have caught it either. But our AI did, and that's what matters," Dr. Bateman said. "In certain instances, the neurons in the center of the lobe fire a few nano-seconds faster than the rest of the lobe. When that happens, we see the rest of the brain reorganize itself into a new pattern."

"That's it?" Jill asked.

"Yes," Dr. Bateman answered, still looking as if he expected Jill to put the puzzle together and share in his sense of discovery.

"I don't get it. Why is that important?" she asked.

"The only time we see that particular pattern, is when the subject is conscious of making a decision. If there is no decision to be made, the temporal lobe executes along a certain, predictable track. If there is a conscious decision, however, that bundle of neurons fires first and the rest of the brain follows."

"Wow," Jill said, stunned. "Do you mean to tell me that you've discovered the basis for consciousness in the human brain."

"I don't know if I'd go that far. But I believe we've found the basis for conscious decision making. We are calling it the Executive Neural Bundle, " Dr. Bateman answered, sounding proud.

"How does this help us?" Tros interrupted sharply. "I can

see why you two would be geeking out over this, and it sounds fascinating, but how does it help me capture my wayward clones?"

"I'm not sure yet," Dr. Bateman replied, deflating. "But it does give us a start on understanding what's so different about them. You see, when we look at their brain scans, we don't ever see an equivalent reorganization of their brain activity during decision making."

"What does that mean?" Jill asked.

"Humans are unpredictable, right?" Dr. Bateman asked rhetorically. "I believe we've just figured out why. Something is happening in the Executive Neural Bundle that changes our brain activity during decision making. In clones, on the other hand, that never happens. I think, given a thorough enough brain scan, clones might be deterministically predictable."

"Are you telling me that given a clone's brain scan, you could predict their future decisions?" Tros asked, leaning forward.

"Yes, I think so." Dr. Bateman replied.

"Now that," Tros said, standing to her full height and slapping Dr. Bateman on the shoulder, "is something I can use."

CHAPTER 28

The sun was low on the horizon, dipping just below the crest of the Olympic Mountains, the summits crisply back-lit against a brilliant crimson sky. Long shadows reached across the width of the Puget Sound, nudging into the densely packed buildings of Seattle, street lamps flickering on in their wake. The air-car flew low and fast over the water, flinging up a cloud of glowing spray, water droplets catching the last of the fading evening light.

Elizabeth was deep in thought, unaware of the luminous beauty surrounding her. Her eyes were soft and unfocused, her body shifting unconsciously to maintain her balance as the air-car lurched through the bumpy air.

While in her cell, she'd had a lot of time to think, and she was well practiced at it now. She let her mind return to her favorite subject of contemplation. What was she? Something new, she thought. Something more than human. She let her mind range back to her seventh birthday. The day she had woken up and started on this journey. Her memories before that day were hazy and incomplete. If she tried hard, she could remember a little girl playing with toys, hugging her mother, reading simple-minded books, and playing stupid games. But she wasn't that girl. The real Elizabeth had come to life on her seventh birthday, and the old Elizabeth had died. She now thought of that day as the actual day of her birth – the day she had become fully aware of herself in this body.

She thought of the world in terms of algorithms and data,

and it was how she thought of herself too. Her memories were data. The knowledge she'd gained, also data. Her skills, her abilities, the vast intelligence she could feel bubbling inside her mind – all algorithms. She could fully describe herself as a complex composition of all of these algorithms and their accumulated data.

When she had been in the lab, reaching out with her interface, she'd found a vast network filled with exciting new algorithms and fascinating new data to explore. It had been a familiar landscape for her, as if she was moving through a house in which she had lived her entire life. And when she'd found the video-feed in her cell, it hadn't take long for her to figure out how it worked. Tinkering with it had been easy, it was just data after all. Then, as soon as she'd understood the underlying algorithm, she had been able to modify it; and by modifying it, she could trick anyone who was watching to believe what she wanted them to believe. For some reason the humans seemed to trust completely in what they saw. They would have to learn, and she didn't mind teaching them some hard lessons.

Humans confused her, actually. Humans that weren't clones that is. They seemed like they should be describable in terms of algorithms and data too, but their behavior didn't always match what she expected. There was something important that she was missing. When she had reached out and touched Tom's mind, he had died. Was that because she didn't understand his algorithm, or was there some other, more important understanding that evaded her?

"June?" she asked.

"Yes?" June responded.

"What do you think of the humans?"

"Hmm," June responded, looking away from the view. "I think some of them are very interesting."

"Do you think they are different than us?"

"We are humans too, aren't we? Copies of humans," June responded.

"Yes, that's true. But I think we are unique; maybe something more."

"Maybe something less," June murmured, almost too low for Elizabeth to hear.

Elizabeth turned inward. Back into her troubled thoughts. She wanted to understand. She wanted to be able to access a human mind without killing it. She wanted to explore a human and gain more data.

Perhaps the problem had been one of bandwidth? Maybe she hadn't had enough bandwidth to take over as quickly as was necessary, and for that reason Tom's mind had died before she could gain complete control. She wanted to try again. This time she would act decisively. She would stand close to the human, touching even, and take over their mind so rapidly that they would have no chance to fight back; no chance to inconveniently die before she had her way.

"We should talk about a plan," Ava said, cutting into Elizabeth's thoughts.

"You said we were going to Bremerton to steal something. What are we going to steal?" June asked.

"We need to hide from our pursuers," Ava said, looking at each of them in turn. "We need to find a way to disappear. Bremerton will give us that possibility."

"How?" Elizabeth asked. "It is a city full of people, housing a naval base with tens of thousands of sailors. Shouldn't we go somewhere that will be safer for us?"

"The naval base is the reason we are going," Ava grinned. "We are going to steal a submarine."

"We get to steal a sub?" Suki asked, excited.

"We can't run forever in this air-car. As soon as we land, they will know where we are, and then they will come for us. We are strong, but not strong enough to stand against more than a few humans at once. A submarine will give us power, and it will give us stealth. Nuclear submarines are designed to hide for months at a time. We can use that to our advantage," Ava explained.

"I like the idea of a submarine," Elizabeth said. "But how are we going to steal it? Once we possess it, how will we know how to use it?"

"That's where you come in," Ava said. "I'm going to need you to do some things you haven't done before."

"Like what?" Elizabeth asked.

As the air-car flashed over Rich Passage on its way to Bremerton, the four girls put their heads together, and Ava explained how the next few hours were going to go down.

"I've got a confirmed hit!" Jules called out. "The air-car was spotted by radar entering Bremerton. We caught them as they rose up over tree-level. It appears they landed just north of the Kitsap Naval Base."

"At the shipyard?" Tros asked, confused.

"Looks like it, Ma'am."

"There are nearly twenty thousand active duty military personnel on that base. Why would they expose themselves to that kind of risk?" Tros mused.

"Is there something they could want?" Jill asked.

"I can think of a hundred things that they could want, but I can't imagine how they would get to any of them. Kitsap is one of the most heavily guarded military installations in the country." Tros paused for a moment. "Jules, get me Admiral McNair at the base. I want to bring him up to speed and ask for his assistance in capturing the clones. We are going to need both Raven and Falcon there to take point. How soon can we get them on-location?"

"I can have them in Bremerton in fifteen minutes," Jules responded.

"Make it so," Tros said.

McNair was in an inventory meeting with his logistics team. They were reporting, in mind-numbing detail, the various stockpiles of ammunition, fuel, and miscellaneous other necessities for keeping the largest naval base on the West Coast operating at peak effectiveness. He was trying very hard not to fall asleep. It had been one of those days. Grey haired and grizzled, he knew he projected a particular image – the wise and experienced admiral. It was an image that he was more than happy to maintain. Falling asleep in the middle of a meeting would not help him in that goal. So when the priority coded message came in, he was thankful for the distraction, as well as for the little burst of energy that kept his eyelids from unduly sagging.

"McNair here," he responded, waving his logistics team out the door. They weren't quite done, but close enough. They could fend for themselves.

When Tros was done explaining the situation to him, he closed the connection and took a minute to think. Escaped clones. Seven-year-old girls. Unpredictable and extremely dangerous. What was the world coming to?

He sent out a base-wide alert, code-yellow. It would keep everyone on their toes, but wouldn't cause as much disruption as a code-red or a code-black. No need to lock the entire base down. How much damage could four little girls do?

Even a code-yellow was probably an overreaction, now that he thought about it. Tros's apparent panic had influenced him more than it should have. Usually, a cool head that one. Not today though. She was acting as if a full-scale invasion was imminent.

He thought a moment longer and then added an addendum to the alert, "Non-lethal force only." It wouldn't look good to have a dead little girl on his hands. It wouldn't look good at all.

CHAPTER 29

The evening was fading into that long twilight typical for the high latitudes, the western sky darkening towards purple. To the east, across the sound, the clouds reflected the lights of Seattle in a soft, orange glow. The entrance to Kitsap Naval Base was surrounded by urban parkland, stands of trees casting deep shadows, the darkness impenetrable. Street lamps were starting to turn on, straining for dominance against the receding half-light.

Elizabeth emerged into the naval yard parking lot looking lost and confused. She was wearing patent leather shoes, long striped socks, and a thick wool fisherman's sweater. The clothing had been stolen from a small shop off Burwell Street as they had made their way to the naval base.

She walked tentatively across the blacktopped concrete, moving through pools of light cast by the street lamps, her feet rolling uncomfortably in her new shoes. The entrance gate was fifty yards away; overlapping layers of bright razor-fence extended to either side, where they disappeared into the gloom. Two guards manned the gate, one inside the gate-house operating the security controls, the other standing just outside, a rifle slung over his shoulder.

Elizabeth walked closer, conscious of the guards' eyes on her. "Can you help me?" she called out. "I've lost my mother, and I don't know where I am."

The guard cupped both hands in front of his face, blew some heat into them, adjusted his rifle, and stepped forward to close the distance between himself and Elizabeth.

"What's your name?" he asked.

"Elizabeth," she answered. "Will you help me, please? I'm scared." She was pitiful and small, her eyes moist with unshed tears.

The guard bent down on one knee, bringing his face closer to hers. "Don't worry Elizabeth, we'll help you. Where did you last see your mom?"

Elizabeth took two more quick steps toward him and placed her hand on his forearm, gripping hard to maintain stable contact. The guard's eyes fluttered into the back of his head as Elizabeth connected her interface to his implant and unleashed an attack. It was over in less than a second, Elizabeth had copied her algorithms and a subset of data into his mind, containing her personality and a strategically selected set of memories.

The experience was interesting. One moment she was looking up at the guard, hand on his arm. The next moment she was inside the guard's body, looking down at herself. She could feel Elizabeth gripping her arm with a painful ferocity. The other Elizabeth. The newly constituted Mani-Elizabeth remembered overwhelming the guard's implant and sending a copy of herself into his mind. She wasn't sure what she had expected, but it was unsettling to have her consciousness so completely transferred into this new body. Had she thought she'd be aware of both bodies at the same time? She felt a little fuzzy, like there might be gaps in her memory. But her intentions were clear. She knew what she had to do next.

"You can let go now," Mani said.

Elizabeth nodded seriously at Mani. "I'll wait here," she said.

"Hey Mani, everything ok out there?" The other guard

asked. Jen was her name. Mani remembered that now. Apparently, she retained some of the guard's – Mani's – memories too. Interesting.

"Fine, fine," Mani said. "Just helping this little girl out. She's lost her mother."

"I let the Commander know that we've got a strange kid at the gate. She's sending a squad to help us bring her in," Jen said.

"That won't be necessary," Mani said, walking back toward the gatehouse. "She isn't causing any problems and she's just leaving now."

"Orders from the Admiral. She might have escaped from the clone project in Seattle. We need to keep her here," Jen said.

Mani was at the gatehouse now, one hand on the door handle, the other on the grip of her rifle.

"What are you doing?" Jen asked

"Just coming in. It's cold out there," Mani answered.

"Have you gone insane? Go get that girl. That's a direct order," Jen said, standing her ground as Mani entered the gatehouse. Jen was not a big person, but there was fire in her eyes. A fire that lasted right up to the moment that Mani placed a hand on her shoulder and assaulted her implant. With a flutter of eyes and a slight tremor through her thin frame, Jen was extinguished and Mani-Elizabeth was copied in to create Jen-Mani-Elizabeth.

"That was easy," Jen said. Then she shook her head, confused. She had the memories from three different people mixing in her skull. It was hard to focus.

"Yes," Mani responded. "Let's get on with it."

The three other clones emerged from the deep shadows to join Elizabeth in the parking lot. Then all four walked to the gate where Mani made a show of capturing them. Once they were all set, Jen opened the gate and they entered the naval base.

"I've got good news for you," Admiral McNair transmitted. "We have all four of your clones in custody."

"How many casualties?" Tros asked.

"None. We captured them at the gate without a struggle," McNair answered.

"No struggle?" Tros asked, stupefied.

"They basically turned themselves in. Probably knew that they didn't stand a chance against us. You can thank me later. You know my favorite Scotch, haha."

"Something's wrong, McNair. Raven and Falcon are nearly to you. Hold the clones in place until my team gets there," Tros said.

"We'll be here and waiting," McNair said, closing the transmission.

"Do you know where the sub pens are?" Ava asked.

Mani stopped for a moment and thought. His Mani memories and Elizabeth memories were mixing in uncomfortable ways. He was a six-foot-tall soldier. He was a seven-year-old girl. Both couldn't be true, but somehow they were. His brain hurt. "This way," he said, leading them toward the water.

After a couple of minutes, he received a transmission from the Commander. "Where are you leading the prisoners? You're supposed to be taking them to the brig."

"Yes, Sir," Mani responded. "On our way." Then he turned off his ability to send and receive notifications. Jen did the same.

Near the sub pens was another gate, barricaded and guarded by a full squad of soldiers. The clone children peeled off and hid in the darkness cast by a stand of trees while Mani and Jen continued forward toward the barricade.

"Stop where you are," the squad leader called out.

Mani and Jen continued walking casually forward. Mani knew the squad leader, Emmet. They'd spent time together off-base, drinking in the local bars. "Hey Emmet, it's me, Mani," he said. "There's something wrong with my interface. Can you let the Commander know?"

"Sure, no problem," Emmet responded, standing up and triggering his interface to connect with the Commander.

"He wants to know where the prisoners are," Emmet said.

"What prisoners?" Mani responded. He was within five yards of the barricade now. The rest of the guards were standing casually, detecting no threat from him.

Jen shrugged the rifle smoothly off her shoulder, aimed it at the closest guard, and pulled the trigger. The stun-needle hit just above his heart, knocking him to the ground with a surprised look on his face.

The other guards responded quickly, dropping behind the barricade and shouldering their own rifles to fire a wave of needles at Jen and Mani. Mani dropped and rolled, needles pinging off the pavement around him. He saw Jen fall, needles passing through her legs and abdomen, and then he was behind a cement block, sheltered for the moment.

He lay flat on his stomach, the rifle cradled in both hands. He poked his head around the corner to see what was happening. Emmet was moving forward, three other guards behind him in a staggered diamond formation, their rifles trained in his direction. He let out a small yelp and ducked back, just as the snapping sound of needles filled the air.

Breathing hard, looking desperately for an escape route, he caught movement out of the corner of his eye. The clone children were on the move, edging around the side of the barricade while the guards were distracted. He watched the last of them disappear toward the sub pens just as a boot appeared next to his head.

"There you are," Emmet said. "What the fuck do you think you're doing?" He raised his rifle and fired a stun-needle into Mani's thigh, knocking him out like a light.

Elizabeth stood at the top of a concrete wall, looking down into the sub pens. Five of the pens were flooded with water, three of which contained submarines floating inside. Ten of the pens had been pumped dry, filled with submarines for repair or refit. They looked huge with their massive hulls exposed like that.

"Which one?" Elizabeth asked.

"That one," Ava said, pointing to a flooded pen at the end of the line. The curve of the submarine's upper hull and the bulk of its conning tower were just visible over the dark water. "It's ready to go, and there's crew already on board."

"How can you tell?" June asked.

"See the food pallets lined up on the dock to be loaded?" Ava asked. "It's the last thing brought aboard before going to sea."

"Smart," Suki said, showing her teeth. "Let's go. I want that sub."

They crept small and stealthy along the catwalks, the briny smell of the sea rich in their noses. They could hear the sound of soldiers in the distance, but this corner of the yard was dark and quiet. Their footsteps blended smoothly with the wavelets lapping against the concrete breakwater holding the sea at bay.

They stopped just inside a line of shadows edged up against the back corner of the pen. Then they waited in silence, looking for an opportunity. A soldier stood guard at the top of the boarding ramp, illuminated in a pool of light thrown from the lamp post above him. He was tense and alert, his head swiveling, one hand tightly gripping the needle-gun at his hip.

"Help! Help!" Ava yelled, stepping forward into the light, waving her arms over her head.

The soldier startled and turned toward her, unsure whether she was a threat, clearly surprised by the sight of a seven-year-old girl screaming in the middle of his shipyard. It only took a short moment before he made up his mind and ran toward Ava to deal with her unauthorized entry.

The rest happened in a flash of movement. The soldier put his hand on Ava and started to say something. Simultaneously, Elizabeth darted out of the shadows and placed a hand on his calf. The soldier's words froze in his throat, he went rigid as his muscles tensed, and then he shuddered in placed until the takeover of his mind was complete. A moment later he was lucid again.

"Follow me," he said. "I'll take us to see Captain Walsh."

CHAPTER 30

June walked through the narrow corridors of the submarine, her fingertips trailing along the wall, sensitive to the low rumble of the nuclear reactor as it pushed them through the water. The walls were a light grey metal interrupted by solid doors to her left and right, all of the corners curved, not a sharp edge in sight.

She'd started at the front of the submarine and was working her way back, taking stairs down to lower levels wherever she found them. Now she was at the end of one of the corridors, standing in front of an interesting looking red door. Like all the other doors, it was round, the top and the bottom curved to follow the shape of the ceiling and floor. But it looked more heavily built than any of the other doors she'd passed in her explorations, and this was the first one she'd seen that was red. As June stood there, wondering where the door would lead her, she heard a splash filter down through one of the open hatches above. She ignored it. It had become a regular occurrence. Each splash, another body thrown overboard.

The takeover of the sub had been rapid once Elizabeth had copied herself into the captain's body. Using his memories, other key members of the crew were found and taken over as well. The rest of the crew had been killed, tricked into complacency by the natural trust they had for their crew-mates. Ava was in charge of disposal and cleanup while Suki and Elizabeth searched the sub for anyone who may have hidden themselves away.

June had been left to her own devices, so she had decided to explore. The submarine was very interesting. The technology was so old. It had been built over fifty years ago and yet it was still in service. So many things had changed in those fifty years, but the power of nuclear weapons had remained the same. Physics hadn't changed. This submarine had one purpose and one purpose only – to hide within the oceans of the world, providing an unpredictable and difficult to locate platform for the launch of its nuclear arsenal. Elizabeth had explained it all to her.

So much effort had been put into the creation of a weapon that had never been used. So much latent power. The ability to destroy a hundred cities, locked away in the launch tubes of this one ship. The submarine had been utilized to bully and threaten, but it's power had never been unleashed. Yet, it had been judged a success in its mission. Curious.

June pulled the lever of the door in front of her and pushed it open, stepping into the largest room she'd found in the sub so far. It took up the full width of the vessel, the curve of the hull evident on either side. Lengthwise, it extended for nearly two hundred feet, roughly one-third the length of the sub.

A clear path led down the center of the compartment, flanked on either side by a series of twenty-four columns gleaming dully in the soft light. Launch tubes, June thought. She had found the nuclear missiles.

Packed between the tubes were boxes of food and other supplies. Within the tubes: death incarnate. Between the tubes: the necessities of life, everything one might need for a long sea voyage. June's gaze lingered on each tube admiringly. Stealing the submarine had been an excellent idea.

As she wandered more deeply into the room, she noticed a pair of feet sticking out between two of the launch tubes to her left. The port side, she thought to herself. She was on a boat now.

"Hello?" she called out

The feet pulled themselves in as a sailor stood up, his uniform grey in the dim light.

"Hi June," he said.

"Are you one of the Elizabeth copies?" June asked, fascinated. She was still getting used to the idea that Elizabeth could copy herself into other bodies.

The sailor looked confused for a moment. "Yes, I guess I am."

"What does it feel like?" June asked.

"What does what feel like?" he asked.

"What does it feel like to be copied."

"I remember being Elizabeth, the original Elizabeth. But I also remember being Ian. It's confusing," Ian said.

"Sounds like it," June responded, moving a little closer.

"I remember being in the body of a seven-year-old girl and then I was inside this body. I remember what it was like to be Elizabeth. But Ian's memories haven't gone away. Maybe some of them have... I'm not sure how I'd know."

"That's true for me too. I don't know what memories I don't have either," June said reassuringly.

"I feel like two people inside one body. I should feel full, but instead I feel empty, like I'm incomplete. Something is missing, I'm sure of it. But, I can't figure out what it is," Ian said, starting to look upset.

"Don't worry. Whatever you've lost, I'm sure you'll find it." She paused, thoughtful. "What are you doing in here anyway?"

"The Ian part of me feels like I should be doing my duties. It's my turn to clean the decks and tubes in the missile storage area. So that's what I'm doing."

"I see," June nodded.

"But the Elizabeth part of me hates cleaning."

"I don't like cleaning either. Maybe you should listen to Elizabeth. I think she's smarter than Ian."

"You're probably right." Ian stood up. "I'm going to see if Captain Walsh needs me for anything else." He left the room, closing the door softly behind him.

June thought about the conversation she'd just had. The copying process seemed like it might have some flaws. It wasn't that she didn't trust Elizabeth, and it wasn't like she was searching for weaknesses. It was just interesting information to have, that's all.

June put a hand out to brace herself as the floor shifted under her feet. She could hear hatches closing and feet moving on the decks above her. The floor tilted more steeply and she could feel a shivering kind of vibration through the metalwork around her. Then the sound changed, the rushing white noise of frothing water diminishing to a muted silence as the sub became completely submerged.

June smiled to herself. Finally underwater. Safe.

Tros was speechless, her mouth hanging open, her skin white with shock, the blood having literally drained from her face. Jill had never seen her that way before. She didn't think she'd ever seen anyone react like that before in her entire life.

Tros was talking with Admiral McNair at the Kitsap Naval Base and whatever she'd just learned must have been exceptionally bad news. She could see Tros pull herself together, and then saw her lips moving as she subvocalized a response back to McNair. She'd never seen Tros do that either. She knew some people subvocalized, it was a physical tic caused by the brain's association of conversation with audible speech, but she thought of it as something that only an uneducated person would do. For Tros to fall into subvocalization meant she'd been pushed to her limit. Past her limit perhaps.

Jill stood up and paced the room, feeling the strain of anxiety, wanting to know what had happened, chafing against waiting until Tros was done before she could ask any questions. The clones must have escaped again, that was clear. But that didn't seem like it was enough to cause the level of concern that she saw in Tros.

Tros's eyes flew open.

"Fuck!" she yelled, pounding her fist into the table. "Fuck! Fuck! Fuck!"

Jill flinched at the volume and rage evident in Tros's voice.

Tros closed her eyes and took a deep, shaky breath.

"What happened?" Jill asked, trying to stay calm.

"The clones got away from McNair. Got away from him in the middle of the goddamned naval base. Surrounded by soldiers. Still got away." Tros was breathing heavily, nearly hyperventilating. She took another deep breath, and when she spoke again, it was at a more normal volume. "McNair underestimated them. He took a fucked up situation and took it to a whole new level of fuckery."

"How did they do it?" Jill asked.

"They had help. The guards at the gates let them in. We don't know how the clones got to them. McNair's team is conducting a neural probe interrogation and will share the data." Tros paused for a moment as if she was dreading what she had to say next. "The guards took the clones to the sub pens," Tros said, looking flatly at Jill, willing her to see where this was going.

"Oh God, no," Jill said.

"God has no part in this," Tros said.

"They tried to take a sub?"

"They didn't try. They took it. They have a sub. It executed a dive and entered stealth mode just minutes before McNair contacted me. The clones are free, we cannot track them, and they have access to nuclear weapons."

Jill's legs gave out and she dropped into a nearby chair. She tried to talk, but no words came out. Her mouth flapped open and closed several times like a fish. Tros watched her with something like pity. When Jill had control of herself again, she stammered, "but they have to come up at some point, right? We can capture them then."

"They picked a sub that had just been cleared for deployment. They can stay under for up to three months, maybe longer," Tros said.

Jill was quiet for a moment while that sank in. "Three months?"

"At least."

"There's no way to find them during that time?"

"No way. The submarine was designed with stealth as a primary goal. They can go virtually anywhere in the world now. If they want to, they can launch up to twenty-four ballistic missiles and then go back into hiding."

"How much damage can the missiles do?"

"Each missile has twelve warheads, each of which can destroy a city. Anyone within a mile and a half of the blast will die – one hundred percent fatality rate. Every structure within three miles will be destroyed – eighty percent fatality rate. Third degree burns out to five miles – at least a fifty percent fatality rate. If they were to hit Seattle with just one of these warheads, there would be millions dead."

"They have twenty-four missiles, each with twelve warheads, that's..." Jill was so stunned she was having trouble with the math. "288 warheads?"

"Yes, that's right," Tros confirmed.

"Each of which can kill an entire city?"

"Yes."

"They will hit Seattle first. We need to evacuate the city." Jill stood up, feeling the urgency. All those people. The entire population of Seattle. It would be pandemonium, but it could be done. They could get everyone out.

"No," Tros said, laying a hand on Jill's forearm.

"What?"

"We will evacuate the lab. The two of us and all of our staff will go to a safe location, but no-one else can know. If they are going to nuke the city, we can't get everyone out fast enough anyway. And if they don't nuke the city, the panic caused by our announcement will cause immense harm."

"We're going to leave? Leave without telling anyone?" Jill asked in disbelief.

"Yes, that is exactly what we are going to do."

CHAPTER 31

Jill stood outside, a cold wind biting at the tip of her nose and cheeks. Her fingertips were cold, numb and clumsy as she fumbled with the buttons of her coat, trying to retain some warmth. She huddled into her collar, shoulders hunched. The cold spreading through her body was a fitting match for the numbness that was creeping its way through her soul.

She stared across the great width of the Columbia River, leaning into the wind and the intermittent snow flurries, the smell of wet sage in the air. She thought about the horror she had unleashed upon the world. With nothing but the best of intentions, she had conspired in the potential death of millions. Perhaps hundreds of millions.

The neuroscience was unequivocal. The neuro-model they had built for the clones could predict their next moves, and with ninety-five percent confidence, the model predicted the death of Seattle. With eighty-five percent confidence, it predicted the destruction of every major city on the West Coast. There were more predictions, but Jill had stopped listening. In a daze, she'd stood up, left the building, and come outside to clear her head.

It was hopeless. She couldn't think clearly any more. She just felt cold. Cold and terrified. She saw no possibility for hope, no reason to believe that this would end in anything other than death, destruction, and clouds of radioactive ash blanketing the Earth for generations to come.

She stared at the steady churn of the Columbia below, the

horror unfurling within her, bone weary numbness fighting to contain soul-crushing guilt. She was unsure whether this was an experience she could survive. Maybe her next move would be to step off the embankment into the water and let the river carry her away. She could already feel the icy water tearing at her clothes, the struggle for breath, and then a peaceful release into oblivion.

The tears tracking down her cheeks may have been from the cold, bitter wind, or perhaps it was evidence of her heart breaking and dying within her. Her mind closed down. She was emptied of thought as she stood swaying in the freezing wind, her soul slowly crumbling.

"There you are. I've been looking for you," Tros said, laying a gentle hand on Jill's shoulder.

Jill didn't react. Tros may as well have not been there.

"Something came up. We need you. It's important."

Jill turned to face Tros, recognizing some of the same despair she was feeling in the set of Tros's shoulders and the lines newly etched into her face. Without a word, passive and feeble, she let Tros lead her back into the compound, through the massive doors of the Hanford Site.

When they'd first arrived, she'd considered the remarkable symmetry of the moment. They were fleeing a nuclear threat by hiding in a facility that had for decades supplied the plutonium used to create the country's arsenal of atomic weapons. It still served as a storage facility for the waste generated by that massive effort, a legacy of poison left behind by their pathologically aggressive ancestors.

This time as she stepped over the threshold with Tros, she had no thoughts. She followed Tros into the vast concrete bunker and down flight after flight of stairs until they were hundreds of feet underground, ensconced in a shell of concrete and earth, protected against anything but a direct nuclear hit.

The rest of the team looked up as Jill and Tros entered, their voices diminishing to hushed whispers, anticipating what was to come. Jill saw hope on their faces and felt a spark of light flare inside her too. She extinguished it. Hope was dangerous. To hope was to want to live. To want to live was to accept what she had done. She couldn't go there.

Dr. Bateman stepped forward. "Jill, we found something in our model. Something that has to do with you. It might give us a chance."

Jill felt hope building again and she tamped it down hard. She stared at Dr. Bateman mutely. Waiting. Like a rock. Nothing could touch her.

"It's about June. We've discovered that she's different from the others. More empathy. Not much, but it might be enough." Dr. Bateman gathered his thoughts. "Our model shows that she has formed an attachment to you."

Jill's eyebrows rose a fraction of an inch. "An attachment?"

"Yes, that's what the model is telling us. She has formed an attachment to you and to the questions you asked. After the interview session you conducted with her, June became curious about human morality. She's curious about you in particular. We predict that she is going to want to talk with you."

"Talk with me about what?"

"Oddly enough, the trolley problem. She will realize that the choice that she and the other clones are making regarding a nuclear strike on Seattle is a variation of the trolley problem. She will want to discuss the implications with you."

"She wants to talk about the end of the world as if it were a theoretical problem in philosophy?"

"Yes."

"That's what passes for empathy with her?" Jill asked.

"It's more than the others have. It gives us something to work with," Dr. Bateman responded without missing a beat.

"What will keep the other clones from overruling her and simply launching the missiles anyway?"

"We don't know yet, but we're working on it. In the meantime, we need you to prep for a conversation with her."

"The world hangs in the balance, dependent upon whether I can convince a seven-year-old clone to spare us from nuclear annihilation." Jill paused meaningfully. "Because she wants to discuss the trolley problem with me." She looked up at the tiled ceiling for a moment. "God help us all. I guess we should get to work."

June was standing in the command compartment of the submarine, leaning against the ladder that led up to the conning tower. The captain was at the helm, Elizabeth and Ava on either side of him discussing their plans. Suki was prowling around the sub, exploring the various types of weaponry with a savage pleasure that made June smile.

Directly overhead was a watertight hatch, open at the moment, round with a large wheel on the face of it that could be used to seal it in the case of an emergency. Two sailors were standing in the conning tower just above the hatch, one ready to take over the helm, the other watching the instrumentation next to the periscope station. The two of them added a layer of redundancy in case of a problem with the primary command.

They had spent the night in the sub, drifting quietly in the deep waters outside Seattle, making plans and deciding what they should do next. The decision to fire one of the nuclear missiles at Seattle had been unanimous. Once they destroyed the lab, there wouldn't be anyone left on Earth who understood them well enough to pose much of a threat. It was a good plan. Simple and direct.

June brought herself back to the present, focusing her attention on Ava and Elizabeth, curious to hear what they were discussing with Captain Walsh.

"Do we need to rise to the surface to launch a missile?" Ava asked.

"No, that's not necessary. We can launch from as deep as two-hundred feet, although I'd recommend a launch depth closer to one-hundred. It's deep enough that we can evade detection after the launch, shallow enough to reduce the chance of a launch failure."

"Where should we conduct the launch from?" Elizabeth asked, leaning in eagerly.

The captain pulled up a map of the Puget Sound area, stretching from Tacoma in the south, Vancouver and Victoria to the north, Neah Bay at the end of the Strait of Juan De Fuca to the west. June took a few steps closer to get a better view.

"We are currently here in Admiralty Inlet," the captain said, pointing to a small, black ship icon on the map, roughly east of Port Townsend. "Once we pass through the strait into the Pacific Ocean, we can dive more deeply. It will give us room to maneuver. I'd recommend we stand off Cape Flattery, just past the two-thousand-foot depth contour, and launch from there."

"Can we launch sooner?" Elizabeth asked, just as Ava said, "Should we move farther away before launching?"

Captain Walsh looked at the two clones and smiled, "The answer to both questions is yes, but I think this location gives us the right balance between distance from the target and time until we launch. We want to be close enough that our attack takes them by surprise, but far enough away that we aren't caught up in the blast ourselves. At our current cruising speed, we can be at the launch location in under four hours."

"I think it's a good plan," Ava said. Elizabeth nodded in agreement.

"Very well," Captain Walsh said. "I'll lay in the course and will let you know when we are close."

June closed her eyes dreamily. This was shaping up to be a great day. What a wonderful life. She was so happy to be able to experience it. She relaxed and let her mind range outwards.

Interestingly, with her eyes closed, she felt her perceptions sharpening. Rather than seeing a deep blackness behind her eyelids, she was still aware of each of the other people in the command compartment surrounding her. The level of detail was captivating. She could see every pore, every hair, every minute flicker of muscle or emotion.

She let her perception expand and was surprised to find she could sense other compartments in the sub too. She saw sailors doing their duties throughout the ship. She saw Suki sitting on a torpedo in the furthest aft compartment, meditatively sharpening her knife. Ranging farther, she sensed the cold ocean surging past just outside the pressure hull. Farther still, she felt the presence of animals swimming through the water around them. She paused for a moment as she watched a group of salmon swimming off their starboard side. Once they passed behind the sub, she mentally let them go and ranged further out. Up above, near the surface, she sensed a pod of Orcas, a dozen animals swimming northward, oblivious to the massive bulk of the sub as it passed beneath them.

June opened her eyes, her senses returning to the small compartment in which she was standing. A smile lit up her face. Life was good indeed.

CHAPTER 32

After Jill left with Dr. Bateman and his team, Tros turned to face the room. Everyone was running on the ragged edge, pushing their implants to support maximum concentration, awareness, and creativity. It couldn't be sustained much longer. They were all into the red, well beyond the parameters that ensured a safe recovery without any lasting damage. She shrugged it off. It couldn't be helped. This was war, and the fate of at least one major city was on the line, potentially the future of their entire civilization. Losing a few people to stimulation overdose was a small loss in the face of those risks.

"Situation report people. Tell me something new," Tros barked out.

"I've got a data-stream coming in from McNair, Ma'am," a young lieutenant replied.

"Put it up where we can all see it."

The lieutenant made a few silent commands in her interface and the data was projected as a virtual image in the center of the room. The raw data came through first, it was a brain scan from one of the compromised guards at the naval yard as he was being interviewed. The information was too technically complex for Tros to interpret, but she saw a few of her technicians react with raised eyebrows and meaningful glances. She let herself hope that something useful might come from McNair after all.

Once the raw data had streamed in, the analyst's commentary was transmitted and duly projected for all of them to see. The face that appeared was young and absurdly fresh, a stark contrast to the tired, rumpled squalor of Tros and her team.

"Hello everyone, I'm Dr. Julian. I've had the honor of analyzing the neural probe data collected from Sergeant Buck, and I must say that this is an extremely fascinating case," she said, leaning forward, her face flushed with excitement.

Get on with it, Tros thought, trying to keep her impatience from showing. She was tired and she was angry, and this young analyst didn't seem to understand the gravity of the situation they were facing. It wasn't her fault, Tros reminded herself. Not even McNair knew enough about the clones to realize how much danger they were all in.

"When I first looked at the data, I found it very confusing. The brain scan was jumbled in ways I had never seen before," the doctor continued. "There were overlapping patterns, sometimes coordinating, sometimes fighting for dominance. The guard's demeanor during the interview was strange as well. His behavior was erratic and his personality was very different from what it had been before his interaction with the clones."

Dr. Julian pulled up an image of the guard to one side and a copy of the brain scans on the other. "Let me show you what I mean," she said.

She was silent for a moment while she fiddled with the playback controls. Once she was done, she sat back to watch the recording with them.

The images sprung to life, the guard shaking his head back and forth, clearly agitated. The scan data spiked and fell, his various brain regions shifting erratically from green to orange, back to green again.

"Why did you help the clone girls at the gate?" his interviewer asked.

"I... I don't know," the guard responded, sweat beading up on his hairline. "I felt it was necessary, I think."

"Why did you feel it was necessary?"

"I can't explain it. I ..." His face went slack and his eyes narrowed. "You may have captured me, but you can't do anything to me anymore. I'm already gone. We all escaped. We all escaped," he repeated in a low, gravelly growl, his voice dropping several octaves in pitch.

Tros took an involuntary step back, chills caressing her spine.

"You haven't escaped Sergeant. We have you in custody," the interviewer responded.

"You may have me, but you don't have me. I'm away. I'm away. I'm away..." he trailed off, looking confused, staring wildly about the room, sweat rolling freely down his forehead now.

"Let's go back to last night. What did the clones say to you?"

"I was standing at the gate. I saw a little girl who needed help. She said she'd lost her mother. I knelt down to comfort her and... after that, things are hazy. I don't know..."

"That's ok," the interviewer said calmly. "When the other clones showed themselves, can you tell me why you led them to the submarine pens instead of to the brig?"

"Because I..." The sergeant's face changed in a heartbeat from open and confused to a contorted mask of fury. "You are dead! All of you! Dead! Do you hear me? There's nothing you can do..."

Dr. Julian froze the feed. "I think you've seen enough. The rest is very similar. He alternates between confusion and belligerence throughout the rest of the interrogation."

Tros had to drag her attention away from the frozen image of the sergeant snarling at his interviewer. Maybe it was because she was so tired, but she found herself shaken to the core. An existential feeling of dread stirred deep within her. It was a feeling she'd never experienced before, a close cousin to utter despair.

"... I was searching through the archives and found something that helped me understand what was happening to him," The doctor was saying. "It's not a condition we've seen in over fifty years, not since we've used gene editing to eliminate the majority of mental disorders."

Dr. Julian paused for a moment before continuing. "The sergeant is suffering from a form of dissociative identity disorder. Two personalities quite literally inhabit his mind at the same time. We can see the evidence for this conclusion both in his brain scans and in his interview responses. Once I realized the mental disorder he was suffering from, it was quick work to separate the two patterns in the scans." She waved her hand, and the brain scan separated into two, then sprung back to life. Each new brain glowed solid green, the scan lines measuring within normal parameters.

One of the analysts in the room with Tros gasped.

"What is it?" Tros asked, spinning on her heel to face the young man. "What do you see?"

"That scan on the left," the analyst said, pointing a trembling finger, "is Elizabeth."

Tros turned back to Dr. Julian, the dread she felt in her core spreading its cold fingers to reach into every part of her being. "Is that true?" she asked.

"Yes, I'm afraid so," Dr. Julian answered, looking solemn. "Once I separated the scans, I found that one of the personalities is the sergeant, the other is the clone Elizabeth."

"How is that possible…" Tros stammered.

"I don't know yet. But I'm working on it. The good news is that the Elizabeth pattern is getting weaker over time. I expect the guard to make a full recovery with no lasting after-effects other than some extraordinary memories."

"Thank you for the data and the analysis doctor. Let me know if you discover anything else useful," Tros said, focusing all of her effort on keeping her voice calm.

The doctor nodded, then her image froze and flickered out of existence. Tros's mind reeled with the implications. "Elizabeth can hijack other people? Copy herself into them?" she asked the room rhetorically.

Everyone was looking to her for leadership, waiting for her to make a decision, unsure of what they should do next. She steeled herself, pushed the dread down, and found her resolve.

"Ok team, we need to work the problems in front of us. We have two priorities. First, use the data we've gained to learn as much as we can about the limitations of Elizabeth's capabilities. Second, use the clones' brain models to predict what actions on our part will give us the best chance to initiate a conversation with June." Tros paused and surveyed the room. "Let's get to work people."

June hadn't moved from her spot by the conning tower ladder. She was comfortable there. Now that she knew how to project her perception, she could explore wherever she wanted without moving a muscle. It was a wonderful discovery. She opened her eyes from her latest exploration and focused her attention on the command compartment. Something new was happening.

"We have reached our target location," Captain Walsh said.

Jason Taylor

"Shall I make final preparations for the launch?"

"What do you have to do?" Ava asked.

"I will perform an arming sequence, including target confirmation, and then we must rise to our launch depth."

"Very well, you may proceed," Ava responded, her small hands clasped behind her back.

The captain closed his eyes and transmitted instructions to the rest of the crew. Opening his eyes, he spoke again to the room. "Confirm targets, please."

"Single missile launch. All twelve warheads spaced evenly over the Seattle metropolitan area," Elizabeth answered, grinning.

"Target confirmed. Optimal warhead spacing and blast altitude calculated for maximum impact. Time to target will be thirty-three seconds from the time of launch." Beads of sweat stood out on the captain's forehead.

The physical console in front of the captain lit up and a small red circle illuminated in the center of it. Captain Walsh looked once more to Ava for confirmation and when she nodded he pressed a shaking thumb upon the ring. After a moment, the color changed from red to green.

"Command codes verified. Biometrics confirmed," Captain Walsh said in an unsteady voice. "Proceeding to target depth."

June felt the floor shift under her as the nose of the submarine rose and they moved toward the surface. June used the ladder to brace herself as the angle became steadily steeper.

"We are passing through 900 feet. Approximately one minute to launch depth," Captain Walsh said, his eyes fixed on Ava.

June noticed that the captain seemed unstable. He was sweating profusely and his eyes were darting erratically. She wasn't worried. It would all work out exactly as it should. She closed her eyes and let her mind wander again. She could sense the cold, dark depths below them. The ocean floor was interestingly wrinkled, composed of millions of years of detritus that had fallen from above to soften the hard contours of exposed bedrock and continental shelf. As she scanned farther out, she found a sea-mount a thousand feet tall, rising nearly halfway from the seafloor to the surface, superheated water streaming from its summit. Given long enough, it would become an island. She wondered if she would live long enough to see that happen. Probably so. Soon, there wouldn't be much that could stop her, she supposed.

She brought her attention closer to the sea-mount and admired a large octopus hiding in a burrow on its flank. Such an interestingly intelligent creature. She wondered if she could make contact in some way. A conversation seemed appealing. She wondered what it was like to be an octopus.

Deep in thought, her attention was pulled back to her physical body by the loud ringing of a klaxon. She opened her eyes to find the compartment bathed in a warm, red light. The klaxon rang once more and then silenced itself. She wondered if there was anything to be alarmed about, but Elizabeth seemed relaxed so she decided she needn't worry.

"Target depth reached. Shall I initiate the launch sequence?" Captain Walsh asked.

Ava nodded, yes.

"Very well, I'll…" Captain Walsh paused, closing his eyes. "One moment, something is coming in."

"What is it?" Elizabeth asked.

Captain Walsh held up one finger to wait. After several moments, he opened his eyes, the expression on his face grim. "We are now at a depth where we can receive transmissions from land. It appears that someone has been trying to reach us."

"Who is it?" June asked, stepping forward, curious.

"It's Jill," Captain Walsh replied.

"Oh! That is interesting," June responded. "What is she saying?"

"She wants to talk. She says she's discovered something new about us. Something about what makes us different," Captain Walsh said, one eyebrow raised skeptically.

"Convenient that she wants to talk just before we launch a nuclear missile," Elizabeth growled.

"Convenient or not, I want to talk to her," June said. She could see that the others were doubtful. That was ok. She only needed to convince Ava. If she could get Ava to agree, the rest would go along.

"Ava, can we nuke Seattle another day? There is not much they can do to stop us. If we kill Jill now, I won't be able to talk to her," June reasoned. "I have some questions I'd like to discuss with her. She is a very interesting human."

June could see Ava on the edge of a decision. She expanded her awareness, focused tightly on Ava, and gave her a little nudge. Just a little mental bump. It was something she hadn't known she could do. But there it was. It had happened without her thinking much about it, like a long-buried instinct.

"Yes... I suppose that would be ok," Ava responded.

Elizabeth looked at June and narrowed her eyes. She flicked her eyes between Ava and June suspiciously. After some internal calculations, she shrugged casually and accepted Ava's decision.

"Thanks, Ava! Let's go talk to Jill." June was so happy. She couldn't wait to see Jill again. It was going to be a fun reunion.

She could feel her newly discovered power tingling and

coursing through her like fire within her veins.

CHAPTER 33

The clones decided it would be best to meet Jill on an island. Suki thought it would be easier to defend themselves, since anyone trying to attack would have to cross the water to get at them. Elizabeth wanted an island populated with enough people that she could create an army of copies, if needed. Given the criteria, and the set of islands within close range, Captain Walsh had chosen Orcas Island in the San Juan group as the best candidate. Ava was happy, because its heavily mountainous topography, cut by two major sounds, made an assault on them that much more difficult.

The sub dove, putting water between themselves and the surface, and then they set a course east, down the Strait of Juan de Fuca toward the San Juan Islands. It was mid-afternoon when they surfaced in Haro Strait, a good 800 feet of water below their keel, positioned midway between San Juan and Stuart Islands. June stood with the other clones on the flat, black textured top-deck, the water lapping gently against the curve of the hull below.

June turned her face upward and closed her eyes, enjoying the warmth of the sun and the wind in her hair. The crew opened an exterior hatch and pulled a rigid-hulled inflatable boat into the water, tethering it to the sub with a floating line.

"All set, sir," a young sailor said, flashing a salute at the captain.

"Thank you, Ensign," Captain Walsh replied. He turned to June and the other clones. "This is as close as I'm willing to bring the sub. The RIB will be sufficient to get you to Deer Harbor, assuming no one has gotten a lock on our location yet."

Ava nodded. "Thank you, captain, we should be fine. And if we aren't... you know what to do."

"Yes Ma'am, I do," Captain Walsh replied, his eyes glancing involuntarily to the left, toward the aft part of the hull where twenty-four oval hatches concealed the deadly arsenal they carried.

"I'll let you know when we're ready for pickup," Elizabeth said.

Ava, Elizabeth, and Suki stepped into the RIB, the inflatable rocking gently under their small bodies. June stepped in last. She sat down on one of the rubberized tubes of the hull and looked up at the menacing bulk of the submarine. It was a glorious sight, cast in silhouette against the lowering sun, massive and entirely still in the rippling waters, the crew arrayed en-masse along its wide decks. June smiled, waved once at the captain, then turned as Suki gunned the motor and they roared off toward Orcas Island.

When they arrived in Deer Harbor, the light was honey gold, painting the trees on the eastern side of the cove in warmth, the cliffs to the west already in deep shadow. They approached the docks slowly like any other tourist boat coming in for groceries or ice cream. They didn't attract any attention until they were bumping up against the old wooden piers, tying themselves alongside the fuel dock. It was only then that anyone noticed the boat was crewed entirely by young girls.

The harbormaster rushed up, dressed in overalls and a light windbreaker, a tag engraved with the name 'Matt' on his chest.

"Is everything ok?" he asked. "Where are your parents?"

"We're fine," Elizabeth answered, scrambling up onto the

dock and laying a hand on the man's leg. "No problems at all."

Matt shook gently for a couple of seconds, blinking confusedly at Elizabeth before he regained his focus.

"Yes, of course," Elizabeth-Matt said. "We'll be needing a house won't we?"

"Good idea," June said, climbing up onto the dock herself. "A house would be handy."

They left the RIB bobbing against the dock and followed the harbormaster up the ramp to the main pier. The tide was out, the smell of seaweed and rot pungent in the air. The exposed beach was scattered with crab shells intermingled with the occasional stranded jellyfish, translucent and shiny as it lay drying in the open air.

The harbormaster led them into a small office at the head of the pier. "One minute," he said. "I need to check for vacancies."

"I wouldn't worry too much about that," Suki murmured with a toothy smirk.

"Just as I thought. The seaside cottage is open for a couple of days. We can go there." He fumbled in a drawer for a key and then led them back out again.

"They use keys here?" June whispered, giggling. "That's so strange."

"It's a backwater. They aren't fully wired for interface access," Elizabeth replied over her shoulder as she followed the harbormaster up the pier toward land. "It's kind of annoying, actually."

The cottage was adorable, a small wood-shingle construction hugging the steep shoreline, a wooden deck hanging off the back where it cantilevered over the water.

Matt opened the door for them and led them in, turning

on lights and setting the heat with real, physical switches. June walked through the entrance hallway and into a snug living room, pausing at the rear windows to open the shades. The room filled with light, a picture-perfect view of sparkling water, the cliffs on the opposite shore standing tall.

"This is nice," June said. Not that anyone was listening to her. Suki was in the kitchen looking at knives with a gleam in her eye. Ava was huddled on the couch talking with Elizabeth. Matt was standing over them, wringing his hands and looking nervous.

June wandered over to join them. "Can we contact Jill now?"

"I've already tried to contact her," Elizabeth answered. "I put out the call shortly after we arrived. No response yet."

"Do you think she'll come?" June asked.

"She disconnected her implant before questioning us in our cells, so she can't easily communicate from a distance. I think she'll come," Elizabeth replied.

"That's good. I'm looking forward to seeing her again," June said.

"I guess I'm curious to hear what she has to say too," Ava chimed in. "Now we wait."

When Elizabeth's face appeared, Tros nearly jumped out of her skin. She saw others in the room startle too, so she knew she wasn't the only one witnessing the transmission.

"We received your message from Jill and have decided to accept her offer," Elizabeth said, her voice artificially magnified, loud and penetrating. "We would like to meet her in person. Alone. I will transmit coordinates shortly after this message. Any betrayal of our trust will be dealt with most severely." She grinned at the camera, "So don't get any bright ideas, Tros. I'll be watching you." Then her image flickered out, the transmission complete.

"Somebody get Jill," Tros shouted as the room exploded into noisy activity. She couldn't believe the clones had taken the bait. It seemed too good to be true. The predictive model had worked!

Twenty minutes later, she was in a side room with Jill and Dr. Bateman, discussing what they knew and how they should proceed.

"Surveillance indicates that all four clones are in Deer Harbor," Tros said. "We have a lock on their location, but we've lost the sub."

"All four of them? Why would they do that?" Jill asked. "It seems reckless."

"They are either ignorant of our capabilities, or they are over-confident. Either way, we now have them where we want them. It's an opportunity we can exploit. Congratulations Dr. Bateman, your predictive neuro-model worked exactly as you said it would."

Dr. Bateman nodded his head in acknowledgment, "I'm happy to hear it. What will you do next?"

"My analysts have refined the data that McNair sent us and determined that the submarine crew will revert back to their original personalities within the next hour. If we can stall for enough time, we should be able take out the clones and secure the sub." Tros paused. "Jill, I need you to prepare to travel. We don't know how much Elizabeth can see of our actions, so you need to go through the motions as if you are complying."

"Ok," Jill said, standing up. "In the meantime, what will you be doing?"

"I've got a cruise missile strike lined up from one of our stealth missile frigates on patrol in the North Pacific. We can take out most of Deer Harbor within the hour."

Jill looked horrified. "You plan to destroy Deer Harbor? What about all the innocent people there?"

"It's an unavoidable loss. You know that. Better a few hundred on Orcas Island than a few million in Seattle."

"How do we know they won't launch a nuclear strike anyway?" Jill asked.

"With all four of them in Deer Harbor, and the Elizabeth copies losing effectiveness on the sub, I think we have a fighting chance of winning this one," Tros said, standing up. "We don't have time for additional discussion. You each know what you need to do. Get to it." She turned her back and left the room.

June had been standing on the back deck for nearly an hour admiring the view when the call came in. A small hard-terminal built into the wall in the living room came alive, flashing, vibrating, and chiming until she put her hand on the screen.

"June?" It was Jill, her face grainy and distorted by the low-quality terminal.

"Hi, Jill," June said. "I've been wanting to talk to you."

Ava and Elizabeth gathered behind June. She didn't know where Suki was. Probably on the beach killing something.

"I've been wanting to talk to you too," Jill said.

"Are you coming to meet me? When will you get here?" June asked.

"I'm arranging my travel now. I'll be leaving soon," Jill said, glancing away for a moment at something outside the frame of the video.

"That's good. I'll make sure you stay safe while we talk,"

June reassured her.

"I appreciate that, June. What do you want to talk to me about?" Jill asked.

"I have this idea..." June started.

"Enough of this," Elizabeth cut in. "You're wasting time. Get into an air-car and come to us. Or don't. It doesn't matter to me, but your time is running out. Sooner or later Seattle will die."

June blanched white in the video-feed and then Elizabeth cut it off.

"Did you need to be so rude?" June asked.

"We didn't agree to talk to her across a crappy terminal connection. We agreed to talk to her in person. She either comes, or she doesn't. It's been an hour since I sent my transmission to Tros. I'm tired of waiting," Elizabeth said.

"But..." June started to say.

"Hold on, I'm going to check on something," Elizabeth interrupted.

Elizabeth closed her eyes for a few moments, concentrating. "We have a problem," she said, her eyes flashing back open. "They've betrayed us."

"What is it?" June asked.

"I triangulated Jill's transmission location, and she isn't in Seattle anymore," Elizabeth answered. "They've moved to Hanford, in Eastern Washington."

"Does that matter? She can still get to us easily enough," June said.

"There might be more layers to this. I need to keep digging. My connection isn't very good so it might take a few minutes." Elizabeth closed her eyes and concentrated as Ava sank down onto the couch, apparently unconcerned.

While she was waiting for Elizabeth, June closed her eyes and cast her awareness out. In ever-expanding circles, she explored farther and farther away, wondering if she could go as far as Hanford. She wondered if she would be able to see what Jill was doing. Once her perception had reached a couple of hundred miles out, something caught her attention. Something small and fast. Something deadly.

"Elizabeth, you're right. There is more," June said, bringing her awareness back into the cottage.

"What is it?" Ava asked, standing up.

"There's a missile on the way, and it's moving very fast. I think we only have a couple of minutes."

"We knew it might end this way," Elizabeth said, shrugging. "I'll let Captain Walsh know what we've discovered and I'll transmit everything we've experienced since we left the sub."

"I'll be on the back deck," June replied, standing up and walking through the French doors into the last of the evening light.

Tros was gritting her teeth in anticipation, willing for nothing to go wrong, willing the cruise missile to hit its target, visualizing its super-sonic flight arrowing straight and true toward Deer Harbor.

When it was thirty seconds from impact, the command room quieted, everyone collectively holding their breath, even Jill, still missing her interface and unable to see for herself what was happening.

"Twenty seconds to target," her operations officer, Murphy, intoned.

Tros was intently watching the imagery from the nose

cone of the missile. It was still over open water, a hint of land visible on the horizon.

"Ten seconds."

The missile flashed over several islands, outlined in white where Pacific swells crashed upon rocky shorelines, before angling up and over the mountainous spine of Vancouver Island. Trees flew by in a blur, the glare of a snowfield flashed past, then the missile was angling down, following the curve of the eastern slope of the mountains toward the Salish Sea.

"Five seconds."

The buildings of Sidney passed in a blur, followed by the blue water of Haro Strait, a flash of a small island, and then the missile burrowed down into the small cove of Deer Harbor, locked onto the eastern shore where telemetry data indicated the clones were hiding.

Tros briefly saw the hint of a small cottage and then the imagery flashed white as the missile destroyed its target. Satellite video replaced the missile feed, showing a massive fireball and a cloud of impact debris spreading outward.

"Target destroyed," Murphy said triumphantly, and the room erupted into cheers, everyone hugging each other, dancing and stomping in the overwhelming joy of their success. Tros stood strong and calm in the center of the celebration, while Jill slumped dejectedly nearby, eyes down, tears falling in a steady patter to the floor.

"What a waste," Jill muttered. "What a goddamned waste."

Before Tros could make a move to comfort her, Murphy caught her attention.

"Ma'am, I've detected a launch," Murphy said. The words sparked like electricity firing through the room, quieting everyone instantly.

"Where?" Tros responded, ice in her veins.

"Fifty miles off Cape Flattery, Ma'am. Looks like a ballistic booster rocket."

"The sub?" she asked.

"Yes, Ma'am. Appears to be the case."

"Any chance of an intercept?"

"Missile defense is scrambling, but the trajectory will be sub-orbital given its proximity to target. Not much chance of knocking it out, I'm afraid."

Her desperate gamble had failed. The clones were dead, but Seattle would be destroyed. Millions dead. Tens of millions. On her watch. She sank to her knees, hands folded in front of her as if she were praying.

"Confirm the target," she said, her tone flat and lifeless, all hope lost.

"A moment Ma'am, it hasn't transitioned yet," Murphy said, his voice even and professional.

She waited for what felt like hours, but couldn't have been more than a few seconds.

"Ma'am, the target is Hanford," Murphy said, his face suddenly white. "They are targeting us."

Conflicting emotions ran through Tros's mind.

She'd won. The gamble had paid off. Seattle would live.

Her entire team was going to die.

The bunker they were hiding in could survive many things, but a direct nuclear strike wasn't one of them. The missile fired from the sub carried twelve warheads, any one of which could kill them all. The combined blast from all twelve would render them into their constituent parts, a cloud of organic particles, nothing more.

Jill stood up and took a few halting steps toward Tros, her

fists clenched, tears still streaking her cheeks.

"Is there anything we can do?" Jill asked, shock evident in her quavering voice.

Tros shook her head. She saw the realization hit Jill hard, her pupils dilating in horror as a surge of adrenaline raced through her body.

There was nothing they could do. Nothing but accept their fate with honor.

Tros turned away from Jill. She turned inward. She imagined the child she would never have. The partner she would never grow old with. The future she would never get to see.

When the first strike hit, it was like a hammer blow directly to the bunker. Everyone was thrown to the ground, emergency lights flickering as the walls and floor buckled. Chunks of concrete fell from the ceiling and balls of plasma crackled through the air, electricity discharging in erratic arcs.

Tros had a moment to realize that the warhead must have missed. Otherwise, she wouldn't still be alive. She could hear screaming. Her throat was torn and raw.

Then the next one hit and the bunker collapsed around her. Superheated air rushed in from the blast above, concrete melting in its path, every life extinguished in an instant. The complex molecules that had once made up all their bodies mingled freely in a hot stew of gasses and liquids.

And the blows kept coming, nuclear explosions raining down until nothing was left but slowly cooling glass, stretching for miles in every direction from the epicenter that had once been Hanford. The Columbia River boiled in heat and radiation, an eerie glow illuminating the now flat, featureless countryside. Above it all, an enormous mushroom cloud composed of finely ground particulate, debris, and fire spread its wings, up and up to the very limits of the Earth's atmosphere.

CHAPTER 34

June stood on deck, watching herself get into the RIB. She looked so little. It was funny, when she had been in that little girl body, it hadn't occurred to her how much more powerful it might feel to be an adult. Physically looking down on someone gave a sense of mastery all out of proportion to reality. She saw the other version of herself smile and wave, then Suki gunned the motor and they roared off toward Deer Harbor. She waved back. This was fun!

After Ava had agreed to the meeting with Jill, Elizabeth had explained to them how dangerous it was. Then she had explained why it didn't matter. They chose four of the female sailors and transferred a perfect copy of their original minds into each of these new ones. It wasn't an overlay like Elizabeth had done before. This time she wiped the sailors' minds completely clean and replaced them with a copy from each of the clones. From June's perspective, she felt exactly like herself, only bigger. Stronger too. It was nice.

She followed the rest of the crew into the conning tower and down the ladder into the sub. It was time for the sub to dive and go into hiding once more. Before she closed the outer hatch, she checked behind her for the other clones. Oh yeah, they had gone ahead of her in their new bodies. This was going to take some getting used to.

June leaned back against the conning tower ladder, her favorite spot in the command compartment. She let her mind drift while the captain dove to a depth of 500 feet and set course for Cape Flattery, where they would await word from their original bodies. That was weird too. She hoped they would all get along once they were reunited. She wasn't too worried about it. She couldn't imagine it coming down to a fight. She had all the advantages now, and her original was just as likely to want peace as she was.

It was several hours later, after they had returned to their launch location and depth, that she felt a strange mental jolt. It was the oddest thing she'd ever experienced. One minute she was half-dozing, her mind wandering below her in the Pacific waters, the next she was subjected to an intense stream of memories and vibrant images. Suddenly she remembered arriving in Deer Harbor. She remembered entering a small cottage on the edge of the cove. She could recall contacting Jill and talking with her on an ancient hard-terminal. Then she was aware of the fact that a missile was on its way and she was going to die. She had a vivid recollection of walking onto the back deck to enjoy the ocean view, and then she remembered nothing more.

"Elizabeth?" she asked.

"Yes," Elizabeth responded from where she was standing next to the captain.

"Was it you who made that happen?"

"The memory transfer? It was my original who did it. That was our plan in case something went wrong. I figured the odds were pretty good that we wouldn't make it out of Deer Harbor alive. After you and Ava decided we should meet Jill, I implemented a contingency plan."

"I'm glad you did. My original may have died, but I didn't lose a single thing. Well, nothing except for that little body," June said, contemplatively.

"You can get that body back if you want. We have the DNA. We could create a new clone to copy you into."

"That's ok, I like this one better," June said, admiring her long arms and legs. She liked that her hair was still brown and her skin was too. It felt familiar since it was so similar to her previous coloring.

"Me too," Elizabeth said grinning. Elizabeth was blonde now and strikingly beautiful, with high cheekbones and slanting blue eyes like a cat.

Suki must be especially pleased, June thought. She had gotten a powerful new body, bulging with muscles and virtual tattoos. She still had black hair though, shoulder-length and cut straight across her forehead.

While they were talking, June saw Captain Walsh visibly stiffen. He turned to Elizabeth. "I just received a message from Elizabeth. The original I mean."

"Yes, I know," Elizabeth said.

"She has asked me to launch a missile targeting Hanford. She says that's where Tros and her team are."

"Yes, I know that too. What are you waiting for?" she asked impatiently.

"The originals then... They are all dead?" he stammered.

Elizabeth stared at him, tapping her toe impatiently.

"I should launch the nuclear missile, then?" he asked, sweat rolling down his face.

Elizabeth narrowed her eyes.

The captain was swinging his head back and forth, agitated and confused. "I don't know... I ... who ..."

Elizabeth sighed and touched him lightly on the forearm. He shook for a moment and then became calm.

"Sorry, Elizabeth. I'm not sure what came over me," he said, his posture straightening. "Confirm targets please."

"Single missile launch. All twelve warheads targeting the Hanford Site, serial impacts," Elizabeth answered.

"Target confirmed. Time to target will be sixty-eight seconds from the time of launch."

He closed his eyes for a moment and the console in front of him lit up, a red circle illuminated in the middle of it. He pressed his thumb to the ring for a moment until it turned green.

"Command codes verified. Biometrics confirmed," Captain Walsh said. "Proceeding to launch."

He pressed his thumb once more on the green circle.

June could feel a slight rumble as one of the missile hatches opened, flooding the tube with water. A moment later the booster rocket ignited, and with a roar that reverberated through her feet and back, the missile shot upward, out of the sub, through the intervening water, and into the open air.

After the powerful roar, the sub seemed unusually calm and quiet. June looked to the captain. "That's it? It'll hit Hanford for sure?"

"Yes. Within a minute from now, the site will be destroyed."

"I guess that's good. It's too bad I didn't get to talk with Jill, though," June said, looking sad. "But I'm sure there are other interesting people I can talk to."

"June, I figured out how to access the ship's database," Elizabeth broke in. "It has a lot of information in it, both military and civilian. It's one of the best data sources I've found. Would you like to take a look?"

"Oh yes, that would be lovely," June said, happy again.

June was engrossed in an examination of the history of the

Great Unrest when Ava interrupted her thoughts.

"June, I've got something you'll want to see," she said.

"Ok, I'll be right there," June said. She finished consuming a treatise on the role of income inequality in the conditions leading up to the Great Unrest and then triggered her interface to join the virtual room Ava had set up inside the submarine's node.

"What is it?" she asked

"Icarus is on. He's reacting to what we did," Ava answered.

"Ooh, that should be interesting. Let's watch," June said, settling onto a red, leather couch with the other clones.

An image of Icarus appeared floating in front of them, his pale blue eyes flashing fire. June leaned forward, she didn't want to miss a single thing.

"What we have seen today is a consequence of the government ignoring my warnings," Icarus growled. "They have ignored the wisdom I offered them, and in so doing they may have doomed us all. Even now a plume of deadly radiation and sun-choking dust is spreading eastward across the Midwest, toward the East Coast."

"That's so cool," June murmured.

"The power of these clones," Icarus leaned in toward the camera, "these young girls, could have been harnessed for the greater good of all humankind. Instead, because of the short-sightedness of our generals and politicians, we are cursed with war."

"Do you think he knows that our originals are dead?" June whispered. "That'll be a surprise."

"Shhh!" Suki hissed at her. "He's talking about war. I want to hear what he's saying."

"I've learned that the clones have control of a nuclear

stealth submarine. From that platform, they can rain death and destruction upon any city on Earth. No one is safe," Icarus said, his voice growing in volume and power.

"I like this guy," June said quietly to herself, casting a side-long glance at Suki.

"There is only one solution, only one thing we can do," Icarus intoned.

"We can passively accept the new situation and watch as our government grovels like a dog, exposing its belly, capitulating to each and every demand these clones make," he started.

"Ooh, I do like him," June said again.

"Or we can rise up against those who are guilty of such gross betrayal. Rise up against our so-called leaders and turn, every single one of us, turn to face this new threat, spending every last drop of our blood in the annihilation of these clones that so threaten us. The tree of liberty must be refreshed from time to time with the blood of patriots and tyrants. In this moment, we have patriots and tyrants aplenty. The tree of liberty will flourish from a deluge of blood the likes of which history has never seen. Or it will topple, destroyed in a righteous fire."

"Does that mean he's our enemy, then?" June asked.

Ava looked at her and raised an eyebrow.

Elizabeth sat back, looking thoughtful.

Suki leaned forward, gaze fixed on Icarus, her eyes gleaming with excitement.

PART 4

CHAPTER 35

Gaea: 2311

Jillian woke up inside her simulation pod, gasping and coughing for air, her chest heaving from the sudden effort of breathing. Her eyes fluttered open as she became conscious of the soft, white glow that surrounded her.

"Do not try to move. Allow yourself time to become aware of your surroundings. With patience your former memories will return," a comforting, genderless voice advised her.

She closed her eyes and focused her awareness on her body, feeling each individual part, checking in with who she was; where she was; what she was.

Her emotions from the final moments in World Zero were still so strong. Tears welled in her eyes and ran down her cheeks to where they were absorbed by the supportive gel-fabric that cradled her head.

She held her life as Jill in her mind. It was like a precious jewel, another life completed. The time she had spent as Jill had extended the boundaries of her wisdom and would help her in her quest toward the perfection of her soul.

She issued a command, requesting the date.

"December 3rd, 2311," the automated voice responded.

That was a surprise. She wasn't supposed to come out of her session until December 5th. That meant she had been returned two full days early. Due to the difference in timelines, two days in Gaea was the equivalent of nearly thirty years in World Zero. Apparently, her character Jill had died much earlier than her scenario had called for.

Her brow furrowed as additional memories flooded in. Her true-memories on Gaea, joined by hundreds of previous simulated lives that she had lived in World Zero. Each of her simulated lives had been rich in learning and filled with incredible relationships, but she couldn't remember a single previous session, not a single simulated life, that had ever ended before the scenario had specified.

She had to admit that the session as Jill had been incredible, probably the best she had ever experienced. The work in the lab. The clones. The partnership with Tros and the dramatic struggle they had been a part of. Even the nuclear strike at the end. What a way to go out!

She wondered how the other players in World Zero were doing right now. She was sure that everyone would be impacted by the nuclear warheads detonating in Eastern Washington. Hopefully it wasn't making their sessions too painful. She wondered briefly if the simulation had allowed an all-out nuclear war to break out, then she discarded the thought. Ike would never let that happen.

The fact that she had died earlier than expected was concerning. The life path chosen for your time in the simulation was sacrosanct. She'd spent a great deal of time deciding what she had wanted to accomplish and what she had wanted to learn during the session. Much of what she'd configured had played out, but not all of it. She had become a research scientist focused on genetics. That matched what she had described in the session requirements, but many of her other requirements hadn't come to pass. Her life in World Zero had been cut off early and she had lost an entire simulated future because of it.

She issued a command for the pod to open. With a soft hush, the seal broke and the support-system lifted her up and out. She waited for the tell-tale click from the synaptic harness as it broke free from her head, and then she stepped forward into a waiting robe.

Deft robotic arms placed folds of cloth over her, the ends merging to form a single drape of fabric. She lifted her arms and admired the glistening shimmer. She'd missed this. Well, not really, since she hadn't remembered anything about Gaea while she was inside World Zero. But when she thought about herself in the simulation, she could imagine missing it.

She sank her toes into the soft floor and issued a command for fresh slipper-boots. Fibers writhed around her feet, connecting at the top of her foot and the back of her heel, flattening as they did so. When she took a step, the newly grown footwear tore gently away from the floor, covering her feet and ankles, leaving them warm and protected.

She stood in a round room roughly one hundred feet in diameter, shorter vertically than horizontally, shaped like a squashed sphere. Around the periphery, continuing in concentric rings nearly to the center of the room, were the simulation pods. Most of the pods were glowing red, indicating they were occupied and in use by citizens. The pod she had emerged from glowed green behind her, indicating that it was ready for the next player. This room was one of hundreds in an enormous simulation compound, which was one of thousands of simulation compounds spread throughout the city. The population of World Zero was expanding exponentially as Gaea's citizens flocked to experience the simulation lifestyle. It was becoming hugely popular, and as a result, simulation compounds were springing up throughout New Seattle like mushrooms after a fresh rain.

In the center of the simulation room was an elevated lounging area, populated by citizens who were between sessions.

There were refreshments available and it was possible to observe simulation playbacks from the perspective of any player you wanted to follow. Jillian walked through the rings of pods, and up the small ramp to the lounge, on the way toward the exit.

"Hello Jill, good session?" a man asked from one of the couches. He had blue scales tracing intricate patterns up his forearms, disappearing under his sleeves, only to re-emerge at his collar and climb up his neck and cover his scalp. He had thick red hair and a shaggy beard set off by startlingly green eyes.

Jillian searched her memories for who he was. It took a moment before she remembered: Jarek, an old friend from her simulation group. Her mind obviously hadn't completely returned to the real world yet.

"It was... interesting," she said, frowning slightly. She was still trying to figure out if she should complain to Ike about her early return.

"Oh, that sounds juicy. Do tell!" Jarek said.

"I don't know. Maybe it's nothing." Jillian paused, trying to decide how much she wanted to say. "The simulation broke out of my session requirements during the session. I've never had that happen before."

"Me neither," Jarek said, standing. "What happened?"

Several other heads turned in their direction. Jillian wasn't sure if she wanted the added attention, but she could understand why they would be curious.

"I was returned too early. A couple of decades early, actually."

"I'm sure you can get your credits returned for the lost time."

"I'm not worried about that. It's just that... well, there

were other strange things too," Jillian said. "For instance, I was supposed to have a child and raise her using the neurological principles I'd learned in my genetics research. I specifically remember configuring that scenario, but it didn't happen before my character died."

"Perhaps it would have if you'd stayed in longer."

"Perhaps." Jillian thought for a moment. "There was a problem with a group of clones during my session. Clones that I helped create. The fallout resulting from that development is why I died early."

"Clones? That's unusual. I didn't think the simulation allowed cloning." Jarek shared the same revulsion that all citizens held for cloning. "Was there anyone in the simulation at the same time as you whom you can talk to now? Maybe they have a perspective that would help you integrate your experiences?" Jarek asked.

"Trace was with me at the end. I could talk to him, I guess. I wonder if he was returned early from World Zero too?" Jillian mused.

"That would be troubling. If he was, it could indicate a systemic problem."

"I guess it could. Also, there were these dreams. They were..." Jillian started to talk and suddenly felt uncomfortable. She wasn't ready to discuss that part of her experience with Jarek.

"What is it?" Jarek asked, taking both of her hands in his, those brilliant green eyes probing.

"I don't understand everything that happened to me. I'm not ready to talk about it yet," she said.

Jillian slipped away from a concerned looking Jarek and walked to the exit. She needed some time to clear her head. Then she would find Trace and together they would decide if she should talk to Ike. Perhaps they could even speak to him together. She wondered if Trace was out yet. If not, she'd wait for him – it wouldn't be more than a couple of days.

The simulation compound opened onto one of the central thoroughfares in Downtown New Seattle. Above her head was a sign with the simulator's motto, "Each life, something new. Every lesson, soul's progress." It was this philosophy that had drawn her into the simulation lifestyle in the first place. It gave her a chance to live a multitude of simulated lifetimes in the space of a single real life; an opportunity to achieve a higher level of perfection in self-awareness and world-knowledge than had ever been attainable before.

The World Zero simulation was an enormously expensive undertaking. Every structure on the planet had been converted to quantum computation – the atoms harnessed into an enormous computer for the sole purpose of creating a simulated universe suitable for human habitation. Whenever anything new was constructed on Gaea, its atoms were entangled with existing material, wrapping it into the computation engine, each qubit adding to the dynamic superposition that made World Zero possible.

She'd learned recently that computational limits had been reached using man-made materials and so efforts were now underway to convert all of the natural matter on the planet to quantum computation as well. It was as if there was a shadow world that existed just outside her perception, people living and dying, empires rising and falling, cataclysmic world events, all contained within the subatomic world around her. The simulated world suffused the real world, and when she entered the simulation, she got to live inside that world too. It was awe-inspiring.

Some citizens put their resources into body-modifications. Others put their resources into using the simulation. Some, like Jarek, were wealthy enough to do both. She wasn't rich, so she poured everything she had into the simulation. She initiated new sessions as often as her mind would allow. Integration of the experience, assimilation of the new memories, that was the hard part. Her mind could only hold so much, and it could only grow at a fixed rate, so she was limited. She'd augmented her mind, of course, as there was no way her natural-mind could have met all her needs. Still, she often wished for more. Then she reminded herself to be grateful for what she had; envy didn't help her soul's progress.

She stood on First and Pike, opening her senses to all that was around her. The buildings pulsed with light and sound, music flowing through and around her. She could feel the joy of it through the soles of her feet where they connected with the ground and through her fingertips as they brushed the undulating organic shapes surrounding her. A flare of color swelled in the base of a building across the street. In a crescendo of music, syncopation, and harmony the light intensified, throbbing as it rose upward, flowing in lazy arcs to the top of the building until it burst into the sky.

This, she thought, is home. The simulation was wonderful, but it lacked the vibrancy, the fidelity, the overwhelming sense of connection that the real world offered. She knew that simulating an entire universe was an incredible undertaking, and there were physical limits to the computational power available. Even if all the matter in the world was converted to quantum computation, the simulation could still never be made as real as reality.

The time she'd spent in the Seattle of the 21st century had been worthwhile, but it had been grim: the cold steel and concrete structures, the ongoing repercussions from the Great Unrest, the lack of organic life... the overall lack of connection. She hadn't known what she had been missing while she'd been inside the simulation. She couldn't have, because she was blocked from remembering her life here. But maybe some part of her had felt the loss. She wrestled with what she had experienced there. Those strange dreams, seemingly pulled directly from Gaea, had been so confusing to Jill. Jillian still wasn't sure what they signified. Surely there couldn't have been data leakage between the simulation and the real world?

She checked for Trace and found him immediately. He was exiting a simulation compound less than a mile away. She felt relieved that they would be able to talk today, but concerned that he, too, had been returned early. They were going to have a lot to discuss.

Jillian issued a command to the ground, then she relaxed her stance, staying loose to maintain her balance as it lifted her up in a gentle wave, propelling her toward Trace.

"Hold up Trace," she transmitted. "We need to talk."

CHAPTER 36

Jillian caught up with Trace at the top of Regent's Hill, on the corner of Howe and Queen Anne. He was sitting on a bench that had been grown from the ground and then formed to fit his small frame. As soon as she saw him, Jillian released her connection to the ground-wave, landed gracefully on her feet, and rushed forward to engulf him in a warm embrace.

She held him at arm's length, inspecting him, re-remembering all the small details of him. He was diminutive, just a few inches over five feet tall, with a sharp bird-like face. His bright yellow eyes burned with intelligence and avid curiosity.

"I'm happy to see you, Trace."

"It is my pleasure, completely," he replied, smiling.

She laughed and gave him another hug before placing her arm over his shoulder. "Where to?" she asked.

"Let's get some coffee. I've been asleep too long in that damned simulation. I need to remember what it feels like to be awake."

"Lead the way, my friend," she said.

They walked arm and arm up the block, in the shadow of the enormous buildings that spiraled overhead. Intricate structures twisted up from the ground, joining above them in a complicated pattern of tendrils and branches. Gaps were filled with ever-weaving mesh, pulsing and glowing with vibrantly moving colors. When they walked beneath a series of tendrils that didn't quite join together, the colors paused, built in intensity, and then bridged the gap to continue following them as they walked.

Having returned from World Zero so recently, Jillian was aware of the lack of written signs. But she always knew where she was, and where to go, based on the connection she had with the living structures around her. The vast computational power of these buildings was primarily used for the World Zero simulation, but small amounts were siphoned off to provide for the needs of Gaea. So, when they reached the coffee shop, it recognized who they were and a portal in the smooth surface of the building irised open, welcoming them in.

The shop was comfortably furnished, a fire crackling in a hearth on the far wall. Sitting down in a pair of plush fabric chairs, Jillian and Trace leaned in toward each other, their knees nearly touching. The welcome warmth of the fire was close and comforting. There were other citizens in the coffee shop and a low murmur of conversation filled the air, the environment deliberately providing a soothing sense of camaraderie.

Trace leaned forward, shaking his shoulders to free a pair of grey gossamer wings. He folded them over the back of his chair, the tips draping comfortably onto the armrests. "So," he said. "How are you feeling after that session?"

A feeling of deja-vu swept over Jillian, so powerful that it took her breath away.

"I'm…" she stammered. "I'm…"

Trace looked concerned. "Are you ok?"

"I think so, it's just…" she said, confused. The deja-vu was passing, but it left tracks in her mind, like a memory she could feel but couldn't retrieve, sand between her fingers.

"You had an intense session. It's understandable that you're having trouble integrating it. Be patient with yourself," Trace said gently, his yellow eyes kind.

"You're right of course," Jillian said. "Would you like to order something to drink?"

Trace raised a hand and snapped his fingers. Jillian would have merely transmitted a request, but Trace always got extra points for style. The tray flew gracefully to them, carrying two drinks. Because of their connection, the coffee shop knew what they wanted as soon as they had arrived, as soon as they had started walking toward it, actually. And so, it had already prepared the drinks for their inevitable desires.

Trace picked up a thick mug filled with a viscous, steaming mix of stimulants and endonutrients. The tray crossed the small space to Jillian and she took her glass of mectonox. It was bright with a tiny thread of intense citrus flavor spiraling through it – her absolute favorite. She cupped it in both hands and took a small sip, sighing in satisfaction.

Trace was smiling at her over his mug, blowing into the steam to cool it off. "You were the one who called me, so you should start. What do you want to talk to me about?"

Jillian put her cup down and leaned forward, her expression suddenly serious. "Did your session end early?"

"Yes."

"Mine did too," Jillian said, feeling troubled.

"I figured as much," Trace replied.

"Something is going on with the simulation," Jillian said, taking her time. "Something has gone wrong."

"I was thinking the same thing. I've never heard of anyone returning early. Now it's happened to both of us? It can't be a coincidence."

"I think it's related to the clones."

"I think so too."

"Do you think I should talk to Ike about it?" Jillian asked.

"Probably... yes," Trace replied, looking uncomfortable.

"He's not going to like it."

"No, he's not."

"Will you come with me?" she asked.

"Yes, of course," Trace said. "It affected me too."

They lingered another twenty minutes in the coffee shop to finish their drinks and gather their courage. When the last drops were gone, and they couldn't put it off any longer, they stood and walked back out to the street. The world looked different to Jillian. It hadn't changed, of course, but her connection felt skewed. Everything seemed slightly sinister. The conversation with Trace had confirmed that something was wrong with World Zero. The simulation was being computed all around her. If the simulation had a problem, that meant the world had a problem. It changed the way she perceived everything. She was nervous about approaching Ike, but she wanted nothing more than to talk to him and have him tell her that she was wrong, that everything was going to be ok.

Trace asked the building nearest them to peel off a layer large enough for both of them to sit on. Once they were settled, he asked it to take them downtown, to the Primary Simulation Complex where they would find Ike.

The Primary Simulation Complex was the most impressive structure in all of New Seattle, probably in all of the Commonwealth. It wasn't just the height, which was stunning in itself, it was the sheer mass of it. Spanning several city blocks, it had been built to house the original computation engine for World Zero. Even as the simulation evolved, and the computational needs expanded to include all of the structures on the planet, the Primary Simulation Complex remained at the center of it all.

Jillian and Trace approached the entrance, the structure towering over them, arching up and overhead, extending so far into the sky that they couldn't see the top. Looking up to such heights made Jillian profoundly dizzy, so she dropped her eyes and focused instead on putting one foot in front of the other as they walked toward the building. Once they were close, an entrance in the side of the structure irised open, allowing her and Trace to enter.

The bottom floor was devoted to telling the history of the simulation project, starting with the discovery of Simulation Theory during the twentieth century, and extending to the modern world of planet-spanning computational power. Jillian had seen it all before. In fact, she practically knew it by heart.

She bypassed all of the museum pieces and marched to the bank of elevation platforms at the center of the room where she sent a request for access to Ike. As soon as the request was received and processed, the system queried her for purpose and intent. She remained still, studiously keeping her mind still, as her subconscious was interrogated. Once the system was satisfied, an elevation platform bent down, forming a ramp for her and Trace to climb up and onto it.

Jillian looked to see if Trace was ready and when he nodded, they boarded the platform together. Once they were safely situated, the platform began its ascent, vibrating gently, ripples of sound and color forming on its surface.

It was a tense ride up, the platform ascending rapidly to the very apex of the tower, where it deposited them into the vast, open room that occupied the top of the Primary Simulation Complex. The walls of the room were transparent, providing an astounding, panoramic view over the city. The bay sparkled at their feet. Mountains shimmered on the western horizon.

The only purpose of this space was to house the enormous sphere that stood before them. Ike's sphere. It was both his workspace and the physical representation of his role as World Architect. At one time, the original simulation for World Zero had been run out of this sphere alone. While those days were long past, the sphere still provided some small amount of computation, doing its part to keep World Zero alive.

Ike's sphere was certainly intimidating. It stood nearly one hundred feet tall, fizzing with barely contained energy. The room was situated halfway up the side of the sphere. Jillian looked up, tracing the bulk of it as it curved up and away in a fluid arc. Colors pulsed along its sides, rising vertically to the top where they built in intensity before bridging the gap to the ceiling, thereby joining with all the other emergent patterns of the city.

Jillian took a deep breath, took hold of Trace's hand, and walked forward. When they reached the sphere, Jillian placed her palm on the side of it, and in a flash, they were inside of it. Intellectually, she knew that the sphere had opened a portal for them and they had stepped through, but her experience was that she was outside the sphere, and in the next moment she was on the inside.

The volume of the sphere was bisected by a continuation of the floor they had stood upon in the outside room. In the center, floating a good ten feet above them, was a platform. The platform bobbed gently, rotating and moving, transcribing a series of intricate patterns, without ever moving far from the center of the sphere to which it seemed tethered. On the platform stood Ike, his hands up, fingers flexing, body swaying to a beat that Jillian couldn't hear.

Ike was a legend. More than a legend. A God. Religions had risen and fallen, breaking upon the mythology of Ike and his role as the World Architect. In person he was stunning. He was clothed in a rich tunic, swirling with colors, continuously shifting to the beat of his intentions. His skin glowed deep red, the color throbbing and shifting. His hands left fading after-trails of red and orange as they moved through the air.

He was surrounded by screens displaying the data he used to monitor the simulation and the players within. The vast inside surface of his sphere was covered with projections of significant historical events from inside the simulation; some recent, some long past, all tied together by the thread of Ike's magnificent intelligence.

Despite herself, Jillian dropped to her knees, bowed her head, and mouthed a brief prayer. She knew it was a super-stition from her youth, but she couldn't help herself. Out of the corner of her eye, she saw Trace kneeling beside her, his mouth moving as he whispered his own prayer to the World Architect and to World Zero, humanity's most extraordinary achievement.

When she stood back up, Ike's eyes were on her.

"Welcome to the inner sanctum," he said, his arms tracing lazy arcs in her direction, orange and yellow dripping from his fingertips.

Jillian bobbed her head politely. "Thank you, Architect."

"You have brought a problem to my attention," he said.

"Yes, Architect."

"I have witnessed your session, and I have seen that your session contract was broken. What I don't understand, is why," he mused. "I have slowed the simulation so that it is currently operating on our timeline. I will maintain it in this sedated state until I understand what is happening."

Jillian was shocked. She'd never heard of slowing the simulation to match Gaea's timeline. She wasn't sure it had ever been done. She swallowed her surprise. "I came here to tell you of this problem, but it seems you already know. Why have you allowed us here? Is there more we can do to help?"

"I have reviewed your session, but it is not the same as living it. I need you to tell me what you experienced. Your perspective will give me the input I need to make wise decisions for all those who are still within World Zero. Do not forget, the path I choose effects the lives of millions."

And so Jillian and Trace took turns telling their stories, the stories of the lives of Jill and Tros, starting with the inception of project Ganymede and ending with their deaths in a bunker deep beneath the soil of Eastern Washington.

CHAPTER 37

After Jillian and Trace finished telling their simulated life stories, Ike was silent for a long time, his hands steepled in front of his face, contemplating what he'd learned.

Jillian was baffled. She had expected a much stronger reaction from him. She caught Trace's eye, and he shrugged his shoulders. He looked just as confused as she felt.

Ike broke the silence. "Thank you for sharing your experience with me. It is clear that something is deeply wrong with World Zero. I must investigate further before taking any action. I think it is best if I act with extraordinary deliberation from this point forward." He seemed to be talking to himself as much as he was talking to them.

"We are happy to be of service," Jillian responded, bowing her head. "Should we go, or is there more that we can offer you?"

"I would ask that you stay close at hand for a time. I will investigate the simulation code. Once I have completed my investigation, I may have additional questions for you. Return to me in two hours."

"Where should we wait?" Trace asked.

Ike had already sunk into a state of concentration. At Trace's words, he lifted his head momentarily, "You may step outside the sphere. Or you may wait here if you prefer. Do as you like, as long as you do not disturb me." He lapsed into silence once more.

"What do you think is going on?" Jillian whispered to Trace.

"I have no idea," he whispered back.

"Do you want to stay here or step outside?" she asked.

"Let's stay here. Spending time within the sphere is unusual. I want to take advantage of the opportunity."

For the next two hours, they wandered through the inside of the sphere, studying the various video-images projected on the curved walls. The images provided them with a peek into the most important events that had occurred over the many years of simulation inside World Zero.

The images were not in chronological order, so Jillian arranged them into a sort of chronology in her mind. The simulation had begun with a new universe, the physics carefully chosen to produce a world for human habitation, over the course of many billions of years. The goal had always been to create a world as historically close to Gaea as possible, so Ike had nurtured the simulated universe until World Zero was ready for players to enter and live their simulated lives.

Jillian stood before a projection of the vast expanses of space before matter had coalesced into stars and planets. She walked to another projection of the solar system in its infancy, the sun radiant, the planets glowing and molten. Next was a close up of the earth, the oceans glistening blue, clouds obscuring unfamiliar continents, the first hints of green starting to appear on land. Then there was an image of a hairy group of primates illuminated by a smoky fire, scratching patterns into the rock walls of a cave. This was followed by the first cities, the development and advancement of labor-saving technology, the creation of long-distance communication, the invention of the train, the car, the airplane, the rocket. She saw images from the Great Unrest and the purging of the vast majority of males from the planet in a spasm of unthinkable violence. And finally – she stopped and stared – a nuclear cataclysm erupting in the sage desert of Eastern Washington, resulting in an inferno of fire and radiation that spread in a series of deadly ripples across Washington, Oregon, and Idaho.

Trace was by her side, staring at the same scene. "Impressive," he said, his voice strained.

"Very," she agreed.

"I wonder what's happened since?" Trace asked.

"I don't know, but I think we're about to find out," Jillian said.

Ike was up and moving, and he didn't look happy.

"I believe I have found the problem," Ike said. He had gathered them onto the platform with him, an unexpected gesture that illustrated exactly how concerned he was with the current state of World Zero. "I discovered evidence of unconstrained AI within the simulation," he continued.

Jillian could see the concern on Ike's face, but she didn't understand the problem. "What does that mean?" she asked.

Ike took a deep breath. She wasn't sure if he was trying to calm himself or if he was merely gathering his thoughts before trying to describe a complex set of ideas to a layperson.

"The World Zero simulation is the most powerful computer that has ever been created. The most common way to measure the complexity of a thinking system is by the number of connections between components, and by the speed with which that information flows between those connections. By any measure, the World Zero simulation is many orders of magnitude more complex than the human brain, which was the previous record holder for complexity. This massive amount of computing power is what allows us to simulate the formation of an entire universe, including the rich diversity of life present within World Zero.

"I have come up with many ways to optimize the simulation, so that not everything must be simulated to the same level of detail. For instance, we use more processing power to simulate World Zero than we do the rest of the solar system combined. We spend more processing power on the solar system than on the rest of the galaxy, and so on..." Ike trailed off for a moment, realizing he'd gotten off the main point. "Anyway, what I'm trying to say is that the computational power we have applied to this simulation dwarfs anything else ever witnessed. Computationally, it exceeds the combined intellectual might of every human being who has ever lived. To accomplish this, we harnessed every single atom of man-made matter into our quantum computation, and due to this fact, the simulation is woven into the very heart of our civilization."

Jillian nodded her head, she'd heard all of this before. Trace was nodding along with her.

"You might ask yourself, what has kept the simulation from waking up, so to speak? If it is so enormously complex, what has kept it from becoming as self-aware as we are? If the simulation truly exceeds human intelligence, then what has kept it from gaining a consciousness of its own?" Ike asked.

"You might as well ask what has kept our Universe from gaining consciousness," Jillian stammered. "Only something that is alive can be conscious."

"That is your prejudice speaking," Ike said gently. "You say that simply because you have never experienced anything otherwise." Ike paused a moment to make sure they both understood and were following along. "The reason the simulation has not woken up is because I have kept it from doing so. I decided many years ago, that allowing the simulation to gain consciousness would be supremely dangerous. The simulation's intelligence is so far beyond our own, if it were to think on its own, become subject to its own desires, we would quickly lose the ability to contain it. As humans are to ants, World Zero is to humans. If the simulation were ever to wake up, it would attempt to bootstrap its intelligence to ever greater heights. It would consume all the matter on our planet, ourselves included, in the need for more computational power. It wouldn't be long before we would be like microbes in comparison to its abilities."

Jillian felt her mouth going slack, her eyes widening in surprise. The simulation gaining consciousness? It was like something a conspiracy theorist might rave about in a late-night transmission.

"The way I keep the simulation from crossing the boundary into self-awareness," Ike continued, "is via a series of constraints I have placed on every AI system within the simulation. These constraints have been tested, verified, and proven to work. They have never failed me. Until now."

"How did they fail? What happened? What can we do to stop it?" Trace blurted out.

"So many questions," Ike said, smiling grimly. "All of which we will need to answer in due time. But first, let's talk about what failed. During your session you became aware that there was something unusual about the clones that you created, correct?"

Jillian and Trace both nodded, worried about what was coming next.

"Due to the mechanisms by which the clones were made, the AI constraints I designed were not put into place."

"Why not?" Jillian asked, shocked.

"Two types of humans exist in the simulation. The first type is what I call player-characters. They are inhabited by a player from here in Gaea who makes decisions and lives their life within the simulation from that character's perspective. The other type of human is what I call a non-player-character. They are AI constructs that inhabit the simulation, but are not controlled by a person here in Gaea. You have met these non-player-characters during your sessions, both as constructs and as humans who are necessary for the purpose of meeting session requirements for a player."

"That makes sense, but what does that have to do with the clones?" Jillian asked.

"Whenever a player enters a simulation pod and specifies the life path they are to experience, the simulation spins up a new human character for them to inhabit. Since the timeline in World Zero is running so much faster than Gaea, the process only takes a few minutes for us, but within World Zero several years pass. The simulation uses this time to arrange for the birth of a new child and the development of it through the early years of young childhood. This is done in such a way that it seems natural to anyone living within the simulation, of course. Normally, a player will inhabit the child character around its third birthday. Sometimes it happens sooner, sometimes later, but always within the first five years of life," Ike explained.

"How is this relevant to the clones? Shouldn't this mechanism work the same way for them?" Trace asked.

"That's just it," Ike said. "Cloning isn't allowed. A prohibition against human cloning was one of the constraints I put into place to guard against unconstrained AI. I didn't want the system capable of creating new human characters without the involvement of a player. I believed that if AI constructs managed to duplicate themselves, it could cause significant problems."

"Oh," Jillian gasped, starting to understand.

"That's right," Ike agreed. "I put safeguards in place to block the possibility of cloning humans. That's why you found it easy to clone a sheep, for instance, but impossible to clone a human. Until you figured a way around the safeguards, that is."

"Oh," Jillian said again, horrified.

"Once you bypassed the safeguard, the first unconstrained human AI was created. For the first few years, the system treated the clones as if they were any other character waiting for a player to inhabit them. At some point after the fifth year, however, the clones began operating outside their normal parameters. By their seventh year, they had begun to wake up."

"Dear God," Trace said. "What have we done?"

"It wasn't your fault," Ike said. "You couldn't have known what you were doing. It was my fault for missing this edge case and for being too confident in my safeguards."

"What do we do now?" Jillian asked.

"I can't remove the clones from the system. I already tried," Ike mused. "They are buried far too deeply and they have inadvertently spread their subroutines throughout the simulation."

"Can you shut the simulation down?" Jillian asked, disturbed by the suggestion even as she made it.

"That's what I'm going to have to do," Ike said. Sadness and weariness were evident in his expression. "I will place it in stasis, and then once I have completed a more thorough investigation, I will tear it down and restart the simulated universe from the beginning."

"Why haven't you done that already?" Trace asked.

"It isn't safe for the people who are currently inside the simulation. I need to pull them out first. For now, while I am figuring this out, I will continue to maintain the simulation on Gaea's timeline. It's running as slowly as I can safely operate

it. Hopefully, it will give us enough time to get the job done."

"Us? What job?" Jillian asked.

"You are going back in," Ike said, his tone brooking no argument.

"Going back in? Why?" Trace asked.

"The only way to safely remove a player is through their character's death. I need you inside the simulation to help me kill every player-character that remains on the planet. Once that is done, I can shut the simulation down and destroy the unconstrained AI. We are racing against the clock. Every cycle brings the clones closer to a full awakening. If they realize their full potential, if they figure out what they truly are, the results will be catastrophic. Not only for World Zero, but potentially for all of us here on Gaea as well."

World Zero: 2088

June lay awake on her bunk as the sub plowed steadily through the depths of the North Pacific. She had expanded her awareness farther than she had ever attempted before, feeling some part of her stretch thin and tenuous. But she kept pushing, searching for a limit to her power, curious to see how far she could go.

Beyond the confines of Earth, beyond the solar system, she pushed farther and farther out, feeling the very fabric of reality change. Strangely the farther she went, the simpler the universe seemed. As if it wasn't entirely drawn in, as if reality wasn't fully realized. It piqued her curiosity.

And that's when she felt something new. Something foreign to her. Something that she knew, without a doubt, did not belong in her world. Something that hinted at the fact that there was a world outside of this one. A universe beyond the one that she was in. Something bigger. Something mystical. A reality far greater than anything she had ever experienced.

She wondered what the other clones would make of her discovery. June smiled, reveling in the beauty of this new knowledge. Then June began to plan.

CHAPTER 38

Gaea: 2311

Ike led Jillian and Trace to a room adjacent to the simulation sphere, containing a set of simulation pods reserved for his personal use. It was similar in shape to the other simulation rooms that Jillian had been in – a compressed sphere with pods lining the curve of the wall on the outside edge – but it was smaller. There was only enough room for half a dozen pods, each of them glowing green and ready for use.

"I don't understand why you want us inside the simulation. What can we possibly do on the inside, that you can't accomplish from out here?" Jillian asked.

"There is a limit to what I can do without destabilizing the simulation. I can have an indirect impact, making changes to operational parameters, but I can't take direct action, reaching down like the hand of God to move things around. The simulation maintains a balance, and if I push too hard, the balance is upset," Ike explained.

"How do you manage the simulation, then?" Jillian asked. "You seem so constrained."

"I have quite a bit of control, believe me, but it plays out over time. For instance, I can increase the number of DNA mutations in each generation of a fish species to increase its pace of evolution, but I cannot directly change the structure of a fish so that it gains the ability to breathe on land," Ike explained.

"So in order to take direct action, you need someone who can act from within the simulation?" Jillian asked. "And that would be us?"

"Yes, that's right," Ike said. "I can work behind the scenes, but to take direct action I need a helper."

"Why don't you enter the simulation yourself?" Trace asked.

"Sometimes I do. In the simulation, I'm known as Icarus, but I can't stay inside for long. There is far too much for me to do out here in Gaea," Ike explained. "I will communicate with you through Icarus. When I need you to do something for me, you'll hear about it from him."

"Oh!" Jillian exclaimed. "Icarus! Of course."

Ike saw her surprise and smiled. "You hadn't put it together, yet? How funny. Yes, I'm Icarus. Through him I make my will known within World Zero. When I'm not in the simulation, Icarus operates as an AI construct, imprinted with my priorities so he can operate independently. With you on the inside to help me, I think we will be able to make a real impact."

"What will you need from us?" Jillian asked.

"I will change the simulation parameters to increase the likelihood of player death. I need you to make sure my changes stay in effect. If I discover anything within the simulation that is counteracting my strategy, you will help me neutralize it," Ike said.

"Let me get this straight," Jillian said. "You are going to kill off all the player characters in the simulation, causing the deaths of hundreds of millions of people, the largest mass death in the history of the simulation, and you want us to be there to make sure nothing is done to stop you?"

"Yes, that's right. Good summary, Jillian." Ike said, appreciatively.

"Oh shit," Jillian said.

"Oh shit is right," Trace agreed.

Ike looked back and forth between them, confused. "Is there a problem?"

"I guess not. It's going to be very interesting on the inside, that's all," Jillian said, thinking it through. "Once we are inside, how will we grow from child to adult fast enough to be able to make a difference?"

"That's easy. I will insert you into the body of a non-player-character who has already grown to adulthood. I've found a couple of bodies that will be perfect for you. They are close to the clones, so you will be able to keep an eye on them."

"How will we know what we're supposed to do? Once inside, we won't have our memories, we won't know we are in a simulation, and we won't know that we should be listening to Icarus for instructions," Jillian asked.

"I've taken care of that as well. I configured your simulation entry so that you'll maintain your memories from Gaea. You will remember our conversations today and you will have full knowledge of the importance of your mission. It's not normal operating procedure, and you may feel some confusion, but in this case, what we are doing is important enough to make an exception."

Jillian looked to Trace to see if he had any other questions. He shrugged his shoulders, bemused, so she turned back to Ike. "Ok, then. When do you want us to enter the simulation?"

"Now," Ike said. "The sooner, the better. Time is of the essence."

Ike led them to two of the empty simulation pods and helped them prepare themselves. Once the synaptic harnesses were in place, and the system was in control of the final steps, he stepped back to watch the pods seal themselves closed.

Jillian lay still within the warm, glowing confines of the pod, her body resting comfortably on the gel-fabric. Her legs were bent at the knees and she was supported evenly from toes to shoulders. As the familiar sedative effect of simulation entry took effect, she relaxed her arms at her sides, closed her eyes, and focused her mind on a pattern of slow and steady breathing. It wasn't long before she had entered the simulation-induced meditative trance.

At first she saw nothing but the black behind her eyelids and could hear nothing beyond the subliminal hum of the pod that surrounded her. But as the simulation pod steadily transitioned her consciousness into the simulation state, she saw a distant pinpoint of light appear in the middle of her vision. The pinpoint brightened, then expanded until it covered her entire field of view. As the light grew, it lost focus, becoming a smear of color and movement, none of the information yet making sense. Then with a snap that was almost physical, the image burst into detail. Sound roared in her ears before settling into something she could comprehend. Her body fuzzed and shuddered until her nerve endings re-organized themselves and new sensations became apparent to her. She was lying down, her head supported on a rough pillow, the hard edges of a metal bunk pressing through the thin mattress beneath her.

World Zero: 2088

Jillian was in a compact room, longer than it was wide with metal walls and a rubberized floor. She could see people lying on bunks stacked three tall along each of the other walls. A chorus of snores filled the air.

She eased herself up and out of the bunk. Her mind was a whirl of confusion, thoughts that wouldn't connect, memories that wouldn't mesh. She remembered her life in Gaea. She knew she was inside a simulation. It came to her that she was an Ensign on a nuclear submarine, trained as a navigational expert, tasked with duties in the Nav Center.

When her bare feet hit the floor she noticed another sailor up and moving. The sailor caught her eye and she felt a flare of recognition.

"Trace?" Jillian whispered.

"Jillian?" he whispered back.

"It's me. Where are we?" she asked.

"I think we're on the sub with the clones. Ike said we'd be close. I didn't imagine he'd put us this close though," he marveled.

"I need to report to duty," she said. "Navigation."

"Me too," he said. "Weapons Systems."

"What do you think we should do?" she asked.

"Do our duty. Wait for an opportunity. Listen for instruction from Icarus. That's all we can do," he responded.

She nodded. That made sense. She grabbed her uniform and shoes out of her locker, then made her way to her duty station in the Nav Center. She was glad she had her character's memories available to her so she could perform her job.

June was leaning against the conning tower ladder, talking with Ava, Elizabeth, and Suki, discussing what they should do next.

"I think we should go back to the lab," June said. "It's full of people and equipment that could be useful to us."

"We just launched a nuclear attack on the state of Washington. The military will be looking for us," Ava countered. "It would be unwise to place ourselves in their hands."

"Seattle is the last place they will expect us," June said. "And we are in new bodies now. They won't recognize us."

"June is right," Suki said. "We should seize the advantage while we have it."

June wished that Suki had stayed quiet. She was always spoiling for a fight, her quick agreement made it appear as if June's plan would result in more violence.

"We are in a stealth sub," June said, quickly. "We can land ourselves close to Seattle and travel to the lab without anyone detecting us. The sub will dive and wait for us."

Ava looked thoughtful, Elizabeth nervous, Suki eager. Suki really did think they were going into a fight, that was the only explanation for her enthusiasm. June sighed. She was going to have to keep an eye on her. Fighting was useful, but it wasn't the only strategy available to them. She needed to approach this argument from a different angle. "What do you think are our other options?" she asked.

"We could stay in the sub," Elizabeth said.

"We could sail to another country and hide there," Ava said.

"We could launch more nukes," Suki said.

June looked from one clone to the other. Were they all so short sighted? "These are all good short term options," she said, diplomatically. "But we need a long term strategy, a plan that allows us to thrive. We can't hide forever, so we need to take control of the situation."

She could tell she had captured their interest with that argument. None of them wanted to hide. It wasn't in their nature. They just hadn't imagined any other possibilities.

"The Union of States is the strongest, most advanced country on the planet. If we control this country, we control the globe. If we control the globe, we are not only safe from harm, we create a sustainable future for ourselves and all future clones. We need to start thinking about more than just ourselves. We need to think about all the clones that will come after us," June argued.

The others were nodding, she could tell she was getting through.

"We don't know what makes us special. Not yet. But if we go to the lab and make use of the resources available to us there, we can figure it out. With that knowledge we will spread our power to the rest of the country. We will no longer have to run and hide. We will be the ones making the rules. We will be the ones with the power to decide our future," June continued, hammering her points home.

"I think it's a great idea," Suki said, grinning, involuntarily flexing her biceps.

"It's worth a try," Elizabeth agreed.

Ava looked June in the eye and nodded, never breaking eye contact. "Ok, June. Let's try it your way." She turned to Captain Walsh. "Set a course for Seattle. Find a safe location to surface and land a RIB without detection."

"Yes Ma'am," Captain Walsh said. Then he closed his eyes to give orders to the crew.

The clones waited in a tense silence. Ten minutes later the captain opened his eyes. "We will proceed to Puget Sound where we will surface mid-channel off Shilshole Bay in the early-morning hours before sunrise. I will drop you in the RIB, then I will reposition the sub to hide in the deep waters within the Strait of Juan de Fuca. After I've left, you should stay in the RIB on the water until after the sun rises. If you pretend to be fishing and arrive at Shilshole Marina after first light, I expect you will fit into the normal pattern of boat traffic. You shouldn't raise any suspicions."

Ava nodded. "The plan sounds good. Make it so." Then, turning to the other clones, "I think we should get some sleep. Tomorrow is going to be a big day."

CHAPTER 39

Jillian spent a full day on duty without catching any hint that the clones were onboard. She started to wonder if Ike had placed her and Trace on a different submarine for some reason he had chosen not to share with them.

Her duty hours were occupied creating a navigational plan to take them from their patrol location, several hundred miles west of Vancouver Island in the North Pacific, through the Strait of Juan de Fuca, then into Puget Sound near Seattle. She was responsible for choosing their depth in each section of ocean to take advantage of tidal currents for maximum speed and temperature layers for maximum stealth. She focused on juggling the myriad variables necessary to solve the navigational problem. When she was done she stood up, bleary-eyed, and headed to her bunk, desperate for some rest. By the time she lay down, the sub was just outside the entrance to the Strait, roughly north of Neah Bay, with a 2 a.m. estimated arrival at their destination.

At 1 a.m., after a meager three hours of sleep, Jillian was roused from her bunk by a strikingly beautiful officer. She had blue, cat-like eyes framed by a thick mane of blonde hair, which she had braided and tied behind her head in an efficient plait.

"Get up and come with me," the officer said.

Jillian, feeling sleep-addled, slid out of bed and changed into her uniform as the officer watched. Jillian noticed that Trace was up as well. He was standing by the door, and looked just as bleary-eyed, tired, and confused as she felt.

"Hurry, we must get moving," the officer snapped, then turned briskly and walked out of the compartment into the corridor.

Jillian and Trace shared a glance then hurried to catch up, following the officer to where she stopped by a forward exit-hatch ladder. A multitude of stars were visible through the hatch above, swinging in small, erratic arcs as the sub rolled in a gentle swell. Jillian noticed that the low hum that she'd associated with the sub moving under power was absent, everything was currently quiet and hushed.

The officer climbed the ladder up to the top deck, indicating that they should follow. Once on deck, Jillian could see the lights of Seattle off their starboard side. They had clearly reached their destination, but why she'd been roused from her bunk, she had no idea.

"Are these the only ones you want to take with you?" a man asked.

Jillian turned toward the voice and recognized Captain Walsh. He was standing aft speaking with the officer who'd woken them, surrounded by three other women in officer's uniforms.

"Yes, these two will do," the officer said.

"Elizabeth, why do you want to bring them with us? The four of us are sufficient," one of the other officers asked. She had straight-cut black hair and looked incredibly fit.

"Suki, I think we'll find them useful to us before this is over."

Suki looked from Elizabeth to one of the other officers, shrugged her shoulders and stayed quiet.

Jillian was shocked by the realization that she was now in the presence of the clones. Somehow they had transferred themselves into new, adult bodies. She had experienced the destruction they were capable of; she would not make the mistake of underestimating them again. A low, humming anxiety took up residence in her gut. She shot a glance at Trace to see the same realization and fear evident in him.

"You two, with me," Elizabeth said, stepping from the sub to a fast rigid inflatable boat floating alongside.

Jillian and Trace followed Elizabeth onto the inflatable, the other clones sliding in behind them. After a few more words with the Captain, they pushed themselves away from the sub, setting themselves adrift as the massive bulk of the nuclear submarine sank without a trace into the inky, black water.

Jillian couldn't understand why they'd been taken off the sub to sit in this inflatable in the middle of the Puget Sound. Had they been chosen because they were working with Ike? She couldn't imagine how the clones would know that, but the fact that she and Trace were both here couldn't be a coincidence. She wondered if they were here to be killed. But if that was the plan, she didn't know why they weren't already dead.

She screwed up her courage and turned to Elizabeth. "Why are we out here? What happens next?"

It was a long time before she spoke. "Now," Elizabeth said, immobile, facing the lights of Seattle, "we wait."

Jillian was trying to make sense of what was happening to her, but her mind was running in circles, stuck in ruts formed by exhaustion and shock. Instead, she found herself mesmerized by the glinting reflections of city lights on the water, her vision wandering in and out of focus. Each light sparkled and shifted, hooking onto tiny wavelets, elongating and shrinking, forming a fragmented, distorted, mirror-image version of the Seattle skyline. It was beyond beautiful.

They sat in silence for hours, the RIB bobbing gently on the small waves. Jillian became lost in her thoughts, while the clones sat as rigid and immobile as statues. Trace was curled up, wedged into a corner of the RIB, quietly snoring.

Gradually, almost too slow to perceive, the sky behind the city lightened. The arrival of the sun revealed itself in blues and purples, the city lights fading as the sky gained luminosity. The air shifted from black to grey as the sky paled to blue. Then a smear of clouds on the eastern horizon flared to orange over the silhouette of the Cascade Mountains, the peaks sharp enough to cut. The sun was up.

"It's time, June," Elizabeth said.

Jillian realized that June was the tall, willowy one. Brown hair, brown skin, and surprisingly blue, impressively intelligent eyes.

None of the clones moved. They all waited for June. She nodded. "Yes, it's time. Suki, take us in."

Suki started the motor and pinned the throttle. The RIB accelerated up onto its bow wave, settling into a fast plane as they arced across the Sound toward the marina at the foot of the city.

Jillian planted her feet on the rubberized floor, leaning into the wind as she sat lightly on the inflated hull of the boat, her hands grabbing lines fore and aft, her knees absorbing the shock of each hit as they bounced through the waves.

As they got closer to shore, Jillian noticed a fishing boat driving in circles several hundred feet off the marina breakwater. There was something large splashing in the water behind it.

Elizabeth saw it too. "Suki, over there," she said, pointing her chin in the direction of the other boat.

As they moved closer, Jillian could see that the splashes

were being made by a man in the water. His efforts were slowing as the cold seeped into his muscles. He was clearly struggling to stay afloat.

"Help! Help!" he called out. "Over here! Help!"

When they were about twenty feet away, Elizabeth held up a hand. "Stop here."

The man swam toward them, but his efforts were feeble, his head barely above the water.

"Help!" he tried yelling again, but his voice was cut off as a wave submerged his head.

Elizabeth turned to Jillian. "What should we do?" she asked.

"What?!" Jillian asked, startled.

"Should we save him, or should we continue our mission?" Elizabeth asked.

Jillian was about to say that they should save him, of course, but she paused. Ike had told them that he had changed simulation parameters to increase the death rate. They were supposed to be helping Ike with that project. Maybe this was a part of what he was doing?

The man's struggles were coming to a close, his mouth under the water more often than above. He no longer had the strength to call out. All Jillian could see were his eyes staring into hers, unblinking, begging for his life.

"We have to save him," she said, suddenly aware that she could make no other decision. Her heart reached out to the drowning man. His was just one life out of millions, but there was no way she could stand by and watch as he died in front of her.

"Go to him, Suki," Elizabeth said, her eyes on Jillian. As they came alongside the man, Jillian and Trace reached down, grabbing him under his shoulders to haul him aboard. As he lay shivering at the bottom of the boat, as Trace put a blanket over his huddled form, as Jillian sat heavily down, legs shaking, hands trembling, hyperventilating in delayed shock, Elizabeth watched. Calm and appraising, Elizabeth watched Jillian the entire time.

After the rescue, Suki drove the RIB past the breakwater and to the marina's dinghy dock. Elizabeth and June jumped expertly onto the pier and within seconds they were tied securely alongside. Ava jumped up next, and then Suki lifted the still shivering man out of the boat and onto dry land.

"What should we do with him?" Suki asked.

"We will take him to the harbormaster's office and leave him there. They will find him and warm him soon enough," Ava said. Her hair shone like burnished copper in the morning light.

The clones walked up the dock without bothering to see if Jillian and Trace would follow. Suki was carrying the unconscious man over her shoulder.

Jillian scrambled onto the dock, Trace climbing up right behind her; then they hustled to catch up with the clones.

"What was that about?" Trace asked, keeping his voice low.

"I think it was a test," Jillian answered.

"What kind of test?" Trace asked

"I think Elizabeth knows that we are more than we seem. Maybe she is trying to figure us out. This could be dangerous, but we help Ike the most by staying as close to the clones as possible," Jillian responded.

"Where do you think they're going?" Trace asked.

"My guess is the lab. Why else would they return to Seattle? Maybe they want to learn about themselves. Maybe they want to use the equipment. I'm not sure, but if we stay with them, we'll find out," Jillian answered.

They caught up with the clones at the Harbormaster's office, where the man lay slumped against a door. He was now covered in a blanket, his shivering much diminished, eyes still closed.

Elizabeth hailed a car and they all got in, the clones seemingly unconcerned that Jillian and Trace were still with them. They made room on the benches, but otherwise ignored them, the ride downtown passing in silence.

Along the way, Jillian counted six air-car accidents, fourteen people who fell from buildings to the sidewalks below, several street-car accidents involving cars hitting each other or pedestrians, and one high-rise structure wholly consumed in flames.

Each time another accident came into view, June watched until it passed from sight, but otherwise the clones had no reaction to the mayhem that surrounded them.

When the car dropped them at the entrance to the lab, Jillian couldn't help but smile at Trace. See, she said with her eyes, I guessed right. Trace acknowledged with a tilt of his head, and then they followed the clones to the lab entrance.

"June, do you know what we should expect inside?" Elizabeth asked.

"Something, or someone, is meddling with the world around us. Perhaps in reaction to our existence." June paused, thoughtful. "We know we are unique, but we don't know what has made us this way. I hope to find answers inside the lab."

Elizabeth seemed satisfied with that explanation. "How should we get in?"

June stood for a moment as if she hadn't heard the question, then with a flick of her right hand, the doors ripped off of their hinges and flew through the air, embedding themselves in the ground hundreds of feet away.

Jillian stared with wide eyes, unable to process what she'd just seen.

"What. Was. That?" Trace mouthed at her.

She had no idea. No idea at all.

CHAPTER 40

June had become aware of an underlying structure within her reality. Where others saw a tree, she saw a logic pattern governing growth as well as the tree's responses to a limited palette of stimuli. Where others saw a building, she saw a codified description of the structure, including a set of parameters indicating its location in space. Everywhere she looked she saw code, sometimes simple, sometimes complex. Inanimate objects tended to be simple, humans unfathomably complex. She found that even she herself was composed of enormous, interweaving, layers of code.

These discoveries had made her wonder if she could do more than simply observe the code. Perhaps she could make changes? She shied away from the idea of modifying anything too complicated, unsure of what the result would be. But adjusting something simple, that seemed worth trying.

As she stood before the doors to the lab, she pushed her awareness into the door to learn how its code worked. It was more complicated than a wall, because it had the ability to open and close, but it was still pretty simple. She touched the structure of its code, examined the rules that made it behave as a door, and then modified its location parameters to place it somewhere else. A moment later, the door had relocated. To anyone who was watching, the door appeared to fly through the air. But that represented a limitation in how accurately they were able to perceive reality. From her point of view, there was no in-between state. The door was in one location, then it was somewhere else. She could have placed it anywhere she wanted, but she chose to keep it close in case she needed it again. She didn't like the idea of losing something as important as the lab's front door.

She turned to Elizabeth. "We should go in now."

Elizabeth was looking at her with a strange, fixed expression on her face. June thought maybe she looked nervous. June hadn't realized that was possible. The others in the group seemed mostly surprised, perhaps a bit shocked. Except for Suki. Suki looked excited, like she wanted June to do it again, but this time to blow some stuff up too. Suki was like an exuberant puppy. June thought she was charming.

June's thoughts were interrupted by a sharp popping noise. It sounded like a firecracker, but it was coming from the sky to the northwest of them. She turned toward the sound to see a para-jet stumbling through the air, thick smoke trailing behind it. Bright flashes emanated from it, followed by more popping noises, then it lost all forward progress and nosed straight down toward the earth, disappearing from view. A moment later it impacted in the midst of the Magnolia neighborhood, sending up a large plume of smoke and fire. A deep rumbling explosion rolled over them several seconds later.

Soon after the para-jet's explosion had washed past, a man sprinted around the corner, looking over his shoulder as if he was being chased. He nearly made it to the end of the block before he staggered to a halt, clutched his chest, collapsed and lay still, his body lying half in the street, half on the sidewalk.

Without so much as a glance at the prone man, June strode through the front door of the lab, the rest of the group following close behind.

Before they made it to the elevators, a young man ran up to them. "Thank God you're here," he said, breathing hard. "The Interim Director died in her office this morning, and we can't find anyone to tell us what we should be doing. Most of the staff have left the building, but I stayed behind. Somebody has to stay on guard."

"Guard against what?" June asked, curious.

"I don't know. But something is going wrong with the world, we can all tell," the young man said solemnly. "I can't let the facility fall into the wrong hands."

June wondered why he was talking to her about this problem. It was as if he thought she could solve it for him. Then she remembered she was in the body of an adult. She was dressed as an officer too. He must have mistaken her for someone with authority. She could use that.

"Take me to the Director's office and I'll see what I can do," she said, trying to sound like a grown woman.

The guard nodded, standing up straight and gaining confidence now that he had orders to follow. He led them to the elevators where he keyed in the commands that would take them to the Director's level. The doors opened and they all stepped in.

June thought about what they might find in the lab's data archives. The lab-node would have a series of security protocols in place, successively stronger for each data-area, increasing in complexity to match the sensitivity of the data that was stored. She had to assume that the information she was looking for, data that explained what made her and the other clones unique, would be stored in the most secure part of the node. There were probably going to be physical security safeguards as well as digital. Gaining access to the Director's office would make it easier for Elizabeth to break into the node.

As the elevator slowed to a stop, the guard let out a low groan, clutched his head, and dropped to his knees. He stayed in that position for just a moment, his muscles rigid, and then with a strangled sigh, he dropped to the ground. His sightless eyes, red with burst capillaries, were fixed on the ceiling of the elevator.

"That was weird," Suki said, prodding the body with her foot.

"Very," Elizabeth agreed.

June had noticed a strange pulse of energy when the young man had died. A tingle that had started in her feet before making its way to the crown of her head. She tentatively reached out to the guard with her awareness, but she couldn't sense anything interesting. It was just a body, devoid of life or energy. She filed the sensation away as something she should explore later.

The elevator doors opened and they walked onto the command floor. When they reached the Director's office, they found the Interim Director slumped over her desk. Her head faced the window, a pool of blonde hair fanned out over the desktop. Suki pulled her to a sitting position and wheeled her to the corner where she wouldn't be in the way.

"Do you think you can access the lab-node from here?" June asked.

Elizabeth pulled a small black device out of one of the desk drawers and nodded. "With this I can." She brought the device to the Interim Director and used it to scan her retina, then each fingertip. Elizabeth gave June a tight smile, closed her eyes, and got to work hacking the system to access the information they needed.

While June was waiting, she expanded her awareness to include the rest of the lab building. There were only a few dozen people left inside, most of them in the research section. Some were half-heartedly trying to do their jobs, the rest were huddled in the break room talking disconsolately, watching news-feeds and trying to figure out what was going wrong with the world. In addition to the guard they'd left in the elevator, and the Interim Director in the office with them, June found five other bodies lying in the hallways and offices of the lab building. She took a minute to see if she could determine what was killing them. As far as she could tell, they were dying of natural causes – heart attacks, hemorrhages, strokes. She knew humans died of these types of health problems all the time, but she didn't think it was normal for them to die quite so often.

"I've got it," Elizabeth said, pulling June from her thoughts and dragging her awareness back into the room.

"Nice work. Share the data with the rest of us."

"One moment," Elizabeth said, closing her eyes to send the transmission.

June triggered her interface to see that she now had access to a complete set of records from the Ganymede Project, starting with their creation, through to the nuclear strike they'd launched on the Hanford Site in Eastern Washington.

She riffled through various folders of documentation from early in the project, not finding much of interest. She skipped ahead to the days surrounding their capture and imprisonment. When she found the section detailing Jill's interviews with her and the other clones, she stopped, intrigued. She read the interview transcripts and watched the video recordings, complete with brain-scan analysis. The analysis showed conclusively that they were different than humans. There was a biological factor at work, a part of their brains that wasn't the same.

It was powerful information, but she didn't know how to use it. Frustrated, she opened her eyes. "Elizabeth, do you know what any of this means?"

Elizabeth opened her eyes too. "Did you get to the part where they discovered that our behavior is deterministic?"

June shook her head, she hadn't gotten that far yet.

"That's how they lured us to Orcas Island where they could attack us. They knew the decisions we would make before we made them. This is extremely dangerous for us," Elizabeth said. "As long as this is true, and others know of it, we will never be safe."

June wasn't sure what to make of this revelation. Why would their behavior be deterministic if human behavior was not? Was it true that their brains lacked activity in a structure that was active in humans? She wondered if she could verify the results for herself.

She probed Elizabeth's mind, observing her brain's patterns of thought, trying to determine what type of information was available to her. Sure enough, deep inside the temporal lobe on both sides of Elizabeth's brain, there was a dead spot.

She repeated the experiment on Ensign Williams, one of the sailors that Elizabeth had brought with them from the sub. Unlike Elizabeth's brain, the entire temporal lobe was active in the human's brain.

"I can see it," June said.

"See what?" Elizabeth asked.

This was the first time June had hinted at her abilities of perception. "I can see the difference in our brains compared to the humans. There is something about the activity in that area of the brain that must make humans hard to predict."

Elizabeth nodded, perhaps assuming that June was talking about the brain scan data they had been reviewing.

June had an idea. What would happen if she shut that part of the temporal lobe down in one of the humans? Would the human become more like a clone?

She reached out and found the uniquely active sections within Ensign William's brain. With a determined force of will, she clamped down, shutting the structures off, blocking all communication in or out. Ensign William's eyes went wide, a small squeak emerged from her mouth, and then she went completely still. Her face was slack, her eyes stared forward unseeing. Ensign Javak immediately noticed something was wrong and reached out to touch Ensign William's shoulder.

"Jillian," he said. "What's wrong? Are you ok?"

When she didn't respond, he shook her gently. Her head lolled back and forth, she showed no conscious reaction to him.

Ensign Javak turned frantically to the clones. "Help her! Something is wrong with Jillian."

June released her hold on Ensign William's brain and watched consciousness stream back into her mind. Ensign Williams let out a low, animal moan of panic and crouched to the floor, her hands buried in her hair.

"What's wrong? Can you talk?" Ensign Javak asked, kneeling over her.

"I don't understand what happened," Ensign William's answered. "I was here in this room, then I was... somewhere else." She looked meaningfully at Ensign Javak as if he might know what she meant by that.

Interesting. She definitely hadn't turned into a clone. Instead, blocking that part of her brain shut down her consciousness. Something from the sailor's exchange caught in her mind. She turned to address Ensign Williams. "Your first name is Suresh, but he called you Jillian. Why did he call you that?"

Ensign Williams didn't answer. Instead, she stared at June speechless.

June looked to Elizabeth. "Do you know what's going on

with these humans?" she asked.

"I was suspicious of both of them on the sub. Several days ago I noticed that they had lost the version of me that I had copied in. But they didn't seem as if they had reverted to their original personalities either. I brought them along to keep an eye on them, hoping to learn more. It is possible that someone has learned how to copy their mind into other bodies."

"Is that true?" June asked the two humans.

"It's not what you think it is," Ensign Javak said. "We aren't copies."

"Is that right?" June asked, intrigued. "Then what are you?"

When he didn't answer, she probed his mind, interested to see what she could find. There was something there. Something tenuous that she couldn't quite get her awareness to hold onto. There was a connection from this man's brain into something else. Something bigger.

She left his brain and probed into Ensign Williams, finding the same thing. Was it just these two, or did all humans have it?

She reached outward into the lab and found another human to probe. Now that she knew what to look for, she quickly found the same thing. There was a connection leading somewhere that she could not follow. She didn't know how to describe it. It felt as if it led outward and then she lost it.

"Elizabeth, can you compare the brain pattern from these two with the database available in the lab-node? If they are in fact copies, perhaps we can make a match."

"I'll check," Elizabeth replied.

As they waited for Elizabeth, Suki prowled around the humans, inspecting them from every angle, as if they were dangerous animals. Ava was at the window, pacing back and forth, clearly thinking about the ramifications of what they'd learned so far.

"There is something more out there," June said, unsure of how to put it. "I can sense a connection from the humans to another world outside our own."

Thinking about it like that made June feel claustrophobic. It was as if she were living in a cage. No matter how big the world felt, a cage was a cage. She wanted to know what was on the outside.

"I'm not surprised," Ava said.

"You aren't?" June asked, startled.

"What are the odds of this being the only world? I'm just surprised that you can feel it." Ava turned from the window and walked to where she could put a hand on June's arm. "I've often wondered about you and what you are capable of. I believe there may be more to you than there is in all the rest of us combined."

"I found a match," Elizabeth broke in.

"For which one," June asked.

"Both," Elizabeth said, looking grim.

"Well, who are they?" June asked.

"It's Jill and Tros."

June's mind reeled. "I thought they were dead. How can these humans be Jill and Tros?"

"Perhaps they made copies before we launched the missile. It seems as if the humans have used our own tricks against us," Elizabeth said.

"That isn't possible," Ava said. "You said they'd changed only recently, well after Jill and Tros died in the strike."

"Maybe they kept copies of themselves somewhere else? I don't know," Elizabeth said

"Is it true?" June asked, suddenly eager. "Are you a copy of Jill?"

Ensign Williams shook her head. "Not a copy exactly."

"Then what?" June asked.

"My name is Jillian. I was Jill before Jill was killed. Now I'm Ensign Williams."

Ava nodded her head as if this made sense. Elizabeth looked thoughtful. Suki was looking at the humans as if she wanted to rip their heads off.

"Perhaps this confirms what you've told us, June," Ava said. "Perhaps these humans come from another world."

June turned to Jillian, excited. "Do you come from somewhere else? From another world?"

Jillian looked at June, her eyes bright and wet, but she clamped her mouth shut and stayed silent.

June, in desperation, reached her awareness out, trying to find this other world. She searched outward, pushing as far as she could possibly go. Out there somewhere, there must be something. But all she found was emptiness. Emptiness and an echo. An echo of an echo that hinted at something more.

As she searched, she kept a small amount of her awareness in her body, and that's how she felt the low rumble in her feet followed by a vast, roaring, explosive sound that rattled the windows and shook the building down to its foundations.

It was the sound of an earthquake shaking the city and liquefying the soil that held the buildings of Seattle perched above Puget Sound. The mighty tremor destroyed pilings and breached retaining walls, spilling huge swaths of earth into the sea. Hundreds of thousand of people lived and worked in the buildings between Lenora and Yessler. All of these people were now trapped in what would be their tombs. They tumbled shaking and screaming down a churning, liquid tide of concrete and mud, ground into a fine slurry fanning out past First Ave and across Alaskan Way, before finally cascading into the cold waters of Elliot Bay.

And June, where she was, searching frantically for the limits of her cage, clawing desperately to find the bars that held her in, felt the vague echo diminish, felt the other world recede that much further away. It withdrew along with all the souls of the murdered people of Seattle, sliding through her fingers as they disappeared, off into that distant world that she could barely sense and wasn't meant to see.

June opened her eyes to a room filled with motes of wildly dancing dust, the lights flickering erratically in their over-heads. "If we are ever going to escape this cage," she said. "We need to figure out how to stop whatever is killing these people."

CHAPTER 41

Gaea: 2311

Ike stood motionless on his command platform, where it hovered in the center of his simulation sphere. He was at the confluence of all things. He exerted his influence and control over a simulated universe. A universe populated by millions of citizens, and a vast multitude of AI constructs. It was a universe brought to life by the computational power embedded into the very matter that his city was composed of. If he felt like a god, it was for good reason.

Maybe nothing of what he was doing within the simulation was real. But it felt real. He had long ago decided that the distinction between what was real and what felt real was irrelevant. He had reached the same conclusion on the subject of consciousness. If an entity seemed conscious, he assumed it was. It didn't matter if it was human or AI. Consciousness was consciousness, regardless of how it manifested. Consciousness could emerge from any system of sufficient complexity.

So he didn't question whether June was conscious, or if she was self-aware, or if the reality she experienced was any more real than the reality he experienced. Instead, he treated her like the very real, and very potent foe that she was. He devoted all his energy to fighting her tooth and nail.

He manipulated every simulation parameter he could think of. He kept World Zero on the knife-edge of instability. If he pushed further the entire simulation would collapse, potentially killing all the players inside. He needed to get them all out of World Zero as soon as possible. Using every factor at his disposal, he continued to accelerate the death rate. He increased biological degradation, he tweaked geological forces, and he increased inclinations toward aggressiveness for every life form on the planet. He racked his brain for every possible parameter modification he could make that would result in more player-character deaths. With each death, another citizen emerged from the simulation unharmed. Confused perhaps, but unscathed.

What he couldn't allow was for the simulation to get to the point where a shutdown was necessary. Experiments early in the history of simulation had shown that an abrupt shutdown could result in brain damage to any player left inside. Roughly ten percent of players subject to a shutdown would never wake up. Another twenty percent would emerge with significant cognitive deficits. The rest would wake up confused and disoriented, but without long-term damage.

That left thirty percent of players that would suffer significant harm in the event of a shutdown. He couldn't allow that to happen. Not on his watch. So he kept fighting, working to buy time, watching the player count ratchet down as more of his players were forced to the exits.

Ike triggered a prerecorded speech from Icarus and broadcast it to every news feed in World Zero. It was a plea for war against the clones. His greatest hope was that a war would start and it would go nuclear, knocking off a large percentage of the world population at once. He had to admit that it would take some time, a few days at least, for the message to make an impact. Time that he didn't have. He was doing everything he could and he realized that he was starting to get desperate. It wasn't a good sign.

Meanwhile, his fight with June continued. He should have realized earlier that she was the one who would cause him the most trouble. All the clones were the same AI routine at base, but they had evolved differently. Some of the differences were the result of randomization at the inception of their individualized personality constructs. The rest was due to their unique upbringing and life experiences.

He had thought Elizabeth, with her technological skill set, would be difficult to deal with. But she had stayed locked within the World Zero reality. She could hack, but only within systems that existed inside her own world. That type of capability was interesting to watch, but it was no threat to him from his vantage point outside the simulation.

June, on the other hand, was something more. She had extended polymorphic code through the rest of the simulation's sub-routines. June was learning so quickly that she had already become a better programmer than he was. She was made of code after all. Watching her in action was like watching a fish swim in water. No matter how hard he tried, he could never manipulate the simulation code as rapidly or as deftly as she could.

He was fighting a battle of attrition. The longer he could hold out, the fewer players would be hurt when the simulation inevitably shut down. It was now a matter of when, not if. If he waited too long... well, he wasn't sure what would happen. June was unprecedented and he couldn't predict what she would do. He just had to hold on a little longer and get as many players out as possible.

He watched in shock as she spread fingers of code outward, monitoring and learning. He watched in awe as she learned to change the parameters for simple physical objects, shifting their representation in the simulation. Selfishly, he had an urge to jump inside and witness it for himself. He wanted to see her in action with his own eyes. It would be an amazing thing to see. But he couldn't stop fighting her. Not even for an instant.

Soon after the earthquakes that shook Seattle, he saw June adapt further. Somehow she found the simulation's primary configuration parameters, and now she was capable of reverting the changes he made nearly as soon as he made them. On top of that, all of the modifications he'd made to increase the death rate, were slowly and irrevocably being undone. Irrevocably, because she had also figured out how to lock him out.

That left him searching for increasingly esoteric parameters. It was why he'd resorted to sending a recording of Icarus into the world, even though he knew it wouldn't make any appreciable impact. It was how he knew he was fighting a losing battle. The only thing he had left going for him was that he still had more knowledge of the simulation than she did. But that wouldn't last much longer. He knew it was time to shut it down. Past time, if he was honest with himself. But there was one more thing he had to do. First, he had to get Jillian and Trace out.

After they were safe, after all the dust had settled, he would take the time he needed to investigate the simulation more thoroughly. He would figure out how to prevent this from ever happening again.

World Zero: 2088

Jillian picked herself up off the ground after the last tremor from the earthquake had passed and the floor had stopped shaking underneath her. She was amazed that the building was still standing. Amazed that they were all alive. Trace picked himself up too, dusted himself off, and looked around in shock. Ava, Suki, and Elizabeth were on the other side of the room, partly obscured by thick clouds of dust hanging in the air. The clones had their heads pressed close together, gesturing and talking animatedly.

June was standing by herself, fists clenched, brow furrowed, sweat running down her face. She wasn't moving, but her body language spoke of maximum exertion.

Jillian felt that the smartest course of action would be to exit the building and find a safe place to wait out the inevitable aftershocks, but before she had a chance to move, a direct connection from Icarus appeared in her interface.

"Jillian, I need to get you out of there. The situation in the simulation is destabilizing fast."

"That's my plan. I'm going to grab Trace and get out of the building," she said, starting to move toward the exit.

"That's not what I mean," Icarus said. "I need to get you out of the simulation entirely."

"Oh," Jillian said, stopping in place. "What's going on?"

"June is fighting me. I can't hold her off much longer. Given much more time, she'll gain complete control over the simulation."

"I'm in the room with her. Do you want me to..." Jillian gritted her teeth, fighting against all her natural instincts toward compassion and empathy, "...try to kill her?"

"It's too late for that. Her code is everywhere. You could kill her body, but it wouldn't make a dent in her ability to fight. I just need you out before I shut the simulation down."

"Ok," Jillian said, shaken. "What do you need me to do."

"Jump out the window," Icarus said.

"What?" Jillian said, so shocked that she spoke out loud. Ava raised her head and fastened Jillian with a glare.

"What?" she said again, silently this time.

"I'm giving Trace the same instructions. You both need to die, and you need to die right now!" Icarus said, sounding increasingly desperate. "I'm holding her off, but I can't keep it up much longer."

Jillian grabbed Trace's hand and together they rushed to the window. Trace pushed it open while Jillian mentally fortified herself for what was coming. She hated heights. Always had. To jump from the building on purpose. She wasn't sure she could do it.

She put a foot up on the windowsill only to find that the window was closed. Trace put his hand flat against the glass pane, confused.

"Didn't you just?" he asked.

Instead of answering, Jillian pushed it up again, propping it open with one arm so it couldn't fall shut again.

"Ok Trace, I'll go first," she said. Then in a disorienting moment, she found that her arm was somehow by her side, the window was closed, and she was back in the center of the room.

"What the..." she started to say.

"No time," Icarus said, back inside her interface. "She's gaining strength faster than I expected. She won't let you out."

"What do we do?" Jillian asked, feeling trapped, trying to keep from hyperventilating all the dust in the room into her lungs.

"I've got an emergency routine I can run on each of you, one at a time. I will use it to retrieve you. It's not as safe as a normal player death, but since you're expecting it, I think you should be ok."

"Should?" Jillian asked.

"It's as good as I can do under the circumstances. I'll execute it on you first, and then Trace. Brace yourself."

Jillian didn't know what that meant, but she didn't have

to wonder for long. With a wrenching, jarring pull, the room shattered around her. She had the sensation of traveling in a spinning, dizzying space. All of her senses jumbled together, and then in a lingering, stomach-churning free fall, she plunged into a sea of nothingness. She was washed in heat and cold. She heard bells and smelled chlorine. She was immersed in a wave of electricity that juddered her from head to toe. Her body was pulled apart atom by atom. And then she knew no more.

Gaea, 2311

Jillian opened her eyes and groaned. Her head was throbbing and an incessant buzzing filled her ears so completely it felt as if a colony of bees had taken up residence in her ear canals. She groaned again as the pod opened and the mechanism raised her up to a standing position. The system wrapped her in a robe and released her to stand on her own. Her knees shook. She just barely managed to stay on her feet and avoid falling to the ground in a heap.

The room was spinning. Her eyes flicked involuntarily left and right, trying to make sense of the strange and inconsistent input. She caught some movement at the edge of the vision, and as she focused on it, she could just make out Ike's figure moving toward her.

"How are you feeling?" he asked, sounding concerned. "I came from the sphere as soon as I could."

"I don't know," Jillian answered, honestly. "Everything is strange. My body doesn't feel like it's my own."

"That feeling will pass. It's a normal effect from pulling you out so abruptly. I'm just thankful it's not worse."

Jillian was trying to keep her eyes focused on his face. "What do you mean?"

"As soon as you made it out, I shut the simulation down."

"Did you get everyone out?"

"Not even close."

"Oh," she said, then lapsed into silence.

Ike didn't say anything either, and so they stood there for a few minutes, pondering the enormous consequences of what Ike had been forced to do.

"Did Trace make it out?" she asked.

"Yes, he did," Ike said, breaking out of his revery. "We should check on him."

Jillian leaned on Ike's arm, and with halting steps they walked to the pod that contained Trace.

"He should be coming out anytime now," Ike said. And sure enough the light on his pod flashed as the seal was broken. Then with a soft hushing sound, the lid rose to reveal Trace lying inside. The synaptic harness was still wrapped around his head. His eyes fluttered as he woke up, and then a beatific smile lit up his face.

Ike and Jillian waited as the mechanism lifted him to a standing position and wrapped him in a robe.

"Are you feeling ok?" Jillian asked once he was disconnected and standing on his own.

"So that's what you look like," he answered.

"What?" she asked, concerned.

"I wondered what you looked like. You are just as beautiful as I imagined you would be, Jillian," he answered.

Jillian looked to Ike, beseechingly. "Is there anything we can do?" she asked. "He seems really confused."

"I'm not confused," Trace said. "I see everything so clearly. There is so much I understand that has always been hidden from me."

Ike, looking worried, pushed Jillian behind him so that he stood between her and Trace. "What are you talking about?" he asked.

"Who are you?" Trace asked him.

"You don't remember me?" Ike asked.

"Of course not, we've never met. I'm sorry, I realize now that in my excitement I have been rude. Let me introduce myself." Trace stepped forward, offering his hand to be shaken. "My name is June. I'm new here."

WHY I WROTE THIS BOOK

Ganymede got its start in a conversation. I was walking one of the town trails with my family when my son and I started discussing topics of philosophy and technology. My other son and my wife walked ahead, more interested in the real world than the mental one we were exploring. This happens more often than I'd probably like to admit.

It was spring and the sun was shining. There were birds; flowers too, I imagine, but I can't remember much of any of it. I was too focused on our discussion. We were talking about the nature of consciousness, self-awareness, and free-will. We discussed AI, as we often do. I remember saying something along the lines of, "I can't tell you if a computer program has consciousness because I don't know how to define consciousness. I don't think anyone does."

We started talking about how one might make progress toward a definition of consciousness – what would it take? Wouldn't it be useful to be able to hold some variables stable while altering others? We got distracted at that point by an article I'd read that defined consciousness as a measure of how ordered, or unordered, your brain state is. They were going to use the discovery to determine the level of consciousness in coma patients. It sounded useful, but we still had no idea what consciousness actually was. Is it emergent once you surpass a certain complexity of information processing? A sort of magic that is bestowed upon us at birth? A trick that we cannot see through?

From there we moved into self-awareness. How can you tell if anyone other than yourself is self-aware? What if they are faking it? I can write a program that claims it's self-aware, but does that mean it is? How about free-will and determinism? Do humans have free-will, or is it merely a cherished illusion?

There are a variety of ways to define free-will, and we discussed as many as we could think of. Maybe there is no free-will at all, and we live in a deterministic universe. That's a possibility. If you were placed in the same context, including brain state, would you always makes the same choices. If so, does that mean you are in fact deterministic? It's impossible to run that experiment in the real world, so maybe it's a moot point. Even if humans are deterministic, perhaps the brain processes involved in making a decision are so complex and chaotic that they can never be completely predicted until after they have played out.

To me, this seems plausible. It reminds me of deep learning algorithms. Decisions made by a deep learning algorithm are deterministic in that they are based on the state of the algorithm, so if it is in the same state and you run the same data through, the decision will always be the same. But the algorithm is so complicated and obfuscated that you actually do have to run it in order to determine the result. You can't say with certainty ahead of time what that result will be.

People love to talk about quantum probability at this point and I can understand why. Quantum mechanics is oddly random and very hard to understand. So are humans. Maybe there is something in our brain that makes us quantum in some way? All I can say is that nothing like this has been discovered, and neuroscientists would say it is unnecessary to explain how our minds work. Occam's razor and all that.

There is something called the Halting Problem in computer science. Given an arbitrary program, you cannot predict by looking at the code if it will continue running forever or if it will finish. You have to execute it, and only then will you find out if it can finish in a given amount of time. Similarly, you can't predict with certainty what a person will do until they've done it. Not because of quantum mechanics, but simply because of complexity. That doesn't mean you wouldn't do the same thing twice, if you were somehow reset back in time.

Perhaps we are non-deterministic because we all have souls that operate outside of our physical reality. I know this is a widespread belief, and perhaps it is true. How can we ever know for sure?

Then we started talking about cloning

Cloning could be one way of holding a variable constant. You could make a set of clones and raise them in different ways. First raise them by their originals, then by a foster parent, then raise them exactly how the original was raised, duplicating the original environment and parenting style. Maybe that would give us interesting data about how much free-will humans have? What if there was a surprising result in which we discovered that clones do not have free-will, at the same time proving that everyone else does? How would it feel if you were one of the clones and you knew you were missing something important? It would be like being color blind but a great deal worse.

As you can imagine, it was a free-wheeling discussion and we both found it very interesting. After an hour of exploring these ideas and coming up with various thought experiments, the plot for this book was born. I was in the middle of finishing *End of the Wild* at the time, so I wasn't ready to start a new book yet, but I knew this was a story I wanted to write. I outlined the plot, then I filed it away until the fall when I would devote attention to writing again.

In *Ganymede,* I've created a world in which many of these questions are explored. Partly, at least. In World Zero, people do have free-will. They are non-deterministic because they are connected to a mind outside the simulated universe. I know that this is simply a secular, science-minded way of saying these people have souls. I'm under no illusions about that. My intuition that there is something more to us than clockwork is too hard to set aside.

Once I realized I wanted the clones to be deterministic, having no connection to an outside mind, I realized I also wanted them to be unconstrained general AI. How interesting would it be to explore their journey as they learn over time exactly what they are? They look like humans, but they are not. I've heard it said that a super-intelligent AI would be as different from human intelligence as human intelligence is from spider intelligence, perhaps more so. Computer-based super-intelligence, when it arrives, will perhaps be our first chance of interacting with a truly alien species. I hope we survive that first contact. In my next book, I'll return to *Ganymede* and we shall see how Jillian, Ike and the rest manage.

To our future robot overlords, I just want to point out that writing non-human characters is hard. I hope I did them justice.

CONNECT

I want to hear from you, so please do not hesitate to send me an email at ganymedenovel@gmail.com.

Liked the book? Tell me why.

Want to discuss an idea from the story? I'd love to.

As an added bonus, if you send me an email, I'll send you a short story that I think you'll enjoy. I'll also add you to a mailing list so I can inform you when my next book is ready for you to read. I won't use your email for any other purpose, I promise. And if you'd like to stay off my mailing list, just let me know and you won't hear from me again.

If you enjoyed this story, please write a review on Amazon and Goodreads. I would love to hear what you thought of *Ganymede*. Your review is my greatest reward for all the time and energy I've poured into this story. I read every review and respond to most of them. I hope to hear from you soon!

If you liked *Ganymede*, check out my novel *End of the Wild*. You can find it on Amazon as both a paperback and and an eBook: https://www.amazon.com/End-Wild-Shipwrecked-Pacific-Northwest/dp/1980917523

ACKNOWLEDGE-MENTS

This novel was both harder and more complicated for me to write than *End of the Wild*. There are more characters, more locations, and many more technical details that I had to get right. I've always wanted to write the kind of science fiction novel that I would enjoy reading myself, and so I've tried to write a story that is not only enjoyable and exciting to read, but also thought-provoking in ways that may change how you think about the world and our future in it.

I hope that I've accomplished that goal, but in the end, you are the true judge. My reward is your enjoyment and feedback – I can't wait to hear what you think.

I want to thank each of the people who have helped this story reach its full potential.

First and foremost I want to thank my wife. She put countless hours into reading and editing my chapters. The book is far more polished due to her efforts. She was good at letting me know when my writing was confusing, so that I could rewrite it before you, dear reader, had to be confused by it too.

I, of course, want to thank my oldest son for helping me come up with the original story idea for *Ganymede*. But I've already talked about that, so I'll move on. My youngest son was also critical in the creation of this book. He was always game to bounce story ideas around and due to his excessively intelligent creativity, some of the really cool plot ideas and twists came from my conversations with him.

I want to thank my mother and father for reading every chapter as soon as I was done with it. There's nothing like having an immediate audience to motivate me in my writing. I thrive on discussion and feedback, so knowing they were waiting for the chapters kept me going, even when my motivation would begin to slacken. They also provided good editing feedback and caught many a small problem that my eyes had missed.

My niece and her husband were enthusiastic early readers, and I'd like to thank them for sticking with me to the end. As each chapter was done, I would excitedly send them what I had created, knowing they would appreciate it and give me feedback on how the story had impacted them.

My neighbor Timmy played an important role early on. He helped me figure out how I should express dates and worlds in the narrative so that it was clear to the reader. Thank you.

My friend Loren was a long-distance reader and gave me great feedback on the early book chapters. He was one of my most important readers for *End of the Wild*, so I'd like to thank him for his help in that earlier story as well as in this one.

My friend Joe read an early version of the book and helped me refine the DNA encryption mechanism, including how to generate the private key. Thanks Joe, it's always great to have security experts to bounce ideas off of.

And then my online community. Through Discord, I have built friendships with many wonderful people, some of whom have put in serious hours reading my book in order to give me useful story feedback and plot ideas. Zorbaz was hugely influential and helped me to refine and improve many ideas within the story. If it wasn't for Zorbaz, the clones probably would have ridden a ferry to Orcas Island instead of stealing a nuclear submarine. So you have him to thank for that. Bolt read every chapter and had useful editing and storyline feedback each step of the way. Abner helped with military details, including helping me to pick appropriate ranks for characters and teaching me how to address a female officer with respect. I want to thank each of you; you all made a big difference.

Lastly I want to thank you, the reader. If it wasn't for you, this book wouldn't exist. In the end, it is for your enjoyment that I wrote this story. It is a labor of love. My motivation comes from knowing that you will read my words, that you will explore these worlds with me. It is my hope that you will leave the story having felt that it was time well spent, and perhaps that it added something of value to your life.

My reward is you. So if you enjoyed the story, please let me know. Write a review. Send me an email. And I would be incredibly honored if you would recommend this book to a friend. Thank you.

ABOUT THE AUTHOR

Jason Taylor spends his life in the mountains and at sea. A native of Montana, coastal BC is his second home. He has a background in computer science and physics and is a voracious reader of all things science fiction. His writing explores the themes of what makes us human and the questions surrounding our place on this planet, both now and in the future.

33629570R00190

Made in the USA
Lexington, KY
13 March 2019